Revenge

MW00893281

Contents

Revenge of the Franks

Book 4 in the Norman Genesis Series
By Griff Hosker

Revenge of the Franks

Published by Sword Books Ltd 2016

Copyright © Griff Hosker First Edition

Cover by Design for Writers
Thanks to Simon Walpole for the Artwork.

Dedication

To my first two grandsons, Thomas Hosker and Samuel Hosker.
Have good lives; have long lives. Always remember that your family will
be there for you. You are both the future.
Also, dedicated to New Zealand and its people. You are a strong
people and you will come through this adversity.

PART ONE

The Clan of the Horse

Prologue

Each night I had been dreaming more of late. They did not disturb me but they set me to thinking. I was no Dragonheart nor was I a galdramenn who could see into the future. My dreams did not foretell our future but they showed what was on my mind. Since my son, Ragnvald, had been born recently my life had changed beyond all recognition. Being married had changed me but when I looked down at my son I knew that I had left a mark on this earth. He was part of me. He was not Norse. He was like the others who live in Haugr; he was a mix of Frank and Norse. My wife, Mary, had been the daughter of a lord. She had noble blood. Taken as slave by my clan I had freed and married her. It was one of the better decisions I had made. I had been born the son of a poor Norse farmer who had been taken into slavery. I had escaped. What would the future hold for my son?

My dreams were of my son and I riding horses across the land of the Franks. It was the land of the Franks at the moment. We held a tiny part of it but we were growing as a clan. Soon we would need more land and the land of the Franks would shrink. I had not attacked the Franks. They were Mary's people. The King of the Franks, Louis, was losing his grip on the land. That was partly the fault of warriors such as us. Danes and Norse came to raid. The Franks left the coastal and river areas where we raided. If there was empty land, then we would take it. That was how I captured my new home. Riven by civil discord there had been no order until we came. Now there was order, peace and prosperity.

I was Jarl Hrolf the Horseman. I was young to be a jarl; I knew that but my people, the Raven Wing Clan, had chosen me. We were the remnants of the clan which had followed Jarl Gunnar Thorfinnson and his drekar Raven Wing. That drekar was now sunk. Many people thought it was unlucky to use the name of a dead ship for our clan. That was not for me to say. Older warriors, like Harold Fast Sailing and Sven the Helmsman, chose to serve under me. Newer warriors such as Gudrun Witch Killer had sailed from other lands to serve under me. Then there were the Franks who had lived close by my new home. Bertrand was a Frank but he followed my banner. It was *wyrd*.

Now my dreams showed me a new world. It would be a world built by my people. We would sail and we would raid but we would also use horses. Already we had begun to learn how to fight from the backs of

3

horses like the Franks. When enemies came to harm us, they would find a new breed of Vikings. Already the Franks had a name for us. They called us the Northmen; sometimes it was the Northman from the Dragon Ships. It seemed to suit us. Our time on Raven Wing Island had helped us to become what we were. Now that we lived on the mainland I knew that we would change even more. I was lucky. I had a clan who were happy to follow me and to change as I had changed. Born a slave in the land of the Franks I had been freed by the clan of the wolf and I had learned what my destiny was. The visit to the witch in Syllingar had changed my life. Now we would change the world.

Chapter 1

Ragnvald was on his first solid food and was almost walking when the clan held the feast to celebrate our first harvest. We had spent our first year consolidating what we had. We made our home safe and we tilled land. The Franks who had lived here had prepared the fields and we utilised them. Now we reaped the rewards. Our animals had produced young and the ground had borne both fruit and grain. As I rode around my land on my horse, Copper, I was greeted with waves and smiles. They had all followed me from the Raven Wing Island to this new home. We had had to battle the Franks but we had won and we now clung on. Other Vikings had come to take the land from us but we had stood strong. It was not just the Norse who seemed happy to see me; the Franks were equally content.

I reined in at the farm of Rurik One Ear. He was one of my oldest friends. He was a rock in the shield wall and always stood to the right of me in battle. He had taken a Frank as a wife. Agnathia was not young but they made a happy couple. She was now with child. Rurik took this as a good sign. The Frank she had been married to had been unable to sire children. Rurik had yet to father a child and this happy event had changed him beyond all recognition. He had left the Haugr and taken a farm a few Roman miles from our walls. It was a fine piece of land which was close to the sea and within sight of a large forest. He had two slaves who helped him till the land and he also harvested the sea. He was happy.

He stopped work when I reined in. "A fine morning, jarl."

I shook my head as I dismounted, "We are old friends. My name is Hrolf or have you forgotten?"

"I will never forget my friend who stood alone with me on the island and fought off many enemies but now you are jarl. You are due the respect."

I would not win the argument with him. "How is your wife?"

"She will be ready to give birth by the end of the month. She is well."

"We hold the feast of the harvest in six days. It would be good if you would come. Brigid the ale wife has brewed some fine ale."

"Then I will be there. Agnathia is a good wife but she cannot brew ale like Brigid."

I looked at the stacks of wheat he had drying in the late summer sun. "A good crop?"

He shrugged, "It is my first harvest but I think so. The apples are also doing well but our beans are going better than anything else. Even if we have naught else we will have beans for the winter."

I looked south to the distant forests. They were in the land of the Franks. We had avoided hunting in them as we did not want conflict but I knew that many of my warriors wished to augment their diet with the wild boars they knew roamed there. "Perhaps when the leaves have fallen we might take a party and hunt. Many of our men yearn for wild meat."

"That kind of wild meat can cost a high price. Does it do to rouse the Franks, jarl?" Marriage and fatherhood had made Rurik more cautious.

"We hunt; we do not make war."

"But you know what the Franks are like about their hunting and their forests. They belong to their king."

"Then when you come for the feast we will talk of such things. I would not bring danger to you. There are none who live closer to the Franks."

"Do not fret for me. I now have two good horses. I have learned from Hrolf the Horseman. When first I met you, I could barely ride. Now I ride more than I walk."

I reflected on his words as I rode home. It was true. I had the best herd of horses. I had ten of them and two stallions. Already my mares were with foal and my herd would increase. Others had either bought or found horses and emulated me. My people were becoming horsemen. The Franks with whom we lived were also horseman and the change seemed natural like the leaves turning to brown when summer ended. The land we had chosen was fine horse country with soft rolling hills and verdant, rich pasture.

Mary and I spent some time planning the harvest feast. She was a Christian. I had built her a church on the island which was attached by a causeway. She had managed to find a couple of priests who were happy to live on the island and to hold services. We fed and protected them. It seemed a small price to pay for my wife's peace of mind. She worried about what she called her soul… whatever that was. She wanted me to convert but the old ways were in my heart. We did not argue. I could rarely win such arguments but I had tried to assimilate our celebrations with those of the Christians. It was a compromise but it seemed to work.

The end of Tvímánuður was when we celebrated the corn cutting. This fitted in with my wife's church for they also celebrated God's bounty. We married the festivals. It was a happy time for all. It was also the time when many babies were born. Conceived in the long winter nights it was a good sign. The earth and our mothers gave birth at the same time.

Mary handed Ragnvald to a slave to put to bed and she sat before the fire with me. "We are short of spices, husband. It is soon the time to preserve the meats and the fruits."

"You would have me raid for them?"

She shook her head angrily. She did not like us raiding, "No! You can trade! Everything is not about raids. We have coin; let us spend it wisely."

I pointed to the slave who was carrying Ragnvald to his cot, "If we do not raid then how do we get slaves to work in our homes?"

She frowned, "We have enough for now."

"But there will come a time when we will not have enough. And what do we trade? We produce enough food to keep us during the winter. There is little enough to sell. The gold and the treasure we captured from the Franks and the Norse who attacked us is almost gone. Where do we get the coin to improve the church and give to your priests?" I had a wry smile on my face. Mary and the other Christians gave money each Sunday to the priests. They did not grow rich because of it. The coin enabled them to live and augment that which they grew on their island. They lived better than most for my people also gave them a share of our food and our beer.

"We do not need to raid yet." She nodded emphatically.

I had won and I could not resist having the last word. It rarely happened, "But we shall need to raid soon."

With smoked and salted fish, freshly slaughtered mutton and the first of the apples we had a good feast. The ale was amongst the best Brigid had ever brewed. As we filled the last holes with fresh bread and runny cheese we sang songs and told tales of the dead members of the clan. It was our way and it seemed to make them still alive.

Gunnar Stone Face had had more of the new ale than most and he became loquacious. "I will say what others think, Jarl. This is a better home than Raven Wing Island and I never thought to say that!"

Rurik nodded as he cuddled his heavily pregnant wife. "More than that I think it is better than the land of the wolf."

7

I shook my head, "The land of the wolf is a wondrous land, Rurik. They have Waters and Meres and they have mountains. The land is filled with iron and precious metals."

Rurik laughed, "And the fields are filled with rocks! Do not misunderstand me, jarl. I like that land of the wolf but I am saying that this land is perfect. Or it would be if we hunted in the forests."

Gunnar nodded eagerly, "Aye! I wish to hunt in the forest of the Franks! I have heard that only their lords hunt. That is not right, jarl!"

I had hoped to avoid this discussion but Rurik had remembered my words. "We can hunt but we must all be aware of the consequences." Everyone had stopped speaking and were listening to what I had to say. Many of our women were Franks and they understood the laws which governed hunting. I saw fear on their faces. My men, on the other hand, saw hunting as every man's right.

"We do not make war on the Franks, jarl, but if they dispute our right to hunt then they will feel the edge of my sword. We are warriors!" Sigtrygg Rolfsson had grown into a powerful warrior. I knew that he, along with many of my men, wished to make war.

"Then if you are all decided then we will hunt when the last of the crops are collected in."

That pleased the men who cheered and banged their knives on the tables. The women looked less happy about it. Rurik, it appeared, had not finished. He stood and held his hands for silence. "There is something else. I have thought of this each day as I tended my fields. We are no longer the clan of the Raven Wing. It is unlucky to name ourselves after a dead ship and a jarl who is now in Valhalla. The Raven Wing clan died when the drekar died." He had the warrior's attention now. What he spoke was almost sacrilege. "I know what you are thinking but hear me out. We joined the Raven Wing clan when Jarl Gunnar Thorfinnson led us. He is dead along with those like Siggi and Ulf Big Nose." He pointed to Gudrun Witch Killer and Karl Anyasson. "We have warriors who joined us because of Hrolf the Horseman. I took, as many of you did, a Frankish wife. We have changed. We are no longer the Raven Wing clan."

Sven the Helmsman was the eldest of the men and he said, "I agree but who are we? The name of the clan is not something to be changed lightly. Do we upset the spirits and our ancestors by changing the name?"

Gudrun said, "For my part I did not join the Raven Wing clan. I joined the clan of Hrolf the Horseman. I agree with Rurik."

An uneasy silence descended. It was Mary, my wife who spoke, "It seems to me that you have your name already." I saw Rurik frown. "Gudrun Witch Killer has given it to us. We are the clan of the horse."

Sometimes it takes something as simple as that to make a change. Smiles erupted on people's faces. There were nods and then cheers. Bagsecg Bagsecgson shouted, "And I will make the herkumbl for our helmets! That will be my harvest gift!"

His wife Anya shook her head, "Now that is the drink talking!" She was smiling as she said so.

"We will paint the jarl's sign of the horse on our shields!"

"Aye and on the sail! This is *wyrd*!"

It was as though the clan had all gone berserk at the same time. Mary leaned over to me and kissed my cheek. "As you pagans say, husband, this is *wyrd*."

Although I agreed to the hunt I did not allow all of the men to go. We would have looked like a warband. I allowed those who had served the clan the longest. Everyone took it well. The exceptions to this rule were Gilles and Bertrand. Bertrand was a Frank and his local knowledge was vital. Gilles was a horse master and we might need his skills. We took boar spears and bows. I allowed Rurik to accompany us. It seemed right for his land was closest to the woods. The weather, on the day we went showed the change in the seasons. The brisk wind from the south west helped to take more of the leaves from the trees. There were flurries of rain and we wrapped up well in our cloaks. I took my faithful dog, Nipper, with me. His keen nose would detect animals before we did and I rode Dream Strider. He had been my first horse and was still my favourite for there was an understanding between us. I also took three of my more trusted slaves. They would hold the horses. They were all Hibernians. I did not think they would flee. If they were captured by the Franks, their life would be as hard and we were fair to those we enslaved.

The slaves tied our horses to the trees in the eaves of the woods and we entered. As jarl, I went first with Nipper. Bertrand and Gilles flanked me. They had a great responsibility. They would have to protect me should a boar decide to attack us. The rest of my men spread out behind us. Their bows were slung and their boar spears held poised to strike. The wind took our scent away from us. The animals in the forest would be unaware of our approach.

Nipper's nose suddenly made him stop and he went to ground with ears pricked. I held up my hand to stop the line. That was the time when you needed good eyes. Ulf Big Nose had taught me well and I scanned the trees ahead. It was a case of looking for something out of the ordinary. The leaves moved as did the branches. That was to expected but when I spied the branch moving the wrong way, away from the wind then I focused my attention there. It was a deer. It was grazing on the last of the summer greenery. When I spied one it became easy to see the others. I slid my spear, head first into the ground without making a sound. I carefully took my bow from around my back and readied an arrow. My bow was a Saami one. Very expensive it was far more powerful than even a war bow. My men saw me and emulated me. I made the sign for deer and pointed. Along the line there were nods as the clan prepared to moved towards them.

As we moved I watched where I placed my feet. The crackle of a crushed leaf might just alarm them. They were forty paces from us. I could have hit and killed one with my bow but the others just had ordinary hunting bows. They would need to be closer. I went three steps closer and one of the deer raised its head. I froze and it resumed its meal. I pulled back my arrow and aimed at the one I could see. I had no doubt that my men would have targets they could see. They were still moving although I was stationery. One of them made a noise. The deer' heads came up and I released. Even as it turned my arrow smacked into and through its skull. It dropped to the ground. I saw two arrows strike the deer next to it. I had another arrow ready but the herd had fled.

Pulling my spear from the soil I went towards the deer. We had slain four of them. One of them was still staggering, although mortally wounded. Gilles took his knife and ended its misery. Rolf Arneson said, "Sorry jarl. I stepped on a twig and it broke."

Beorn Fast Feet chuckled, "Ulf Big Nose would have made your ears burn for such a crime."

I nodded, "Take the deer back to the slaves and have them placed upon our spare horses. We will venture a little further in." It seemed that our enterprise was going well and we would not incur the wrath of the Franks.

The skies had darkened as more black, scudding clouds rushed up from the south west. They would not bring snow. We had learned that rarely happened in this land but they would bring rain. Life would be unpleasant but bearable. We used the animal trails and the paths which other hunters had cut. I looked to left and right for sign of spoor. Nipper stopped and sniffed. I bent down and saw some fresh boar dung. It was not quite cold. There were wild boars close by. I held my spear above my head as a sign that I had found tracks. I stroked Nipper's head and whispered, "Hunt!" He sped off.

I knew that the wild boars would be trying to eat as much as they could before winter came. If they found some food they would stay close by until it was completely gone. They would be close to where they had left their spoor. Bertrand was the one who saw them. Nipper returned first and that told me that they were close but it was Bertrand who raised his arm preparing to send his spear towards the wild boar he had seen. I did not see it at first and then I heard it snuffle and saw the shrubs move. Bertrand was brave but he had never hunted wild boar. It was a sow and an old one at that. He threw his boar spear and it struck her in her shoulder. She squealed, shattering the peace of the woods. But she had not been mortally struck and she hurtled towards a terrified Bertrand who was already celebrating his success.

"Back!" He turned and then reacted to my voice. He ran. The sow was old but she still moved quickly. I stepped forward. Bertrand ran to my right and I thrust my spear into the side of her head as she passed. I had sharpened the boar spear but, even so, her skull was thick. I wondered if I had the strength and then it suddenly broke through the bone and into her brain. She fell to the side. The rest of the herd had taken flight as soon as she had squealed. The boar charged towards us. My men presented a wall of spears. He stopped and sniffed the air. Perhaps he smelled the dead sow or perhaps the wall of spears was too much. He turned and disappeared after his herd.

I nodded, "I think we have enough meat now! You were lucky there, Bertrand. Next time wait until there is another hunter close by you!"

"It is considered dishonourable, amongst my people, to have help when making a kill."

"But Franks hunt from the back of a horse do they not?" He nodded. "The horse can escape faster than a man!" I took out my seax. "Let us make an offering to Ullr. We were lucky and he watched over us." I sawed through the thick skin of the belly and pulled out the hot intestines and guts. I sought the heart. I found it. It was warm. I raised it in the air, "Take this sacrifice Ullr, god of hunting, in thanks for your help this day!" Rurik and Beorn Fast Feet dug a small hole and we buried the heart.

Rurik slapped Bertrand on the back. "And now, young Frank, use your spear to help us carry this back to the horses. She was an old boar but there is meat a plenty. Gilles. Fetch those guts! They are not to be wasted!"

Beorn Fast Feet helped Bertrand to ram our two spears through the mouth of the sow and then out of her backside. The other warriors helped them to lift the beast. It was heavy. We sang as we rode home. A successful hunting trip is always worth celebrating. When we reached Haugr it was late afternoon. We wasted no time. The men quickly skinned the beasts. Their hides would not be discarded. They had many uses and then the animals were butchered. Every piece of meat and offal would be used. The intestines would be washed and the skins used to make sausages. The hooves of the animals would be melted down to make a glue which would be used by Sven the Helmsman. The bones would be cooked to make soup and then used to make tools from scrapers to needles. We wasted nothing.

Six days after the hunt riders approached from the south and west. The sentry in the gate tower shouted, "Jarl! Franks approach from the south and they are armed!"

I grabbed my sword, helmet and shield and went to the gate. I stood in the entrance. Gilles and Bertrand had their weapons and flanked me. As the word spread other warriors appeared. The walls had eight men and boys already there. They were armed with slingshots, bows and spears. I could now see that there were ten riders approaching us. Ten Franks did not worry me. "Are there any other riders in sight, Erik Green Eye?"

He was in the highest tower and I saw him peer around. "No jarl. The land is clear."

We would talk. The three of us in the gate could deal with at least four of the Franks and my men on the walls would eliminate the rest. I sheathed my sword and slipped my shield around my back. As they reined in I took off my helmet.

The leader was an older warrior. His beard was white and his face scarred. He had leather armour studded with metal plates and an open helmet. His shield had the emblem of a gryphon upon it. The background was a light shade of blue. I had not seen the design before. He looked at me and spoke in the language of the Franks.

"I would speak to the lord here. Go and get him, boy."

Bertrand's hand went to his sword and I restrained him. "Easy, Bertrand. Other men have made this mistake." I looked the warrior in the eye. "I am the one who rules here. I am jarl."

12

He looked surprised, "You?" he waved a hand at the older warriors who stood on the walls. "You command these? How?"

"Did you come here to insult me or to die? Was there something your master wanted to say to me?"

"My master?"

"I do not recognise your shield and you are an old dog! You are not a lord. Your armour is that of a warrior and not a lord. Speak and then be on your way."

He frowned, "I am Jean of Caen and I serve Philippe of Rouen. I am seneschal of the castle at Valauna. King Louis has appointed him as lord of this land and all the land between the sea and Rouen." I nodded. "Your men have been hunting in his forest. Hand over those who took the king's deer and wild boar so that they may be punished. If you do so then my lord may allow you to live."

I smiled, "And the punishment is?"

He shrugged, "It depends upon my lord. Sometimes it is just the loss of an eye or a nose but I have known him take the right hand of a poacher."

"I am afraid that I need both of my eyes, hands and my nose. I cannot accommodate you."

He looked genuinely surprised, "The Leudes of Rouen was appointed here to make sure that taxes were paid and order restored. I warn you that he will not be gentle if you do not cooperate. He will destroy this stronghold."

"Tell your lord that I pay no taxes and I hunt where I please. I wish no harm to your lord nor his people but if he comes for war then he had better be prepared for the consequences. We are Vikings. We bow the knee to no king."

"And who are you, Viking? I would give my lord your name."

"I am Jarl Hrolf chief of the clan of the horse." I said nothing more but I carefully donned my helmet and swung my shield around. When he did not move, I slid my sword from its scabbard. Erik One Hand was on the gate and he shouted down, "I would move, Frank! When the jarl dons his helmet then it means he is ready for war. If he draws his sword, then all of you will die!" He raised his hand and twenty bows and twenty spears appeared on my walls.

The Frank nodded, "Very well. But I warned you."

After they had gone Arne Four Toes joined me, "What happened to the other lord?"

I shrugged, "Perhaps he was not strong enough and King Louis has replaced him with someone who can do the job better."

Gunnar Stone Face shook his head, "You were right, jarl. The meat we hunted was expensive!"

"This would have happened some time. If the king wants taxes, then they would have come here at Eostre for their coin. We will be vigilant. Gilles and Bertrand, ride to the outlying farms and warn them that the Franks will be coming to punish us."

I sounded calm but I was worried. Would they come with enough men to crush us or just enough to punish us? We had poked the sleeping bear. I now had to work out how to make sure it did not devour us.

Chapter 2

I began to ride around my land with mail upon me. Bertrand and Gilles did the same. Most of my warriors had other duties such as their farms or their ships but the three of us had no such duties. I had slaves who watched over my horses. Gilles supervised them but he could afford to be with me for a few days until we had seen the intentions of the Franks.

A few days after Jean of Caen had left we rode south to Rurik. We had heard nothing more and I was anxious to know what was going on close to the borders of our small enclave. Bertrand knew of Valauna for he had been there. The seneschal's words suggested there were men there but Bertrand thought that the castle there was small. He said the town had a wooden wall and there was a stone tower within. He did not thing that think that the Leudes would stay there. Caen was a bigger place. It would take some days for a message to reach him and for him to react. I would see if there was danger. If not, then we would either trade or raid before the winter storms set in.

Nipper came with us for I would need his ears and eyes too. I saw Rurik with his slaves in his orchard, gathering apples for the winter. He wore his sword at his side. He nodded as I dismounted, "You were right again, jarl. The ale got to us and made us foolish. We should have listened to you."

I shrugged, "It would have happened anyway and we ate well. It was *wyrd*." I pointed to the woods a mile or more away. "You are ready to ride when you sense danger?"

"Aye we have horses." He pointed to his cattle herder who had a dog with him. They were by the sea on the grazing by the shore. "Aksel there has a good dog and good eyes. He watches for us. And you?"

"We ride towards their town. I would like to see what size of garrison they have at Valauna. It was a Roman fort in days gone by."

He nodded, "It is not far. In fact, I think it lies beyond the forest to the west."

Bertrand said, "It does."

"Take care, jarl."

"We will."

As we rode I wondered if the Franks would wait until they had a force large enough to quash us completely or come immediately. If they waited until they had enough men, it might suit us for winter would be our ally. The winter would not be harsh as in the Land of the Wolf, campaigning was never easy in winter. Our prudence in gathering in so many crops and procuring an excess of animals might just save my people if this one was harder than the last.

We skirted the woods and followed the greenway. I noticed that, in parts, there were cobbles beneath our hooves. The Romans had built here. Unlike in the Land of the Wolf many Franks used stones to build their homes. They had dug up many of the Roman Roads to build their houses. It made their roads less reliable. We just used the stones from the sea. We harvested that bounty too. We forded the small river which ran from west to east and began to rise towards the distant stronghold. I had no intentions of riding close to it. That would be too dangerous but I wanted to discover if they had mounted men riding the land.

When the greenway entered another wood, thinner this time, we halted to rest our horses. We were only six Roman miles from home but we were halfway to Valauna. Nipper growled as I let Dream Strider drink from the beck. Gilles and Bertrand knew my dog as well as I did and we all slid into our saddles and drew our swords. I left my shield hanging from my saddle until I had seen what danger came our way.

I waved Gilles and Bertrand into the shelter of the trees and waited in the middle of the path. I heard the hooves of the riders as they approached. Nipper had felt the ground move at their approach. I hissed, "Nipper, hide!" My dog disappeared. I sheathed my sword.

The four riders saw me when they were just thirty paces from me. I had seen their movement before they spied me. My stillness, born of long training from Ulf Big Nose, had come to my aid. None of the four had mail. They had the leather studded byrnie with open helmets and javelins held in their arms. They halted ten paces from me and peered around suspiciously. The leader was a young warrior. I think he had been with the seneschal when he had come to the haugr. He must have recognised me. He said, "You are the Viking the Seneschal spoke with when we delivered our lord's ultimatum. Have you come to hand yourself over for punishment?"

"No, I came for a ride in this pleasant wood. Soon it will be winter and not as enjoyable. And you?"

My easy manner disarmed them. They looked at each other. Then the young leader said, "It matters not why you came here. We have you now and shall take you to the castle for judgement."

I drew my sword, "Heart of Ice here disputes that." I leaned down and took my shield. "As there are four of you I may well need my shield too."

"You are arrogant for a barbarian who cannot ride! We are Neustrians and lords of the horse! Take him!"

They split up as they charged at me with their javelins lowered. I saw that the young warrior hung back a little. If they thought to intimidate and frighten me they were sadly mistaken. I kicked Dream Strider in the ribs and he leapt forward. The four of them were too close to be able to use their javelins effectively. Two clattered into my shield; one missed me completely and Heart of Ice sliced through the javelin of the fourth. I wheeled Dream Strider around. The Franks tried the same manoeuvre but their javelins and numbers threw them into confusion. As I urged Dream Strider towards them I shouted, "Now Gilles! Now Bertrand!" My two men had been waiting for my order and they both sprang from cover. They had ten paces to cover but the Franks only heard hooves. Their heads whirled looking for the new danger.

The warrior whose javelin I had sliced in two had drawn his sword. He swung it at my head and I blocked it easily with my shield. I stood in my stirrups and brought my sword across the top of his shield. He fell from his horse. A javelin punched into my back but my forward momentum stopped its penetration. I whipped Dream Strider's head around and brought my sword across the neck of the Frank. The other two were not faring well against Gilles and Bertrand who were both superb horsemen. Gilles lunged at his opponent and found the gap between his shield and his saddle. The sharp sword slid into his body and he fell. Bertrand's opponent, the young leader who had held back a little, turned his horse and galloped off. I saw that Bertrand had caused a wound to his head for there was blood coming from beneath his helmet.

Bertrand looked to follow but I shouted, "Hold! We have done enough! Gilles search the bodies. Bertrand gather the horses." I rode down the trail a short way to make sure that the last man had fled. There was no sign of him. By the time I had returned the helmets, swords, javelins and shields were hung from the saddles of the three horses we had captured.

Gilles held up three purses. "They have coins, jarl."

"Then they are yours. You did well." We left the bodies where they lay. I had no doubt that the Franks would investigate the attack. They could clear their own dead.

As we passed Rurik's farm he came over to us. "I see you found some Franks."

I nodded, "There were four and they chose to fight. Keep an even closer watch, Rurik. You will be the first to hear of an enemy's approach. Do not try to be a hero. Give us warning."

"I will."

We rode the last mile or two to my walls. Gilles ventured, "That encounter may be enough to put off the Franks, jarl."

"No, Gilles. It will not. Those men were sent to scout. They were not important were they jarl?"

"I fear you are right, Bertrand. We will have to bloody their noses a little more if we are to make them let us alone."

The warriors who farmed and lived close by the walls approached us we returned. It was late afternoon. The men who had watched from our walls had been staring all day for a sight of our horses. I dismounted and said to my two men, "Take the horses to the stables and put the weapons, helmets and shields in my hall. We will distribute them later."

My warriors gathered around me and I told them what had happened. "I think they will be here tomorrow. It is just a guess. I do not have the gift of a galdramenn but if they came quickly for a couple of deer and an old boar then they will come that much sooner for three dead men and lost horses."

Einar Asbjornson said, "So we fight?"

"We fight." I pointed to the open ground before the walls. "We fight there, if they come."

Einar frowned, "But what about our walls? Surely we could stay behind them."

I swept my hand around, "We have yet to gather all of our crops inside. There are animals without. If we hide behind our walls they will take what we have. We meet them here. Our boys and archers can man the walls and loose over our heads."

"Do we fight on horses?"

"No Gudrun Witch Killer. Not enough of you have those skills. From what I have seen of the Franks most of their horsemen do not wear mail and their horses are vulnerable. A good shield wall can withstand an attack. We proved that last year. Have the outlying farmers return to the safety of our walls."

Arne Four Toes asked, "And Rurik?"

I smiled, "He will act as a sentry. He has horses and he will warn us of their arrival. I suspect they will avoid him and try to surprise us."

As I went to take off my mail I reflected that the Franks were more predictable than we were. We might have tried a night attack. They would not. I was confident about that. If they did, then their horses would alert us to their presence. They would come in daylight and that meant we would have warning.

There had been a time when my wife would have been worried about such an attack. Now she was less concerned. She had seen the strength of my warriors. "This will just be the start, husband. You know that. Now that blood has been shed it will rankle with the count and the king."

"I know. It will be a test of the resolve of our clan. I am counting on the fact that your people value horses. If we slay their men and take their horses, then they will have smaller numbers to attack us. It takes time to train a mounted warrior. We may hurt them enough to make them sue for peace. We will see."

She nodded, "I will go with the women and Ragnvald. We will pray in the church."

That was the way of the Christians. They relied on their god to aid them. We relied on the strength of our arms and steel. We had arrows and javelins in abundance. We now had three leather byrnies and three more helmets. With our other captured equipment, every man and boy who stood on my walls would look like a warrior. I sent Gilles and Bertrand out early, before dawn. They would wait by Rurik's farm. We had thirty warriors who had stood in a shield wall. All but two had mail byrnies. Then there were another twenty who, like Bagsecg Bagsecgson, knew how to fight. With twenty old men and boys with bows and slings I hoped we would give a good account of ourselves.

Not long before noon Agnathia and Rurik's slaves hurried down the road towards us. "They come, jarl. There are more than fifty of them and they are mounted. My husband and your two young men are watching them."

"Thank you." As they hurried inside I turned to check my shield walls. We had three ranks with twenty men in each line. It meant that there were the ten least experienced men at the rear of our wall. They stood with their backs to the ditch. Our archers and slingers on the walls could easily reach over our heads to hurt the enemy. Rurik, Bertrand and Gilles could bolster the rear line when they arrived.

The three of them reined in. "They are half a Roman mile behind us. Our presence stopped them from spreading out."

Bertrand laughed, "They thought that we had hidden men who would ambush them. They kept looking to their left and right."

"Put your horses in the stronghold and then join the rear line."

They nodded and left. The Franks galloped up and then stopped three hundred paces from my walls. They respected my archers. They spread into one long line. I saw that none, save Jean of Caen, wore mail. Twelve of them wore what Jean of Caen had worn the other day, a metal studded leather byrnie. Jean of Caen had a tunic with overlapping fish scales of metal upon them. The rest were what the Saxons called the fyrd and the Franks the levy. Everyone had a helmet and a shield. Some wore leather armour but most just had a kyrtle and a leather baldric around their chest. Each one carried a javelin. The eleven who wore the metal studded leather had a long spear. They were the ones to worry about. I saw one with a bandage. He was the young warrior from the earlier encounter.

Sticking my spear into the ground I lifted my helmet and stepped forwards with my hands open to show I was happy to talk. Jean of Caen handed his helmet to the warrior next to him. It was the one who had fled us the previous day. The old warrior nudged his horse forward. It was a big horse. I recognised its quality. This was a horseman and, if we fought, it would not do to underestimate him.

His face was angry, "Not content with hunting on the king's lands I see you dared to attack and kill my men!"

I kept my voice even, "Your men attacked me. The four of them charged at me."

"You had an ambush prepared! That is not honourable."

"I had two young warriors with me. The fact that they are better than yours is what helped me to send them to the Otherworld."

He turned in his saddle and said, to the survivor, "There were just three of them?"

The young warrior lowered his head, "There seemed more, father, but it may have been just three. They wore mail!"

His father shook his head and turned back to me. "It makes no difference to me how many there were. You slew three of my men." I said nothing. He looked up at my men. "You think these farmers and pirates can stand up to my horsemen? We will sweep you from the field and then burn your stronghold!"

I moved closer to him so that we could speak without others hearing us. "Brave words from a man with just twelve warriors to depend on. You think your levy are a match for Vikings? I tell you what; let you and I fight here this day. I offer you single combat!"

"You are on foot!"

"I can get a horse. We fight here and if you win then I will submit to your court."

"And if you win?"

"Then you leave us in peace."

He grinned, "You are a brave young fool! Agreed." He thought a Frank could easily defeat a Viking who rode a horse.

"Then tell your men. It would not give me any pleasure to slaughter them if they tried to avenge you!"

He frowned and then turned. "I will fight with this Viking. When I win, he will come back to our castle as a prisoner. If he wins then we leave them in peace."

His men laughed and behind me I heard those who could speak their language shout, "No!"

I turned, "I have spoken. Gilles, saddle Dream Strider."

I walked back to my spear and withdrew it. Arne Four Toes said, "Why, jarl? This is madness. We could beat these easily!"

"I know but we might lose men. More importantly it might bring forth the wrath of this Leudes from Rouen. We are not yet ready to face an army. Let us have small victories. I know we will have to fight him one day but, for the present, let us try to increase our numbers." I smiled, "Do you not think I can beat him?"

"He looks experienced."

"He probably is but the one thing he has never done is fight a Viking horseman! I have fought Franks before. I have surprise on my side. Do not fear. I have no intention of losing." I put on my helmet and loosened my sword in my scabbard.

Gilles brought Dream Strider and I handed him my spear as I mounted. I leaned down and said, quietly, "Watch the one who escaped the other day. I do not trust him. Have your bow ready."

"Aye, lord."

I kicked my horse on and rode to face the Frank. He was smiling. "I have won many battles from the back of a horse, Viking. You are brave. If our positions were reversed, then I would have asked to fight on foot."

"And that is the difference between a Viking and a Frank. I am afraid of nothing. Certainly, not an old man whose son lies to him." I had guessed that the young man was his son but I saw similarities between them. His reaction confirmed it,

He coloured and whipped his horse's head around. I had angered him. It had been deliberate. I needed him to try to show his men that he was still a powerful warrior. I would use my speed and Dream Strider's innate fighting ability. I leaned forward, "Today, Dream Strider, we put into action all that we have practised."

I took him towards the sea. I knew the ground to be firmer there. We halted just a hundred paces apart. He pulled back on his reins and kicked hard. His horse leapt into the air and then he galloped towards me. I said, "Now, Dream Strider."

We cantered towards the Frank. I heard his men cheering. He intended to hit me with such force that the combat would be over before it was begun. He was showing his men that they were superior. I held my spear overhand. The Frank had his couched beneath his arm. I knew that he would punch at me to knock me from my saddle. He was going quickly; too quickly for I saw the head of his spear waving up and down in the air. He held his shield tightly to his body and was leaning forward in his saddle. He expected me to try to do the same as he did. I had no intention of doing so.

I rode Dream Strider directly at the Frank. As I saw him pull back his arm I jerked my reins to the right. His spear hit my shield but it was a glancing blow and caused only sparks as the head hit my boss. I, on the other hand, stabbed down towards his left leg. His shield was held high and he had no mail covering his leg; just breeks. My spear came away bloody. I was able to wheel Dream Strider around far quicker than he could for I was going more slowly. I heard his men shouting a warning as I cantered up behind him. He wheeled his horse and punched his spear as he came close to me. The spear head hit the boss of my shield. Already weakened by the first blow the shaft shattered. I used my spear overhand. His shield came up and he managed to deflect the head. It tore through three of the plates of metal by his right shoulder. We both drew swords.

I knew he had a good horse but mine was better. I had a longer rein to control him because I was able to use my knees. As he swung his sword I used my knees to take Dream Strider away from the blow. Hitting fresh air was a waste of energy. I then backed Dream Strider away from the Frank. His men hurled insults at me thinking this was cowardice. It was not. When the Frank kicked his horse hard I jerked Dream Strider's head to the left. I brought Heart of Ice across the Frank's chest. His hand and sword came up but it was a slow move and his own sword sliced a long cut down his left cheek as my blade hit his.

As I moved past him I swung back hand and my sword connected with his back. His metal plates and the leather held but the heavy metal of my sword hurt him. His back arced. I continued my turn. As he turned to try to see me I could see the blood pouring from the wound in his leg. He was growing weaker. I stood in my stirrups and brought my sword down hard on his right shoulder. I heard something crack and he tumbled from his horse. My blow had not penetrated his mail but I had broken something. I raised my sword and my men cheered.

The son of the fallen Frank suddenly dug his heels into his mount's flanks and hurtled towards me. My back was to him. As I wheeled Dream Strider around I knew I would not make the turn in time. I tried to pull my shield around for defence when there was a sudden blur before my eyes and Gilles' arrow struck the horse in the side of the head. As it fell forward it threw the treacherous young warrior from its back. My men ran forward, angered by the act. Other Franks were helping Jean of Caen to his feet. His son lay prone. He shook his head. "You have won, Viking. I am sorry for my son's actions. It is a shame for that was a fine horse."

Gilles had arrived with his bow in hand, "Think yourself lucky, Jean of Caen. Gilles is a fine archer. He could have slain your son. You will keep your word?"

He nodded, "I know not what the Leudes will say but I will keep my end of the bargain."

His men wrapped a bandage around his leg and placed him on his horse. One of the others draped the unconscious body of his son over the other and they headed south. My gamble had paid off but now they knew that there was at least one Viking who could ride and fight.

Chapter 3

That evening we feasted. The whole clan had been inside my walls and it seemed too good an opportunity to miss. They stayed the night and we ate well. The food we had laid in for a siege would no longer be needed. Everyone wished to talk of the battle that never was. Even though mine had been the only sword drawn in anger no one had failed to show that they were willing to fight and die for the clan. Had Haaken One Eye of the clan of the wolf, been in the Haugr, he might have composed a saga. We did not do much of that and so my men just talked of what might have happened.

Rurik One Ear said quietly to me as men spoke of the blows they would have struck and the glory they would have earned, "Those are the best kind of battles for warriors always win and slay far more than in a real battle."

"Do not be harsh with them, Rurik. They stood outside our wall and were willing to fight to the death."

Beorn Beornsson nodded, "I believe we would have won. I know you favour a horse, jarl, but I cannot see any advantage. Spears keep them at bay and our axes can cut through a horse's leg just as easily as a man's."

"Perhaps but being mounted gives us a much greater range."

Sven brought over a newly filled horn of ale for me, "A ship travels faster. Are we going to sail before winter, jarl or shall I have the drekar drawn up into her cradle?"

I was suddenly aware that everyone was listening to my words. "This would be a good time. We have most of the crops and animals we need and after today the Franks will not bother us until after winter. If we are to go then it must be soon. Aye, we will sail."

Asbjorn Sorenson asked, "Trade or raid?"

The way he said it left me in no doubt what he wanted. I looked around at the faces of my men. My warriors had been ready to fight and they had not even unsheathed their weapons. These were Vikings I commanded. They wanted to fight.

"I can tell what you wish to do Asbjorn. You wish to raid. What are the wishes of the other men who would crew *'Dragon's Breath'*?"

Beorn Beornsson said, quite simply, "Raid! Trade brings a profit but not as much as a raid." He waved his hand around the fire where my crew sat, "You have a young crew jarl but they are warriors all. Let us hone those skills. More warriors will join our clan if we can raid successfully. Then we can trade."

No one argued against it although Rurik was silent. I stood, "Very well then we raid. However, I would not raid the river Issicauna. I do not wish to make enemies of every Frank!" My men laughed. "I have a mind to raid Wessex. King Egbert has successfully conquered Mercia and Corn Walum. His treasuries will be full. Let us relieve him of some of the burden of counting!" Again, my men laughed, "And then we can sail to Dorestad and trade. Dyflin is too far and I would not risk the isles of Syllingar this close to winter."

The cheers told me I had made the right decision. I turned to Rurik, "You said nothing. What is amiss?"

"Nothing save…" he lowered his voice, "Agnathia is not young and she is with child. I would not leave her until the child is born but I am a warrior and I am your oathsworn…"

"Then you can help yourself and me. You will not be of much use when your child is born. You have the power to end life but others bring it into this world. Fetch your wife here into the stronghold and then the other women can help her. You can command in my absence. I am happy that we have many untried warriors who would have faced the Franks but I need someone to command them while I am gone."

He brightened, "I could do that and it would be something I could do with honour. Thank you, jarl."

It took five days to prepare the drekar for sea. Strakes had to be caulked; sheets and stays renewed. Stores had to be prepared and, with a full crew, the ballast had to be carefully balanced. The weather had deteriorated in those five days but the wind was still with us and blew from the south east. It sped us on our way.

The men used the saga of Siggi White Hair and my son, Ragnvald, to pull us away from the shore. It was a good song and it filled our hearts with both pride and the fond memories of Siggi White Hair. He had been as the father to our clan.

Siggi was the son of a warrior brave
Mothered by a Hibernian slave
In the Northern sun where life is short
Is back was strong and his arm was taut
Siggi White Hair warrior true
Siggi White Hair warrior true

When the Danes they came to take his home
He bit the shield and spat white foam
With berserk fury he killed them dead
When their captain fell the others fled
Siggi White Hair warrior true
Siggi White Hair warrior true
After they had gone and he stood alone
He was a rock, a mighty stone
Alone and bloodied after the fight
His hair had changed from black to white
His name was made and his courage sung
Hair of white and a body young
Siggi White Hair warrior true
Siggi White Hair warrior true
With dying breath he saved the clan
He died as he lived like a man
And now reborn to the clan's hersir
Ragnvald Hrolfsson the clan does cheer
Ragnvald Hrolfsson warrior true
Ragnvald Hrolfsson warrior true

By the time we had cleared the coast and headed out into the open sea we were warmed up and we were optimistic about our raid. I stood at the steering board with Sven the Helmsman and Harold Fast Sailing. With Siggi Far Sighted at the mast we would have ample warning of any danger. We spoke of Wessex. "We avoid Hamwic. We have been to that well too many times. Their defences will have been improved."

"Aye and the King is likely to be at Wintan-ceastre. That is close by. There will be rich pickings there but all of his thegns and warriors will be there."

"Then let us head around to the Temese. The Dragonheart found many treasures when he raided there. The river has many inlets where we can hide."

I shook my head. "I wish somewhere we have never raided. The place the Welsh call Dwfr on the Dour is a rich port." It was the closest part of the land of the Saxons to Frankia. If we raided there we would have a shorter voyage to Dorestad.

"Aye, there is a little bay to the north which only has a few fishing ships. We could use that and attack over land." Harold Fast Sailing was well named. He had sailed the seas for even more years than Sven the Helmsman.

"Good and it is a short voyage to Dorestad."

Bertrand and Gilles were the two who were the most ill at ease on the drekar. Bertrand was a Frank and a landsman. Gilles was a Viking but he had grown up, like me, as a horseman. I had contemplated leaving them in Haugr but they would have taken that as an insult. They would have to learn to be sailors too. Harold Fast Sailing sat them at the bow. They shared an oar with two of the more experienced oarsmen. I saw them looking, ruefully, at their red raw hands after they finished their first session of rowing.

"They will soon harden. Use the sea water to wash them. It will cleanse them. It will sting but it will be worth it."

I knew that they would have to row again. We would have to edge into the empty bay at night. We dared not use the sails. Even Harold Fast Sailing was not that familiar with the bottom of the sea there.

We laid up that first day close by the southern coast of Wessex. We knew that there were many bays in the ancient land of Haestingas. We avoided Haestingaceaster for Harold thought that it had a wall and might be defended. It had been the main stronghold of the ancient land of the Haestingas. There might be a time when we would raid it but this time we had chosen Dwfr. We used a sea anchor in the tiny bay. In summer, there was a possibility that we may have been seen but the nights were long at this time of year and few people were there to see us. A few years later and they would keep a watch for Dragonships such as ours.

We left after dawn and my crew took to the oars for we had to head east into the wind which was south by east. The furled sails meant we were harder to see. The waves were high, too, which made for an uncomfortable voyage as we crested white topped waves and crashed into deep troughs. Poor Gilles and Bertrand were petrified. Bertrand was a Christian and he kept his cross in his mouth the whole time. We headed out into the middle of the channel between Frisia and Cent. However, once we were far enough north we were able to lay down the oars and let our sails take us the last few miles closer towards the little bay. Harold thought that the few huts there were called Addelam but he was not certain. When we saw the thin line in the distance we lowered the sails and men took to the oars. Until dark it would be just a gentle row. We did not wish to be seen.

The later afternoon sky was already darkening as we headed west with furled sails and my warriors rowing. The wind helped us as did the seas. The ship's boys had been kept busy all day bailing the sea water which crashed over the sheerstrakes and then racing up slippery sheets to trim the sails. Now, with the light fading behind us we headed menacingly into the small bay. We knew it had a shingle beach and that the people who lived there kept a couple of boats on the shore. We would be able to slide up onto the shingle. We would have eight miles to cover along the cliffs. An approach from the land might well catch the men of Cent unawares.

When Ulf Big Nose had died, we had lost our best scout. I had been the scout he had trained but I was jarl. You did not create a good scout. You either found or improved one you already had. Einar Asbjornson had shown that he had scouting skills. He and I would lead the band.

The huts were almost invisible against the cliffs which towered over them. They were a shadowy smudge against the land with the faintest of glows from fires lit inside the huts. Standing by the prow I saw the shapes of two boats drawn up on the beach. Siggi Far Sighted waited with us. He was ready to leap ashore and tether us to the land. Einar and I would be the next ashore. There was no sign of life. Knut the Quiet and four of my men would secure those who lived here. Once taken my crew would guard them on my drekar. The hiss of the keel on the shingle told us that we had landed. Siggi and I slipped into the water at the same time. The huts remained in darkness. No door opened to shine the light of their fires on to us.

The water did not cover my seal skins boots. It had been a good beaching and I took it as a hopeful sign. I kept my sword sheathed and my shield around my back. I would not need either yet. I took off my helmet. It would mask what I could see, hear and smell. I headed south up and along the beach. The shingle sucked at my feet. When it gave way to sand and earth I made better going. I did not look behind me. My band would follow. Einar stood at my shoulder.

"There jarl!" His eyes had picked out the path which wound up the cliff. We had known there had to be one and the gods had guided us to it quickly. The wind and the surf on the shingle took away any noise of the events behind us. If the men in the huts fought us they would die. If not, they would be taken as slaves with their families. Sven and Harold would tell me if they ought to be sold in Dorestad or kept as slaves for our new home. We ascended the path to the cliff top. It twisted and turned up the steep cliffs.

Einar and I waited at the top of the cliff for my men to reach us. The icy wind whipped across the cliffs. The salt spray and drops of rain chilled to the bone. I was grateful for my cloak. Like the warriors of the land of the wolf I wore a wolf skin yet I was not Ulfheonar. I had killed a wolf but I wore the skin beneath my cloak. It was not a mark of honour. I wore it for warmth. I did not delude myself. I was not a warrior like those who followed Jarl Dragonheart. I had other skills. I think that was why the witch had given me my vision on Syllingar. Had she not I might have lived still in the land of the wolf. I would not have met Mary and I would not be leading my own warband. *Wyrd*.

Once together, Einar and I led the band at a steady lope across the undulating turf. The well-worn path was clear to see. I guessed that this had been a path since before the times of the Romans. We spied no one. I did not expect to. Haustmánuður had ended and Gormánuður was upon us. By the end of the month we would be upon the shortest days and longest nights of the year. The Saxons sheltered in their homes making babies and trying to keep warm. We did not mind the cold nor the black nights. They would bring us riches.

We came upon the half demolished Roman watch tower and I knew that we were close to the small port. Once again, we halted. This time it was to adjust our weapons and prepare for war. I donned my helmet, swung my shield around and drew my sword. I nodded to Beorn Beornsson and Arne Four Toes and pointed. They would bring up the rear. I had fought alongside the two since I had joined Jarl Gunnar. I trusted them above all others. They both made sensible decisions and would warn of any danger. It meant I could lead with confidence.

The ground began to descend below the abandoned watch tower. I saw the huts and buildings huddled in the bay. The Romans had built this place and there were many buildings made of stone. They even had a stone quay. I saw the ships drawn up there. They were knarr and small vessels used to carry small cargo. An idea began to form in my mind. We went slowly down the slope watching for any sentries or watchers. Ulf's training stood me in good stead. My nose caught the smell of a wood fire close to the ships. I held my hand up and we halted. I peered into the darkness. A shadow moved and revealed a fire. By its light I saw that there were three men standing watch by the quay. They were watching to sea.

I tapped Gudrun Witch Killer on the shoulder and held up my hand showing five. I pointed to the sentries. He nodded and led four men towards the sentries. I led the rest down the path towards the other buildings. The ones closest to the sea would have what we wanted. They would store food and goods to be traded there. We went slowly. Gudrun Witch Killer and his men soon joined us, having dealt with the sentries. I had heard nothing for the sound of the sea masked most noises. I waved the five of them to the left as we approached the stone buildings. They would open the doors and begin to search for treasure. I waved to the right and other warriors went to search there. I headed toward the warrior hall with my most experienced warriors. At least I guessed it was the warrior hall. It was a Saxon building and had a ditch around it. Set back from the rest of the port it was not Roman. I had twelve men left with me. They would have to be enough to deal with the Saxon warriors who were in the hall.

When we reached the door, I listened. I could hear the sounds of men sleeping within. Men were always noisier than women. I nodded to Einar and pointed, with my sword, to the ground. As I opened the door he moved quickly. A Saxon chamberlain was lying across the door. Einar's sword ended his life before he could utter a warning. As he stepped in the Weird Sisters spun their web. It had been too easy. A warrior rose to make water. The opening of the door had revealed us.

"Vikings!"

Einar leapt forward to slay the man but the damage had been done. I ran beyond him as sleepy, half naked men rose and grabbed weapons. There were the glowing remains of a fire in the middle of the hall and by its light I could make out warriors. We had to strike quickly. "Clan of the Horse!"

My men took up the shout and the clamour of our cries and screams as men died filled the hall. It added to the terror for those who were waking. A Saxon ran at me swinging his axe. He wore just a wooden cross and breeks. I dropped to my knee as the sleepy Saxon swung the deadly blade over my head. I rammed my sword into his middle. He was a big man and I had to cut through many layers. I did not find anything vital and he tried to batter me with the head of his axe as I tried to pull out the sword. The axe head rang against my helmet and his weight threatened to topple me. I twisted my sword in his body and changed the angle. I must have hit something important for my hand was suddenly covered in hot, sticky blood. He went limp. As the axe fell I pushed him from my body.

I saw four men at the far end of the room. One was donning his helmet and mail. The other three were guarding him. That would be the thegn and his bodyguards. "Arne! Beorn! On me!"

Without waiting for them I ran at those guarding the thegn. Gilles and Bertrand were on either side of me. The bodyguards had no mail but they had their swords and shields. I pulled my shield tighter to me and just ran at them. I used my shield as a battering ram. Their swords hit my shield and my helmet but I remain unscathed. One fell to the ground as the other two stepped back. My hand darted out and I skewered the one who wriggled on the ground. Before I could face the other two the thegn's sword smashed against my shield. It was a long sword and the blow was powerful. I left the bodyguards for my men and faced the Saxon.

He was bare footed but he had his byrnie on. His sword was longer than mine and he swung it to keep me at bay while he adjusted his shield. I lunged low down with my sword and his hand flicked down to fend off the blow. He just managed to stop my blade from piercing his leg. The high roof on the hall meant he could bring his sword over his head. It would be a powerful blow, if it struck, but I knew it was coming and I stepped to the side swinging my sword as I did so. My arms were much stronger now. Using a bow each day had made my arms like oak and the blow I struck was so hard that I saw him step back. His left arm was numbed. I followed up, quickly, by punching at his shield with mine. He stepped back again. The fire was perilously close to his legs. When he made the mistake of glancing behind him my sword lunged at his throat. His numbed arm and inattention cost him his life. He fell backwards over the fire. I reached down to pull his body from it. As I did so I saw a golden torc around his neck. I snatched it and turned to view the hall.

Six warriors were still standing together holding off my men. Gunnar Stone Face entered the hall and, swinging his axe, roared, "Let us finish this!"

He ran at the knot of men. My men parted as the wild man swung his long handled axe two handed. They had no mail and he did. They fought bravely and struck his mail many times but his initial attack took the heads of two of them and then my men fell on the rest.

"Well done, wild man! Now collect the weapons and treasure." I held yup the torc. "They are rich, it seems. Bring it down to the quay."

31

Beorn asked, "The quay?"

"I thought we would sail the treasure, grain and slaves around the bay. They have ships there and we can sail can we not? Unless you relish the march back?"

He laughed, "No, jarl. I do not!"

Once outside it we came upon a wild scene. The families in the port had woken and were fleeing as fast as they could. My men, led by Asbjorn Sorenson and his men, were dealing death to any Saxon who stood. Few did and most fled.

I shouted, "Take all that you can carry and fetch it down to the quay! Arne Four Toes, take six men and choose the best two ships for us to take. Begin to load them."

Gudrun and his men emerged with many sacks. "There is much grain here, jarl! They have had a good harvest."

"Put it on the knarr." He nodded. "The rest of you let see if there is anything left to take."

Gunnar Stone Face came down, supported by Harold Haroldsson, "He took a couple too many blows, jarl."

"Is he hurt badly?"

"He will live."

"Take him to the ships."

He nodded and added, "Rolf Arneson has found much treasure and they are bringing it."

I had five men with me and we moved deeper into the settlement. We had sown confusion and I had no doubt that our numbers would be exaggerated. I wanted to keep them moving. I only had seven men with me now but they would be more than enough. We had done what I wished. We had slaves and we had grain. The weapons and the gold were extras which I would not shun. As we moved further from the sea the houses became poorer. Sven Siggison opened a door and an old couple cowered there. "Leave them!"

We needed the young and the fertile. The young boys would become Viking warriors in time and the girls would bear Viking children. We left the old. As we reached the end I heard the sound of hooves approaching. "Shields!" My men obeyed instantly and we formed a line across the old Roman road. Einar Asbjornson was to Gilles' right and Erik Long Hair to Bertrand's left. The sound of hooves drew closer. I saw shadows moving quickly. They were horsemen. I knew not how many but I knew horses. The first three loomed up out of the dark and I stepped from the line and shouted loudly while waving my sword and shield. I had stepped back between the others before the riders knew what had appeared. I had startled the horses. Two reared and one Saxon could not keep his saddle. The other barely did but his horse bolted away the third spun his horse around as another three riders appeared.

Einar stepped forward and despatched the fallen rider. From his unnatural position, I guessed he had broken many bones and Einar did him a favour. The four riders who remain did not have spears. They saw six armed and mailed Vikings before them. They did not know how to deal with us. One urged his horse forward and raised his sword to hit down. Sven Siggison blocked it with his own shield and then hacked sideways at the rider's leg. The sword bit deeply and the rider wheeled away as his leg pumped blood.

Then a Saxon shouted, "Back! Wait for the thegn and the others!"

I said, quietly, "They have more men coming. Let us back down to the ships and leave."

The three horsemen who remained could only watch, impotently, as we moved back to the quay. We did not turn our backs on them. That tempted disaster. I saw them dismount to tend to their wounded. It was a waste for I knew the man with the severed leg would die. A horseman needs a spear to deal with Viking on the ground. A sword just invites death.

By the time we reached the sea I saw the sun rising in the east. Gudrun and his men were carrying the last of the chests and boxes to the ships. I saw that Arne had picked two tubby Saxons ships. They could hold much but they were slow vessels to sail. They were built to carry bulk short distances and not for long voyages across the empty seas.

"Get aboard! The Saxons come!"

I stood with my five men and we faced the land as the last of the slaves and booty were boarded. In the distance, I heard a horn. It was the Saxons. The thegn had arrived and they were coming.

"Ready jarl!"

I was the last aboard as the two heavily laden vessels began to edge away from the shore. The fifteen mounted and mailed Saxons halted and waved their swords at us. They had no way to follow. The wind was still, generally, from the south and west so that, once we had sculled off from the quay we had the wind behind us. I looked in the bottom of the vessel at the booty we had garnered. There were sacks of grains as well as large clay jugs. I guessed they were filled with some type of liquid. There were a couple of goats and some chickens. The weapons, mail and helmets lay scattered around. They had been the last thing we had taken. Then there were the slaves. I saw that my men had been choosy. The women all had seen less than twenty summers. One was suckling a child; testament to her fertility. Then there were nine children. The youngest looked to be five summers old while the eldest was a girl of ten summers or so. We would keep them rather than selling them. It took until the sun had risen in the sky before we turned the headland and saw Addelam and our drekar. Sven would wonder what we were.

Sigurd and Skutal were on the ship with me. Both were fishermen and good captains. "I want the two of you to choose two men and then you will each captain one of these tubs as we sail to Dorestad. It will save us having to offload the entire cargo of the grain and armour. We will carry the slaves on the drekar."

Sigurd groaned, "It will take forever, jarl!"

I smiled, "You have something else you wish to do? Besides we will be going at the same speed. Perhaps we can sell the two vessels in Dorestad. We have no use for them." Our own knarr, '*Kara*' had been built by us on Raven Wing Island and she was a good ship. We needed no other.

When we reached our ship, I had the slaves embarked. Had there been men then we might had had trouble but they were women and were compliant. The slaves captured at Addelam included two men. One was a greybeard but the other was in his twenties. I saw that he had a bandage around his head and was bound. Harold Fast Sailing shrugged, "He was too noisy and violent. I was all for slitting his throat but Sven said we could get coin for him."

I nodded. "We sail at the speed of those tubs and we had better be quick for I think there are Saxons coming."

Even as the two Saxon ships pulled away I saw the horsemen appear at the top of the cliff. The white horse banner, fluttering in the morning light, told me that this was a band of the king of Cent. He might be a subject king of Egbert but he still ruled. They began to descend the path to the beach. We waited until the two Saxon ships were well out to sea before we left. The two vessels would have to tack and forth. The wind was now from the south and west. Sigurd had been right. It would take a long time.

Chapter 4

We did not reach Dorestad until after dark. I had planned on staying the night anyway. But we would now have to guard our slaves as well as the goods we would sell. We found a berth some way from the main area of business. It helped for we were able to keep a better watch on the vessel. Dorestad attracted many captains. Not all were to be trusted. I went ashore with Harold Fast Sailing, Gilles and Bertrand. While we were away my men sorted the goods and weapons out. We would keep the best and sell the rest.

We made our way to the official who took the charges for our mooring. In days gone by this would have been an imperial official but King Louis had lost some of his power. He had lost the taxes which Dorestad brought. The port was now filled with freebooters such as us. As we walked down the quay I saw Danes, other Norse, Frisians and even a lateen rigged boat. Harold nodded at them. "We will pick up news here. Perhaps even some charts."

"See if you can find a buyer for the two Saxon ships."

"We may not get much for them."

I shrugged, "Whatever we get will be more than had we not taken them. Do not worry what price we get, just so that we sell them."

"Aye lord." He would leave us after we had found a tavern. He knew his way around Dorestad.

"What will we do, lord?"

"We, Bertrand, will also find as much news as we can and perhaps see if there are others who wish to settle in the land by us."

"But why?"

"We are few in number. We need allies. When we lived on Raven Wing Island we sometimes had the crews of three drekar. Now we crew one. Our numbers grow but not fast enough. More of those who are like us will give us security." Sometimes the Norns listen and they laugh. What I heard was the cry of a gull which took flight at our approach. Later I would realise that it was the sound of the Norns.

There were a number of ale houses and what they called taverns. They sold food and drink at exorbitant prices. They could afford to. This was, like Dyflin, one of the few ports were pirates like we were could trade. It was the price we paid. They were careful, however, never to rob us completely. The type of men who used Dorestad would respond

35

violently to such acts. We paused outside one. It looked to be a well-constructed building and unlike the others there were no drunken men lying outside the door. "Now you two listen more than you speak. Do not offer offence. The men who drink in these places are rough and violent. They do not play by rules. Here it is the rule of might and not right."

"Aye, lord." They both looked nervous.

I entered and the conversation ended as they all looked at the new arrivals. Our dress marked us as Vikings and the conversation level rose once more although I saw wary eyes watching as we crossed to the empty table in the far corner. It was the furthest from the fire and the least desirable. I did not mind. It afforded me the opportunity to look at the others in the room.

Harold smiled, "I will stand in the corner, jarl. I will learn more that way and I think I have spied a couple of likely customers for the two Saxon ships. If not I will try some of the other ale houses further down the quay."

We had taken Saxon coins from the warriors we had slain. We had money to splash around. A one-eyed man with an enormous belly came over. I took him to be the owner for he carried a bunch of keys on his belt. "What can I do for you? A bed? Stables? Food? Ale?" he leered at Bertrand, "A young wench perhaps?"

I smiled for Bertrand was embarrassed, "Just food and ale if you please. I put a couple of silver Saxon coins on the table. The best you have."

His eyes lit up greedily. He saw a hen to be plucked, "Of course, my lord! I will be right with you!"

I watched Gilles and Bertrand as they took it all in. Gilles had been to Dyflin with me but this was the first experience Bertrand had had of the seamier side of life. "Do not worry, Bertrand, they look worse than they are. We must look the same to them."

"No, lord, they look like they eat babies for breakfast!" I laughed. That was how most of the world saw Vikings. Our appearance was designed to inspire terror. It worked.

The ale arrived, brought by a young female slave. She looked to be little older than Gilles. She winked at Bertrand, "If you wish anything else then just ask. My name is Agnete."

I gave her a copper penny, "Thank you Agnete. We have all we need."

"Your food will be along shortly."

I looked at the various men in the room. Most were captains, jarls or the equivalent. Their men would be allowed ashore but they would not frequent the same alehouses. The others would be even worse than this one. I saw one who looked to be little older than I was. He was unusual for the rest were gnarled looking men with the weather-beaten faces which spoke long days at sea. These were sea raiders and merchants. Like us I think they would enjoy both. The difference was that we raided less now than we had. This had been our first raid in almost a year.

The food, when it came, was filling. It was a mixture of sausages in a rich bean stew. We had not eaten for almost a whole day and we devoured it voraciously. I waved for more ale after we had finished and was unsurprised when the slave girl asked for more coins. Our two silver coins did not buy much.

As we drank I listened to conversations. There was a great deal about the aspirations of King Egbert. It seemed he saw himself as Bretwalda or High King of Britain. From another table, we heard that the son of the King of Northumbria had been killed by Danes. Neither items of news would aid us but it was useful to know such things. It meant, for one thing, that we could raid Northumbria a little more easily. They had some fine churches and monasteries which were filled with books, ornaments and tapestries which we could sell. That might be something we did when the new grass came. Of course, all of that depended upon the reaction of the King of the Franks. If he wanted revenge for our acts, then we might be fighting for our lives.

I was considering heading back to the ship when the young captain, who looked to be of an age with me, stood with his companion and came over to speak to us. He smiled and held out his hand, "I am Fótr Kikisson and this is my young brother, Folki. We are from Hedeby and you, I believe, are the warrior called the horseman. You are the one who followed the Dragonheart."

"I am but how did you know?"

"I spied the horse around your neck and there are few jarls as young as you. Could we join you?"

"Of course, this is Gilles and Bertrand. They are two of my warriors."

Fótr said, "You are a Frank, are you not?"

"I am."

"It is unusual for a Frank to follow a Viking is it not?"

Bertrand smiled. "There are many of us who do so. We recognise a good leader."

"You learned that from the Dragonheart?"

"I learned many things from him. Would you serve him? If you do, then you will become rich."

"Have you not heard? He no longer leaves his land. He has fought off a band of Danes called the Skull Takers. They are a cult which is led by witches."

I saw Bertrand clutch his cross, surreptitiously. "Any who tries to take on the Dragonheart risks his life. I have never yet met a better leader or a more powerful warrior."

Folki's became serious, "I have heard that he is now cursed. Not only did he and his men slay four witches but I heard he went to the lair of a Norn and fought a dragon. One of his men who was with him had his hair turned white." He shook his head, "No I would not wish to follow someone curse by witches and Norns. I was just curious why you left his service."

"I was told by a witch that my future lay in the land of the Franks and that I was to be a horseman. So far the prophecy has proved to be fruitful."

Fótr leaned forward, "You live in the land of the Franks?"

I nodded, "The Bretons took many of the Franks captive and the land was left empty. We took it over and we have lived there for a year."

"We have heard that the Franks have great riches."

"They do Folki."

"Yet they allow you to live on their land?" It invited an answer. He wanted to know how we managed to do so.

"They are not happy about it. We have had to fight them on more than one occasion. But we are still there and our clan, the clan of the horse, grows."

Folki gestured to his brother with his half empty horn, "My brother here wishes to raid the Franks. He has been told there is a mighty river which reaches deep into their land and you can sail a drekar up it."

"The Issicauna. We leave on a piece of land just to the north of it. We did live on an island but this is a better home. We have farms and the earth is fertile."

The two brothers looked at each other. Fótr said, "We would like to raid the Franks."

I smiled, "A Viking does not ask permission to raid."

"We would not wish to encroach on the land you raid."

"We do not raid the Issicauna. We have just returned from Cent. If you raided, then you would not be upsetting me or my mine but I should warn you that the Franks have citadels and strongholds. The Saxons are easier to raid. They do not take kindly to Vikings in their valleys."

"They are poor! We want to be rich and rich quickly. We have forty warriors and we have a reputation."

"What is your clan?"

"We are the clan of the fox and our threttanessa is the *'Flying Fox'*."

"That is a good animal. It is clever and only the wolf can hunt it. I see now why the Dragonheart did not appeal. He is the wolf."

"Aye. There is that. If we raid, we would visit with you. Would that be acceptable?"

"Come as friends and you are welcome. If the shields are on your drekar then you will have a warmer reception."

Folki laughed, "Aye I know. You already have a reputation. Did I not hear that you and one of your crew fought two Hibernian champions?"

"We did. I was lucky."

"Men make their own luck." He and his brother stood. "We will talk with our men but we may well meet again. Where is this home of yours?"

"It is called the Haugr and is on the east coast of the peninsula the Franks call the Cotentin. There is an island and a causeway close by. The church is ours. That too is protected by the clan of the horse."

"I have a good master. He will know it. I am happy that we met."

After he had gone Gilles said, "Is this wise, lord?"

"We have few enough friends without upsetting new ones. This cannot harm us and, who knows, he may also find a home close by and then we would have neighbours on whom we could rely. This is *wyrd*."

We had another horn of ale each for Harold Fast Sailing came back to join us. "I have much news, jarl. I have sold the two ships." He pointed to a pair of Frisians who raised their horns of ale to us. "I suspect they want them for a little piracy."

Gilles looked puzzled, "Piracy?"

I nodded, "Aye, Gilles. They fill them with warriors and then lure in a bigger pirate. It is like covering a wolf in a sheepskin in the hope that another wolf tries to take it. With two of them they would be even more successful. You bargained a good price?"

"I did. I made them think that we wanted them for the same reason. I also learned much about King Louis. I think I know why we have been left alone. He has had some disasters. The Bulgarians have retaken their land in the east. Hugh of Tours and the Count of Orleans tried to conquer the caliphate of Cordoba. They returned home with their tails between their legs. They were outwitted and out fought. They lost many men. Most importantly he has sons who want more power. It is said that there will be civil war soon. King Louis does not have the men to quash us."

I nodded, "That explains why no Leudes led the men who attacked us. This Philippe of Rouen is keeping his soldiers safe and watching to see which son he follows." I drained my horn and left two copper coins. It would do us no harm to win favour with those who ran such inns. We would be returning to Dorestad and I wanted them to think me generous. We waved our goodbyes and headed back to our ship.

When we returned to the drekar we spent some time telling the others what we had learned. The news about the Dragonheart, his battle with the dragon, and the Skull Takers was common gossip along the waterfront. There were various stories; some were patently exaggerated. Some had had the Skull Takers killing the Dragonheart's granddaughter and wearing her skull. However, they all spoke of '*Heart of the Dragon*' sailing to Syllingar and disappearing in a fog before emerging with Ylva, Dragonheart's granddaughter. He truly was the greatest warrior of our age for I had been in that cave and met the witch. To fight her took a courage I knew I did not possess. How could I begin to compare myself with Jarl Dragonheart? And yet the witch had said I would be greater. I slept fitfully that night for my mind was filled with too many thoughts.

It took all day for us to sell our ships and our surplus. We did not have enough time to buy all that we wanted and so I let the crew who wished go into the taverns and ale houses. I made sure that Arne Four Toes and Beorn Beornsson took charge. They would keep the younger ones under their control.

I sat with Sven and Harold. "The drekar with the Dane, Folki, left this morning. The other captains say he is ambitious." Some said he wishes to be you or the Dragonheart."

"Me, Sven? I have done nothing."

"You have done more than you know but I think it is the fact that we have survived in the land of the Franks unmolested for so long which is the most important. He has a young crew and they have been successful but the lands they raided were poor. He wishes to be rich."

Harold nodded, "The reasons are immaterial. We know that it is because they have not tried to push us back into the sea but I for one believe that you are clever enough to avoid that anyway."

I was not so certain. I thought that we had been lucky. The sacrifice made by Ulf Big Nose and Siggi White Hair had been the reason we had been able to establish ourselves. All that I had done was to cling on.

"We have done well this voyage. We will not need to raid again for a while."

Harold said, "When we do we might consider Cordoba and the lands around it."

"We have raided there before. Portucale and Olissipo will both be prepared for a raid from us."

"Not those cities. There is a river, the Minho, and it travels from the sea deep inland. I met a captain who had supplied Hugh of Tours when they invaded. The land is not part of the caliphate although there are Moors who fight for the town. It has a great church. They have a bishop. But the most important thing is that the roads there are poor and they use the river to transport everything. Even if we did not raid the city we could wait in the estuary and catch ships coming and going."

"It is an idea but we will not need to raid yet. Besides winter is almost upon us."

"Aye, I will need to take the weed from our keel." Sven thought more of the knarr and the drekar than he did himself. He would happily work in all weathers just to make sure that our ships were seaworthy. We had built them ourselves. Jarl Gunnar had died because he went to the land of the wolf to order a new ship from Bolli the shipwright. We had learned our lesson. What we could not make or steal we did without. Sven and Harold had done a good job in designing two of the most seaworthy and fast vessels that I had ever sailed.

The men returned back in a good humour. They had drunk well and filled their bellies. Some had had women. What more could a warrior ask? The disappointment was that they had told the tale of my fight with the Frank. They had exaggerated. The last thing I needed was to have a reputation. When I had defeated the Hibernian champion it had invited challenges from young men. Now that I was jarl would it invite challenges from other clans?

Sven shook his head when he saw that I was unhappy. "They are proud of you, jarl. You cannot keep them quiet while you perform such actions. It is *wyrd*."

He was right and I could not fight it. I would have to accept whatever came my way.

We left for home on the morning tide. After a couple of days' rest the men were happy to row. We had all made trades and purchases. I had some fine bowls for Mary. She would like them and I had purchased the spices she had requested. Selling the golden torc had given me more money that I could spend. I would be taking coin home to give to her. She like accumulating gold and silver. She always said it was for the days when things went awry. She was a careful wife.

The journey home was a difficult one. We had a storm which blew up from the oceans to the west of us. The crew had to row just to stop us being washed up on the Frankish shore. The slaves were terrified. They were Christians and they huddled around the mast, for it looked like a cross, praying that their god would save them. Perhaps he answered their prayers, I know not, for after a whole day and night at sea we saw the welcome sight of the Haugr. We were home. However, the passage to the wooden jetty was also fraught with danger. The whipped water had white caps. It took a skilful captain to negotiate the rocks which guarded our home. Sven had to edge the drekar through the rocks to tie up next to our knarr. '*Kara*' was pulling at the ropes which secured her to the jetty and we could see that the storm had not been kind to her.

As we began to unload the drekar, Harold went to inspect the knarr. "It has suffered damage in the storm, jarl. We will need to put her in our cradle and repair her."

I nodded. That was disappointing. We normally put the drekar there for the winter and used the knarr to trade during the winter months. "Perhaps that is the price we have to pay for such a successful raid. We come back richer. How long will it take?"

"I cannot be certain but I would say at least until Ýlir."

"Then we will have to mount a guard on the drekar."

"Sven and I will take it in turns with the ship's boys. This is our fault. We were so eager to sail that we forgot to put the knarr in the cradle."

I strode ashore leaving Bertrand and Gilles to help my men unload the drekar. I was anxious to speak with Rurik. Our walls had looked intact but that did not mean that there had been peace for my people.

42

Rurik's grin gave me the answer, "A good raid I see, jarl."

"It was and all went well here too?"

He laughed, "I could enjoy being a jarl! Aye it went well. I took some of the boys out riding each day but we saw nothing." He pointed at the scudding clouds above. "The weather has been a better ally to us than we could have hoped. The only roads which are safe to use are the Roman roads. The rest are muddy and slippery."

"Good. That keeps us safe and we have more than enough supplies for winter. We can sit out Ýlir and Mörsugur behind our walls. We have much news." Just then the new slaves began to enter through the gates. Sven had them carry some of our treasure and I saw Gilles and Bertrand organise them. "Are the slave pens empty?"

"Aye."

"Then we will put them there and feed them until we decide who shall have them."

Siggi White Hair had begun a policy of allocating slaves where there was the most need rather than Jarl's Gunnar's way which had given them as favours to warriors who had fought well. I had continued that. The crew liked it. It meant that if they fell in battle they knew that their families would be looked after. They would be given a couple of slaves to farm their land or work in their home. I went to my hall where Mary and Ragnvald awaited me. My son could now stand, even run a few steps, and he tugged at his mother to bring her closer to me. The droplets of rain in the air made Mary stay beneath the shelter of my roof. Her smile, however was a warm welcome.

"Welcome home, my husband. The Good Lord answered my prayers."

I smiled. Her god was always responsible for our success; at least in her mind. "We have slaves. We will need to allocate them sooner rather than later. The slave pen has no roof."

She nodded, "Old Mivki Haroldsson died while you were away. His wife and daughters will need someone to help them."

The old tanner had been ill before we left. "It was his time. We have two men who might do." I would have to yoke them. The older one, Asser, had been subdued during the voyage but Edward, his son had been belligerent. I would yoke them both and see how they got on. Tanning was hard work but necessary. Along with Brigid and her ale and Bagsecg and his forge these were vitally important parts of our daily life.

Mary saw the sacks of grain. Her face broadened into a smile which lifted the clouds, "And we have grain! You have done well!" She kissed my cheek, "You taste of the sea! Bathe!"

I shook my head. What did she expect? We had been at sea for some days. I had learned the right response, "Yes my love."

Chapter 5

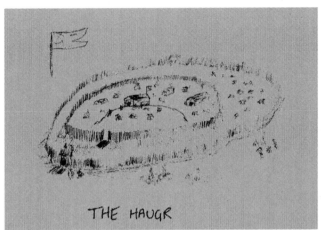

THE HAUGR

We feasted at Yule, through the long nights. The Christians celebrated the birth of their god and life was good. Mary reminded me that our son would be a year old by Mörsugur. When she told me, I frowned. "We are all a year older. What is the significance?"

"My family celebrated such an event."

And so, we made a fuss of Ragnvald. In truth, I did not mind for he was now becoming a child rather than a babe. I could talk with him. I was in constant trouble with his mother for playing too rough with him. "But he will be a warrior! He needs the rough and tumble. When he plays with the other boys he will have to learn to look after himself."

She looked shocked, "He is the son of the lord! He should not play with other children."

"Would you have him stay in these walls and play with women? Would you have him grow into one of your priests with soft hands who cannot defend themselves? He will be a warrior. There are other boys his age. When the weather allows, I would have him play with them."

"But…"

I rarely asserted my authority but I did so that day, "I have spoken!" Then to make it less unpleasant an idea to swallow I added, "And it will keep him from being under your feet."

She accepted my command although I paid for it with a five-day silence. She seemed to think that it would punish me. It did not. At the end, we made up and I think that was when our next child was conceived. Her pregnancy made her worry less about what Ragnvald got up to.

There were other births too. Agnathia gave Rurik a son although he was tiny compared with most of the babies which were born. Rurik did not seem bothered. He smiled, "The women said he was easier to birth and I can feed him up! I will make him strong."

"And what have you named him?"

"Hrolf. If I name him after a warrior such as you, jarl, then one day he might lead his own crew!"

"Hrolf Ruriksson. That is a good name." I gave him a finely made dagger I had taken from the Saxon thegn I had slain. I had planned on giving it to Ragnvald but, with the gold I had from the torc, I decided to have Bagsecg make him one. Until he was bigger it would be as a short sword.

One of my warriors, Bárekr Karlsson came to me. He had taken one of the Saxons as his wife. "Jarl, I would have a farm."

"Aye, that is a good idea. Where do you have in mind?"

"I travelled north and found a bay. It is close enough so that we can take refuge here should our enemies threaten. There is good farmland and we can harvest the sea. My wife's family fished for a living."

I was pleased. I knew the bay well and had often thought it would make a better harbour than the one we used. "That is good and I will give you two of my slaves to work the land for you. They are good men and I thought to give them their freedom. I will give them to you and then you can choose what you do with them."

"You are generous, jarl."

Shaking my head I said, "You have served me well and deserve this opportunity. I ask one thing: have your slaves dig a ditch and build ramparts. We need to defend what we hold." I had said the same to Erik Green Eye when he had taken a bride and moved just north of the Haugr. His farm straddled the road to the old stronghold of Ćiriċeburh. Uninhabited at the moment, it did lie in Neustria.

It was only by little but the land of the horse was expanding. The land appeared as heavy with new life as the women of the clan.

Einmánuður was a time for celebration. It marked the end of winter and the beginning of the new grass. It was when we discovered that Mary was with child. She was not the only one. The longer nights had resulted in most of the women being with child. It was also the time for marriages. Many of my men took slaves as their wives. After three or four moons living as a slave many of them realised that this was their opportunity for freedom and they took it. Our clan was growing.

The well we had started to dig a year since was already much deeper. Now that winter had ended we could send men to work on it once more. It was vital that we had water. We could store food in the rocks beneath the haugr. As Vikings, we knew how to smoke and salt fish and meat. We had barrels of it ready for winter and hard times but if we had no water then we would die. The well drew closer to water each day. In the summer, we would dig pools for the sea to cover. When the hot summer sun got to work, the water would disappear and we would be left with salt. The bay was perfect for salt gathering.

Sven, Harold and their crew took our knarr to Dorestad. Many of the men wished to buy things for their new families. Sven and Harold could be trusted not only with their coin but to buy what they needed at a good price. As the ground had dried out I took Bertrand and Gilles to ride beyond Rurikstad. He had not reported any danger over the winter but I decided to investigate the road to Valauna. Another family, Finni Jarlson and his new bride, had chosen to farm close by Rurik and I wanted them all to feel safe.

We did not wear mail and I rode Copper. Dream Strider and Night Star was busy covering mares. We had had another five foals born over the winter. Soon I would be able to mount all of my men. Only a handful took to their horses as well as I might have hoped but I had an idea that when they grew the children born of a Frankish mother and Viking father might have more natural ability. For the present I was happy. If danger came we could ride to war mounted. I was happy for my clan to fight on foot but our mobility was important.

Now that we knew the road we rode hard and headed for Valauna. My dog, Nipper, acted as our scout. This time we reached the woods which were less than a mile from the Frankish walls and were able to view it. Bertrand had told us that the Franks called their walled homes castles. They differed little from our Haugr. I saw that they had a ditch and a wooden palisade although the bank was fortified with stones. It was a good idea for it would stop the rains from washing away the soil. They had towers at the gates and around the walls too. I saw one stone built building inside the walls which rose above the walls. There was a standard flying there. It was the gryphon.

"Bertrand, what is that beyond the walls? You see, where the standard flies."

47

"That would be the hall of the Seneschal or the Leudes if he is close by. It has walls. There may be a ditch around it too, lord."

I nodded.

Gilles said, "That would be hard to take."

I turned to him, "And why would we need to take it? What would we want it for? It is far from the sea."

Gilles said, shrewdly, "But if we held it, lord, then we could control all of this land hereabouts."

"You are right but with only forty or so warriors that would be beyond us."

As we rode back Bertrand said, "But, lord, if Fótr and his crew joined us then we might have enough."

"We know not if Fótr would relish such a raid and I fear we would lose to many of our men. Your people, Bertrand, have many such strongholds and they have many warriors. We are better, one to one, but they outnumber us. I will choose my battles and this one is not worth fighting. Not yet anyway."

However, he had planted a seed in my mind and I stopped at Rurikstad on the way back. The horses needed resting and I was able to speak with Rurik and Finni. "I worry about your isolation here."

"We have horses, jarl and can reach your walls easily."

I nodded, "Hitherto the Franks have given us warning but what if they do not? I would have you and Finni make your hall into a stronghold." I pointed to the palisade and small ditch which ran around Rurik's farm. "We will make your ditch deeper and use the spoil to make a mound as high as the palisade you have now. The sea is close and there are many rocks. Have your slaves fetch them and then add them to the base. I will have my slaves cut timber for a taller palisade. With wood on top of the rocks and raised mound it will make it hard for an enemy to take this quickly."

"That is all very well, jarl, but we have but two men and our slaves. How could we defend the walls?"

"There will be more who wish to settle here for this is the most fertile of lands. We need to build you a tower which abuts against your hall. If we have an entrance which is only reached by ladder, then your family could shelter within and when the outside walls fall you could fall back here. With a ditch around it and a bridge then you could hold out."

Finni nodded, "Aye and if we had a ditch all around Rurik's hall then it would drain the water. Remember how wet it was this winter, Rurik? Agnathia would be happier without the mud in the hall."

Rurik nodded, "I am convinced, jarl. I have a son now. He needs protection."

And so, the first of our new outposts was begun. It was not completed until high summer for Finni and Rurik had crops to sow and animals to tend but we learned much from its building.

Fótr and the *'Flying Fox'* arrived at the start of Harpa. There were no shields on show. I went to the jetty as he approached. We now had rope buffers to protect ships from damage when they tied up. We had learned from the damage to *'Kara'*. Fótr had told me that he had a good master aboard and it showed in the way the drekar was edged, gingerly around the rocks which guarded our anchorage. I went with Arne Four Toes, Gilles and Bertrand to greet him.

He stepped from his drekar with his arm held out, "See jarl, no shields. It is good to see you." I nodded. He waved an arm at the Haugr. "A fine stronghold. This is a good home. As we approached I could see why you chose it and the approach from the sea is not easy. It would be hard to surprise you."

"Thank you. Will you and your crew be staying the night?"

He shook his head. "We sail at sunset. I am anxious to raid the Issicauna. My master, Formi Formisson, wishes to speak with your captains about the river and I would know where the settlements are."

"Then I will show you my charts. If you wish to copy them then you can do so. Gilles, find Harold and Sven fetch them here. Bertrand, go and tell my wife that we have guests. Come, we will go to my hall and I will tell you all that I know."

My wife had been brought up as a lady and she knew how to entertain. I could see that she enchanted Fótr as soon as they met. She left us to speak once she had seen that he had all that he needed. "You are a lucky man, jarl! She is a lady. I felt dirty just being in the same toom as her."

I nodded, "I know that I am lucky. I am thankful for what I have." I unrolled the map I had copied from one which Aiden the galdramann had made. We had added details to it. I pointed to the features as I named them. "Here is the Issicauna. There is a large settlement and an abbey on the northern bank. Both the Dragonheart and my men have raided there.

If it is slaves you seek, then there is a small settlement on the south bank."

He shook his head, "I do not wish to draw from a well which has been used. I would go further upstream."

"Then you would need to go beyond Jumièges. We raided there. There was an abbey and a walled town. We took much gold but we have not been further upstream. Here is Rouen. It is a major stronghold and the Leudes is there."

"Leudes?"

"Like a jarl or a prince. He is appointed by the king and has great power."

He pointed to a place just down the coast from us. "And here?"

"The river is one the Franks call the Orne. It leads to Caen where they have another stronghold. I have not been there but those that have say it too is strong to be taken by just a pair of drekar. It would need a fleet."

"Then it seems to me that we need to raid between Jumièges and Rouen. If we find nothing, then I will try this other river. When we have raided, I will return here. I would like to add what we learn to your map."

"Would you like to copy the map?"

"I do not read. I will study it and let my master see it. He will add to the information he gathers from your captains." He leaned back. "While my men enjoy your hospitality, I would appreciate a tour of your home. I am impressed. It looks nothing like the homes we have at Hedeby."

I rose, "It is, as you might say, our style. We took what was already here and improved it."

We spent the rest of the day walking around my clan. I took him to the church too. "You allow the White Christ to be worshipped here?"

I nodded, "The Franks are Christians. They are part of my clan. It does not hurt us to let them worship."

"Is not the gold tempting?"

I shook my head, "It is our own gold! My wife gave it to the church. We would be stealing form ourselves."

I could see that he was confused. That afternoon I tried to explain to him our new life and he still could not understand it. Perhaps that was why we were the only Norsemen who had chosen this life. They left before darkness had fallen for Sven had told them of the vagaries of the estuary. "May the Allfather be with you."

That evening I spoke with Einar Asbjornson, Arne Four Toes, Sven, Gilles and Bertrand. We sat around my table and drank some of the wine we had bought in Dorestad. "I like not this raid, jarl."

"It is nothing to do with us, Sven. Personally, I think that Fótr has bitten off more than he can chew for the Franks now watch the river at the mouth. Unless he is very lucky then he will be spotted. The river twists and turns."

"I fear the result of his raid. The Leudes might think it is us."

Arne Four Toes said, "He might but what of it? We do not answer to him. We acknowledge no king and I would not bow to the wishes of a Frankish horseman." He turned to Bertrand, "No offence!"

Bertrand laughed, "None taken, in fact I am honoured that you consider me a horseman the equal of a Leudes."

The debate went on until late. We all had differing opinions. I saw the hands of the Weird Sisters in this. Had we not raided Dwfr then we would not have sailed to Dorestad and never met the Kikisson brothers.

Our new slaves had enabled us to clear more land and to grow more crops. The palisade around Rurik's hall was almost completed. It was as we were returning from a visit, two days after Fótr had left us that Galti, one of Erik Green Eye's young slaves galloped up on a pony. "Jarl, my master has sent me. A party of Franks is heading from the north."

I nodded, "Let us ride." Gilles and Bertrand, like me, had their swords and helmets but we wore no mail. We would have to meet them as we were. I was not as worried as I might have been for Erik would have sent a more urgent message if he thought that we were in danger.

It was only a couple of Roman miles to Erik's farm which was to the north and west of our walls. When we crested the rise, I saw that there were four Franks and they were speaking with Erik. They did not look as though they had come for war. The four of them all wore the same blue tunics. They had the gryphon on their shields. None wore mail but all had a sword.

I reined in next to them and dismounted. Gilles and Bertrand dismounted too. The Franks remained on their horses. I looked at the one who appeared to be a leader. He had a chain and a seal around his neck. Erik said, "They were asking to speak with you." I saw that he had his hand on his sword.

I smiled at him, "Thank you Erik Green Eye." Then I took my helmet off and said to the Franks. "If you wish to speak with us then do us the courtesy of dismounting. I do not relish getting a stiff neck." I suspect they had done so to show some sort of superiority.

I watched as the leader worked out what he ought to do. He turned to his men, "I will dismount." He handed his horse's reins to one of his men.

"There that is better. Now we can speak as neighbours should, face to face. I am Hrolf the Horseman, jarl of this land."

"Jarl?"

"I am the leader of the clan of the horse. You are…"

"I am Hugo of Ċiriċeburh. King Louis has appointed me lord of that town."

"Good. It was sad what happened to it." The Bretons had raided it and slaughtered most of the inhabitants. The survivors now chose to live with me.

"I am here to ask if those who fled now wish to return. We have a lord who is a Frank. They need not the protection of a barbarian."

Erik's hand returned to his sword. He could speak their language as well as any. "Peace Erik, this Frank does not know that we do not like to be called barbarians." I kept my voice even. "However, if he uses it again then feel free to teach him the error of his ways."

"I came in peace!"

"Then keep a civil tongue in your head lest we remove it."

One of his men said, "Lord, this is intolerable! Let me deal with them!"

I held up my hand, "I have tried to avoid bloodshed but each time I speak to a Frank it seems my very presence on this earth makes him reach for his sword." I walked up to the warrior and stroked his horse with my right hand. He watched my face. I drew, surreptitiously, me seax and said, "I will talk with your lord and not his arrogant puppies." My left hand whipped up and held my seax close to his groin, "One more word from you and you will father no children."

"Raymond!" The leader's voice was high pitched. He was young.

The young man glared at me. I shook my head, "I am easily offended young man and I would lose no sleep if I had to gut you like a fish. I would like an apology!"

He said nothing, "Raymond!"

"I am sorry if I caused you offence."

I smiled and sheathed my seax. "There that is better. Now I am more than happy to take you to my stronghold and let you speak with those who lived in Ċiriċeburh but you can ask one now." I gestured to Bertrand. "Bertrand here lived in Ċiriċeburh and was one of the few who survived the attack from the east.. Bertrand, do you wish to return?"

He laughed, "No, lord! You protect the people. King Louis just taxes them!"

"That is treasonous!" The young leader was outraged.

"No, it is not for we do not acknowledge King Louis. I am the lord of the land around the Haugr." I mounted Copper. "Come let us ride to my home. I am thirsty and you need your question answering." I turned to Gilles, "Ride to my lady and tell her we have visitors." I gave him a knowing look and he nodded.

We headed the short distance to the Haugr. I made conversation with the Frank, "Do you know this area well?"

He shook his head. "My family come from the lands further south. This is a little cold for me."

"My people find it warm. Strange is it not?"

"It is."

"Perhaps you need to dress for the climate. For myself I wear a cloak made of a wolf skin in the winter."

"Wolves? Do they have wolves around here?"

"I have not seen any but this was from the land of the wolf north of the land of the Angles and Saxons."

"You killed it?"

I smiled, "A warrior does not wear the skin of something another has slain. It is not honourable."

We had reached my stronghold. The position of the gate meant that we had to ride all the way around before we reached it. I saw the four of them looking first at the ditch and then at the high walls. When they saw the double gate, frowns appeared. This was a well-made stronghold and not just a simple ditch and palisade.

"Did you make this?"

"The knoll was here already and the people had a ditch but we made it something which we could defend." I looked him directly in the eye, "We are here to stay. We have built our walls to last. This will withstand a long siege."

My wife and Ragnvald awaited us. She had changed into her best garment. It was why I had sent Gilles. Mary always wanted to look her best. To me, she always looked perfect but she said I had low standards. We dismounted.

"This is Hugo of Ċiriċeburh. King Louis has made him a neighbour. This is my wife, Mary."

I could see he was taken aback and was speechless. Mary smiled, "I pray you enter my humble home. I have wine and cheese prepared."

They followed her meekly. "Gilles, see to their horses. Bertrand, we may need you but first round up all those who came from Ċiriċeburh. Do not forewarn them of what will be asked."

"Aye my lord!"

The slaves had given them food and drink, when I entered, and Mary was asking them about their families. I took some of the cheese and smeared it on some bread. Alf, one of the slaves, handed me a goblet of wine. We had taken the goblets from Dwfr. I was now used to wine. It did not fill me up as much as ale. With my men, I drank ale and beer but I knew that Mary would have frowned on that before our guests.

Bertrand appeared and I nodded to the wine. He helped himself. When there was a lull in the conversation I said, "If you wish to ask those from Ċiriċeburh if they wish to return to their former home they are outside."

Mary said, "Return?"

I said, "I believe that King Louis believes we hold them as hostages."

It was a guess but when the Frank coloured I knew it to be true. Mary leapt to my defence, "My husband saved them! He fed through their first winter! They would have died without the help of his people!"

Putting my hand on hers I said, "Peace, lady, let them speak for themselves."

Once outside the Franks were all gathered behind Matildhe and her daughters. "Why have we been summoned, lord? We were busy working!"

"I apologise but this lord has been sent my King Louis to ask you something." I turned, "My lord?"

He began to speak. He tried to speak loudly and only managed to sound high pitched, "I am here to offer you your former home once more. I am Hugo of Ċiriċeburh. King Louis has charged me with restoring my home to its former glory."

He was disappointed in the response. Most laughed while a few of the younger men made disparaging remarks. Matildhe held her hand up, "Curb your tongues!" She smiled but there was no warmth in the smile, "We were left defenceless by King Louis, his Counts and his Leudes.

When we appealed for help none came and our men were slaughtered. When we asked for food and shelter we were told that we had to fend for ourselves. This warrior and his clan took us in. We have prospered. This is now our home. King Louis rejected us… now we reject him." Silence followed her words. She smiled at me and then turned, "Come we have work to do!"

They left the four Franks with open mouths. Not one had accepted the offer. I felt proud of my people. This was a foretaste of the future and it was good. Mary smiled too, "Would you care for more wine and cheese?"

He shook his head, "Thank you for your hospitality but we must return home. It is getting late and…" He tailed off lamely.

"Then do not be a stranger. We are neighbours and we welcome all who are our friends." She went back into the hall.

"Bertrand, fetch the horses."

Hugo of Ċiriċeburh looked nonplussed, "I apologise. I thought you a barbarian and I can see now that I was wrong. You dress and speak differently that is all. I hope we can be on good terms but…" He came closer so that he could speak quietly to me. "Jean of Caen lost a leg. His son, Charles, blames you."

"Does his father?"

"No. He said it was combat and these things happen but Charles… Jean of Caen is my overlord. If he orders me to…"

I nodded, "Then pray he does not for Vikings may not be barbarians but once you begin a war you either destroy them completely or pay the price. Do not make that mistake."

They mounted and left. I felt vaguely optimistic. My people had said the right thing and Hugo of Ċiriċeburh had shown that he had a mind. That I could work with.

Chapter 6

Two days layer the '*Flying Fox*' appeared offshore. Fótr and his brother leapt ashore as soon as it was tied up. Both looked excited. "The day we met you changed our lives, jarl! We are rich!"

I smiled at his enthusiasm, "Your raid went well then?"

Folki said, "We found an abbey! The priests did not even defend themselves! They died on their knees, clutching their crosses! If we had stopped there we would have been rich and not lost a man!"

"You raided elsewhere?"

Fótr nodded, "We found a large village. The palisade was small but the Franks fought fiercely. We lost three warriors. We have all their women and children as slaves. My men scoured the land thereabouts and we captured animals as well as the treasure and holy books from another three churches."

"Aye we only left because the horsemen came. They caught two of my men. We headed down river."

Fótr waved a man forward. He held in his hand a small book, a book of the White Christ. "Here, this is for you. It is to thank you for your help."

I shook my head. "I thank you but your men who died paid the price for that. Sell it and give the money to their families."

"They had no families."

"Then share it amongst your warriors. I would not feel it honourable to profit from a raid I did not lead."

Fótr nodded, "I understand. The tide is with us and so we sail for Dorestad and then Dyflin. We hear they pay better prices in Dyflin for slaves."

"But you have further to carry them."

"We also seek more warriors. With our success, we will have many men flocking to follow us." He clasped my arm. "Thank you again, jarl. We will raid again."

Folki laughed, "After we have bought new mail and enjoyed some of our treasure!"

"You could have made more money from the priests you know."

They both looked surprised, "But why?"

"They can read and are worth much more than an ordinary slave. You sell them to lords who wish a scribe or, if you clever about it, you sell them back to their church. Whatever you get for the books you would have got five times the amount for their priests."

"We thought that because they did not fight back they were fair game."

"They are easy game and that is why we do not kill them."

I had left them with something to think about on their long voyage north.

The evenings were growing warmer and the light lasted longer. It was the time of year when the men sat outside my hall drinking Brigid's ale. She made more money in Skerpla than any other month. She and her husband, Erik One Arm, cheerfully sang as they served us. They did not even mind that we did not drink at their hut! It was all profit. I told them what Fótr and Folki had said.

Audun Einarsson asked, "Should we not do as the clan of the fox did and raid the Issicauna? They made a great deal on one raid. If we raided, we would not lose men to horsemen and villagers!"

"Aye and we would have sold the priests!" Arne Four Toes could not keep the disgust out of his voice. He forgot that we had had to learn to do such things.

I shook my head. "They will be alert for raids for some time to come. They will have horsemen riding their roads and ships watching their rivers. We could raid for I do not think we are in danger from the Franks. If we were then we would not have had an embassy from King Louis."

"We had an embassy?"

"Hugo of Ċiriċeburh was sent to deliver a message from the king. He told my wife that the king sent for him. He had served with some distinction under the Count of Orleans in their Cordoban campaign and this was his reward. The Count would have just given him the title but King Louis wanted him to visit with me and ask for the return of his people. We have given him an answer. I suspect it will take him some time to decide what to do next."

Rurik had had his eyes closed but his good ear had been listening, "Then why not raid Cordoba. It is rich. They wear little mail and they have goods, such as spices, silks and jewels that we cannot get elsewhere."

I frowned, "The Dragonheart raided there and it did not end as well as it might."

"You raided there and it went well, for me." Erik One Arm had been rescued from Olissipo.

My silence was taken as acquiescence. It was not but I struggled to find a good reason not to raid. The real reason was that I enjoyed being with my horses now more than I enjoyed raiding. Yet I was a Viking and I led a Viking band.

"If that is the wish of the clan…?"

The cheers answered me. We would be sailing south. Sven said, as he clapped me on my back, "And we take '*Kara*'. I would not go at the speed of a captured ship this time. If we are successful then we fill the knarr."

Mary was philosophical about the voyage. "At least you will not be enslaving Christians. They are worse pagans than you Vikings. Just do not be away too long. Your daughter grows inside of me."

I laughed, "Ah so you are becoming a witch and know what you will have!"

She clutched her cross, "Do not say such things! We had a boy for you and now I believe that God will grant a girl for me!"

I held her in my arms, "I am teasing and I will be away for a month at most. I shall be here when you give birth. That I promise."

We were fully crewed. We had some of the young men who had not been ready for our raid in Cent. We would have a larger crew. Rurik, now that his son was born was happy to come with us. He was keen to become richer. It was Sólmánuður and the days were long and the weather as good as it was going to get. With winds from the west it meant we could have an easy time south and north. As we had a knarr with us we had to rely on the winds. Harold Fast Sailing captained the knarr with Sigurd and Skutal as his crew.

As we sailed past Raven Wing Island I wondered who was jarl there now. That was a closed door but it had been the beginning of our clan and I could not help but remember the island fondly. There I had first learned to ride Dream Strider. There I had learned to become a warrior and it was there that Mary and I had become as one. The Land of the Wolf was special to me but Raven Wing Island held a larger part of my heart.

We did not plan on stopping. We had enough crew to keep watch on watch and sail through the night. Sven kept us close to the coast. We were the only wolves of the sea. Once we passed the Liga or, as the Franks called it, the Liger then the weather became much warmer. Those who had lived in Orkneyjar found it so hot that they lay on the deck naked. They paid for that with burned skin. I kept my body covered for I had sailed these waters before. Each league we travelled was logged on our maps. When we returned, I would copy them out again and then, if we perished, our families would have a legacy. Our clan planned for the future.

We had decided not to raid Olissipo but try the port north of that great city. Harold Fast Sailing had discovered its location while we were in Dorestad. Now it seemed *wyrd* that he had done so. Tui was known to be an important town. It was on the river which marked the border between the Empire and the Cordoba Caliphate. There was a church there and it was an important trading centre for the area. It was on a river and was further inland than either Portucale or Olissipo. More importantly it was used to send ships with goods traded from the north, south to the caliphates of Africa. We would find much that we could steal. As far as we knew no one had ever had the audacity to raid there. Perhaps we would be the first. I hoped that the Frankish attack would have directed their eyes to the land border and they would be careless about their ports. Harold had also discovered that, across the river there was another port. This time it was a Moorish one, Constrasta. Although there was a Roman wall around it we had the choice of towns to raid. As the river was the border it was unlikely that the two towns would aid each other.

We reached a huge estuary towards evening. Sven was loath to risk the rocky coasts further south. We saw no light on the cliffs above us and Sven took us in to a small sandy bay, slowly. We anchored and went ashore. The breeze was coming from the land and we smelled no wood smoke. That meant it was unlikely that anyone lived on the cliffs. The men collected shellfish and we ate well. I sat with Sven and Harold. The knarr had not held us up and I knew it would prove to be invaluable. We examined our chart. The map we had was crude. We would need to make it better. All that we knew was that it was not far to the south of us but we would have to negotiate an unknown river.

"I would not risk the river at night, Jarl."

"Nor would I wish you to. We will leave here before dawn. The captain you spoke with, Harold Fast Sailing, said that the town was some twenty-five miles upstream. You will sail twenty miles and then we will anchor. The men will need a rest. We send scouts to ascertain the difficulties on the river and then sail after dark."

"It Ulf Big Nose would have been the best choice."

I nodded, "Then we will have to send the warrior he trained."

They looked at each other and then Sven said, "But that is you!"

"Aye."

"You are jarl!"

"Is there a better scout?"

"No but..."

"I have been remiss. I should have been training a scout. Beorn Fast Feet has skills. I will take him and Knut the Quiet." I could see that neither was happy. "Would you rather rip the keel from your drekar Sven?"

"We could sail in daylight."

"And they would spy us and either lock their gates or flee. If they locked their gates, then we would lose many men. We cannot afford that. If the Weird Sisters wish to end my life here, far from home, then we can do little about it. Trust my skills and my sword eh, Sven?"

We set sail before dawn and the men had to row against the slight breeze. The knarr struggled to keep up with us for Harold Fast Sailing had to continually tack. It did not matte for the drekar would lie up while we scouted. None of us wore mail yet for the weather was much warmer this far south. I had warned Beorn and Knut that I would be taking them. They saw it as a great honour. Arne Four Toes and Beorn Beornsson tried, as Sven had, to dissuade me. I was resolute.

When we found the river, the entrance was not as wide as I had expected. That was because a sand spit narrowed it. At its entrance, it was but three hundred paces wide. Once we had passed the spit, however, then it widened to over a thousand paces. Sven was happy. We rowed up the centre of the channel with Siggi Far Sighted keeping a good watch ahead. We saw boats but they were fishing boats. They might never have seen a drekar before but they recognised us as a threat and they scurried out of way and their crews headed ashore. I would worry about them on the way downstream. The land through which we were passing looked wild and empty. I could not see them having the means to send a message upstream.

The river narrowed and there was a large island and secondary channel on the eastern bank. Sven nodded. He seemed satisfied. "This is about twenty miles upstream, jarl and the river narrows. If we drop you in the northern shore, then we can hide here in this channel."

"This is good."

We did not take shields and we were not mailed. We needed speed. Our swords and seaxes would have to protect us against any enemies. We slipped ashore in a deeply wooded part of the northern bank. I had already warned my two would-be scouts what I expected of them. They knew to use their noses and ears more than their eyes. I went first and stepped into the cool dark trees which overhung the river. They were taller than the ones higher up the slopes. The river fed them. There was a well-worn path which wound through them; it twisted and turned by trees which grew larger each year. It meant we could not see a long way ahead. Suddenly lighter patches of the woods showed where the land had been cleared to our left but we neither saw nor heard anyone.

As Ulf had taught me, I stopped every fifty paces or so and listened. I also peered towards the river. It looked deep and clear of hidden rocks. The water was smooth. We could get much higher up the river and there would be no danger. We had travelled about four miles when I smelled people. It was a mixture of smoke, human refuse and food. I sniffed the air and pointed to my two scouts. They sniffed and they nodded. I made the sign to move even more carefully and led them forward. The path straightened out. I saw that the trees had been trimmed; perhaps for wood. The walls of Tui lay ahead.

I left the path and moved into the woods. My men followed me. I saw a hill rising before us and, as we reached the last tree, I waved them to ground. Peering around the tree I saw that there was a natural hill and they had made a palisade at the top. Tui did not look as large as I had expected. I heard a bell sound and looked up. I could just make out a stone tower. I guessed it was a church. There must be a service of some kind. I moved carefully towards the river, always keeping under cover and watching where I placed my feet. There was no one nearby but Ulf had taught me to get into the habit of moving silently. It had helped us many times.

When I reached the path again I saw that there was a stone quay. It looked ancient and would probably be Roman. A path rose to the town. There was a gate but it hung from wooden walls and not stone. I had seen enough and I waved my men back down the path. The sun would soon begin to dip to the west. We needed to be back at our drekar before dark. I had seen how we could assault the town.

We were halfway back and I had just stopped to sniff the air and to listen for sounds when I detected men. It was a smell. It was not our smell. There was a perfumed element to it. I sniffed again and detected horse. Lying down I put my ear to the ground and, in the distance, I felt the earth move as a horse walked towards us. I waved Knut and Beorn to either side of the path and I drew my sword. They copied me. They might not be scouts yet but the two men knew how to hide in plain sight. They used the bushes and undergrowth. I smeared earth on the backs of my hands and my face. They did the same.

I heard voices and the neigh of a horse. Without moving my head I swivelled my eyes to peer down the path. I caught the glimpse of some colour approaching. It was at least one man riding a horse. If I could I would let them pass. If it was more than a couple then we might have a problem. Ulf Big Nose had taught me to deal with each problem as it arose. I would do that. Keeping as still as I could I watched the horse and rider change to a horse, a rider who wore a mail shirt, and three men following. They looked to have weapons. I caught the smell of a dead animal and then realised that they had been hunting. I was relieved for I feared they had seen the drekar and would be coming to warn Tui. We would let them pass. As they drew closer I saw that two of the men carried a small wild boar on a spear.

The horse was a fine animal. It was almost pure white. As a horseman, I wanted it. He was passing me when disaster struck. It must have smelled one of us. It stopped, neighed and reared. The rider looked down and began to draw his sword. He had seen Beorn. Even as he opened his mouth to shout I lunged up with my sword. It went under his arm and emerged on the far side of his neck. Knut had quick reactions and he slashed sideways with his sword, ripping open one of the men carrying the boar. Beorn recovered and ran after the warrior who had turned and run down the path. I advanced towards the second boar carrier. He had drawn his weapons and was ready to fight me. Knut ended his life quickly with a thrust to the back.

I grabbed the horse's reins. The last thing we needed was for the horse to drag the body into Tui. I spoke quietly to it as I pulled the rider's foot from the stirap and his body fell to the ground. "Knut, take his mail and search him. Put the weapons and mail on the horse. When Beorn returns, you can carry the boar back to the drekar." I tied the reins to a branch and, when Knut had stripped the body I dragged it the few paces to the river and dropped it in. The current would take it to the sea. I did the same with the other two bodies by which time Beorn had returned.

"He is dead. I am sorry he saw me."

"Do not worry. It was *wyrd*. Help Knut with the boar. I will lead the horse." I saw that the sun was setting. "Come, we must hurry."

When we reached the body of the warrior Beorn had slain I dropped him into the river. The sun was a red glow to the west when we reached the island. I whistled. A whistle sounded in return and then the drekar began to cross the river. I took the saddle from the horse. It was tempting to take it back for it was a magnificent beast but I feared it might cause us too many problems. The wonderfully decorated leather saddle would have to be the only trophy I took home. The drekar pulled up and I said, "Give a hand to carry the boar and these weapons."

Arne Four Toes said, "You had time to go hunting?"

As Knut handed him the weapons he said, "You ought to scout with the jarl, Arne. It would be an eye opener."

While the boar was carried aboard I took off the halter and reins and slapped the horse on the rump. It headed down stream towards the sea. I suspected that it would eventually return home and I assumed that would be Tui. By then it would be too late to alert the men in the town. As we pushed off I went to the stern and waved for Harold to come to the bow of the knarr. "The river has no rocks. Stay in the centre. There is a stone quay. I saw but two small ships there."

He waved and Sven said, "Is it far?"

"You were right in your estimate. It is just over four Roman miles."

I went to don my mail as did Knut and Beorn. The rest of the crew already had their war faces on. By the time I was ready we had passed the place where we had ambushed the warriors. We sailed into darkness and Siggi Far Sighted kept a good watch. The bends were gentle ones. This was neither the Issicauna nor the Liger. I smelled the Moorish town to steerboard and knew that we would be close to Tui soon. I still did not know what sort of watch they kept. Whatever it was we would have to deal with it. I was confident in the men I led.

When Siggi signalled to head away from steerboard I knew that we were close. As we turned the bend in the river I saw the lights from the buildings. They were tiny but showed that we were close. I walked down the centreboard and one in every two men rose. The others would row until we reached the quay. The twenty who followed me would be the ones who would gain us entry not this border town. We ghosted to the stone quay. They had neither watch nor light. There may have been men on the two ships which were tied up but I could not tell. As soon as we touched the stone I leapt, with Siggi Far Sighted, on to the stone quay.

While he tied up the drekar I ran towards the two ships which were tied up. Gilles and Bertrand were right behind me closely followed by Rurik One Ear and Arne Four Toes.

I ran to the farther of the two ships and leapt aboard. Two men rose, sleepily. They were Moors. I did not need help. In two blows they were dead. I stepped off the boat and saw that Arne and Rurik had dealt with the other. My men were waiting for me. I raised my sword and led them to the gate. There was a ditch but they had left the bridge over it. Einar Asbjornson and Erik Long Hair had brought their bows and they ran with me. I saw shadows moving across the top of the gate. We halted, in the dark, forty paces from them. Erik and Einar took aim and their arrows struck the two sentries. They fell, with a dull thud, into the town. We did not have long. The alarm would soon be given. We ran across the bridge. Bertrand and Gilles held Gilles' shield for me. I stepped on it and they lifted me into the air. I grabbed the top edge of the wood as I heard a cry from within. The alarm had been given. I dragged myself up.

I saw that there were two men running towards me from the tower to my right. I swung my shield around and ran towards them. The fighting platform was just wide enough for two men but the two who ran towards me had no shield. I did. One swung his pike at me. My shield took the blow and I kept moving. He fell, screaming, to his death as my shield connected with his body. I rammed my sword into the middle of the other. His falling comrade had stopped his swing from making contact with me.

I turned and saw that Bertrand and Arne Four Toes were leading Gilles and Erik Green Eye down to the gate to open it for the rest of my band. I clambered down the ladder and felt something strike my back. Whatever it was had been heavy. Luckily my shield had saved me again. I stepped to the ground and saw four warriors with spears and shields run towards me. Arne Four Toes appeared at my side. We locked shields as the four ran at us. One spear hit my shield while a second glanced off my helmet. I swung my sword across the faces of the four and they recoiled. Perhaps they had expected to be lucky with their blows. As they stepped back Arne and I stepped forward and lunged under their shields. I hit one in the groin. He fell wriggling and writhing to the ground. Arne's caught one in the knee. He too fell. There was a roar behind me as Gilles and Bertrand opened the gate. The two men who were stood before us made the mistake of looking beyond us at the horse of warriors who emerged through their gates. They died.

I pointed with my sword, "Arne, take men left!"

"Aye jarl. You ten, with me!"

"Rurik, take men right!"

"Aye jarl, you with me!"

"The rest follow me. There is a church and, I am guessing, a hall. They are our targets!"

Tui was not large but they had some buildings which had two stories. When people began hurling things at us I said, "Asbjorn Sorenson. Take two men and clear these houses."

The warriors who had fled us had joined others and were now standing outside the church. There were no openings through which they could hurl objects but there were six men at the top of the bell tower. They had bows and sent arrows our way.

"Shields!"

We held up our shields as we ran at the men standing before us. They had spears and shields but no mail. Gudrun Witch Killer led ten of my newer warriors and his oathsworn to attack them. I looked around the square. There was a hall but the door gaped ajar. The warriors had come to defend the church. As the last of the defenders were slain I shouted, "Now, Gudrun! Break down the door."

Karl Anyasson and Beorn Tryggsson both had axes and they ran at the barred door. They began to hack at it. Suddenly something was thrown from the top of the tower. It was boiling water. Had my men not been wearing helmets it might have caused mortal wounds. As it was the liquid scalded both their hands and their faces. Erik Long Hair and Einar Asbjornson appeared and sent arrows at the tower.

Gudrun was angry and he took the axe dropped by Karl and began to hack at the door. In five blows it gave way and, brandishing the axe, he led his men inside. I said to Karl and Beorn, "Get back to the ship. Sven has some of Aiden's salve. It will ease the pain."

"We can still fight!"

"No, you cannot! Now obey orders. You can help Sven and Harold."

Even as they left two bodies were pitched from the top of the tower as an enraged Gudrun wreaked revenge on those who had scalded his oathsworn. I entered the church. It had linens and candlesticks as well as fine plate on the altar. I now knew of such things from the church of my wife.

"Take those objects back to the ship. Bertrand and Gilles, come with me." As we left I saw the priest's butchered body on the floor. His head had been severed by Gudrun Witch Killer. Rurik and Arne appeared with their men. Their swords were bloody. "Many escaped through another gate. They have fled north."

"Then we can expect company. Rurik bring your men with me. Arne, you and your men search the houses. Gudrun and his men are dealing with the church."

Once inside the hall I could see that the lord and his men had left it suddenly. I had not seen a lord amongst the warriors were fighting. He must have fled. My men knew how to search. While some checked the contents of chests others went to less obvious places such as hidden cavities beneath the wooden floor. I knew that we would not find a great deal. Neither the lord nor his lady were to be found. They must had left as soon as the alarm was given.

I turned to Rurik, "Did you find any horses?"

He shook his head, "No, jarl, the stable was empty."

"Come, let us take what we have." I was about to order them to set fire to the hall when I realised that would alert other enemies nearby. We needed to escape before help came. "Gilles, Bertrand, round up the men. Head back to the ships."

It took some time for my two men to find all of the warriors. The now empty town was looted. Warriors returned laden with pots, pans, fine clay pots and all manner of cooking utensils. Others had hams, cheeses and even a couple of fowl. By the time we were ready to sail, it was almost dawn.

"Harold Fast Sailing, sink these two dhows."

"Aye jarl. They were laden with copper and iron ore. We have loaded it on the knarr. Bagsecg will be pleased. There was also a chest of silver."

With what we had taken from the church we had a fine haul.

"Let us leave!"

The current and the wind would take us down stream. My men would not need to row. They took off their helmets and opened the jugs of wine they had found. There was just enough to go around and not enough to make them drunk.

Sven shouted, "Siggi Far Sighted! To the mast head. Keep a look out ahead."

As the agile ship's boy leapt up the sheets and stays Sven said, "I would not have us ambushed by ships downstream. This raid has gone well, jarl and we both know how the Norns like to spin."

"You are right. Until we see the Haugr let us be cautious."

Daylight came and we saw the town of Constrasta to larboard. We had passed it in the dark when we had headed upstream and now I saw that we would have been foolish to try to take it. This had a well defended stone wall. It did, however, look to be a better target than the one we had taken. The current was sluggish but I did not want to have my men row. Who knew when we might need the again. The other reason I did not use the oars was because we the knarr behind. It was barely keeping up with us as it was.

"Jarl what about this boar? Do we eat it?"

"Raw?" I know you like your food Gunnar Stone Face but let us wait until we can cook it. If it bothers you then skin and gut it. When we stop this night, it will be ready to cook."

He happily began to skin the beast. It was not the largest boar I had ever seen but we would all have hot food. Others gathered around to offer Gunnar advice. "The jarl has appointed me as butcher! Let me do it my way!"

Siggi suddenly shouted, "Jarl. On the bank. I can see laden donkeys."

He pointed to the Cordoban bank. We ran to it. As we turned a bend I saw eight donkeys. They were escorted by four drovers and ten soldiers. They were Moors. At the rear were eight men. They looked to be Franks. They were chained and were guarded by two enormous warriors. As we passed the Moors turned and pointed at us.

"Siggi, tell me what they do!" As we turned another bend they disappeared from view. "Sven, take in some sail. I would have us stop soon."

He looked to question me but thought better of it.

"Jarl they keep coming."

"Good." I turned to my men. "We can add to our gains. We will ambush these Moors. There are but twelve warriors. I know not what is on the donkeys but if there are ten guards then it must be worth guarding."

By the time we had slowed enough to pull into shore we had travelled some distance. Harold pulled the knarr in ahead of us and we disembarked. I took twenty warriors, deeming that to be enough. The rest were left aboard to guard the ship. The eastern bank was almost exactly the same as the western bank. There was a trail passing through the trees. The difference was that here they had cleared some sections of wood and that had opened the river in places. We waited beyond one such opening. My men were spread out on either side. I had Beorn, Arne Four Toes and Rurik leading the men who would fall upon the guards at the rear. I kept the rest with me. I wanted no one to spring the trap prematurely.

I could not understand their words but I heard the guards talking as they headed towards us. I would have gambled a gold piece that they were talking about the dragon ship. I doubted that any would have seen such a vessel before. I could also smell them. They did not smell like Franks nor did they smell like us. Ulf had said that the way a man smelled depended upon the food he ate. He had the ability to differentiate between Frisian and Dane, Saxon and Frank. My sense of smell had improved but Ulf had left us too soon. I had still had much to learn.

We were all well-hidden. I had a branch and leaves before my still face. I still had a blackened face from the previous night and I stared down the trail, confident that I would be hard to see. Four warriors now led the column and the rest were spread down the flanks. Obviously, the sight of our drekar had alarmed them. The guards had helmets and a mail vest. Their arms were bare. Their helmets had a nasal and a plume. Their shields were smaller than ours but each had a point sticking from the boss. Four of them, the ones who led, were as black as night while the others, from what I could see were of a lighter hue. I did not know whence these warriors came.

I waited until the first four were level with me. I was swinging my sword as I stepped out and took the two paces to the trail. Bertrand and Gilles were with me. For a big man the leader had quick hands and his sword was out in an instant. On the other side Sigtrygg Rolfsson also stepped forward and swung. My sword was aimed at the Moor's middle but his shield came between us. His own sword lunged at my face. I brought my shield up and then punched. The Moor reeled. I heard a shout as Sigtrygg was wounded. Bertrand's blade found flesh and the second warrior crumpled to the floor holding his stomach.

Without turning I said, "Leave this one to me! Get the drovers and the other guards."

My opponent roared and brought his sword overhand. He was a bigger warrior than I was and I dropped to my knee. My move confused him. He was committed to the blow but I was not where he aimed. He hit my shield and continued to fall. My right hand reached the ground and I left it there as he fell forward and impaled himself upon my blade. He was such a large man that it was his own weight which killed him. I pushed his body from my sword and stood.

Sigtrygg was holding his side, "Where are you hurt?"

"The bastard punched me with the shield. The point went into my shoulder!"

"Get back to the ship. Karl the Singer, strip these bodies and take their mail, helmets and armour to the ship."

Sigtrygg added, "Aye and their shields!"

I hurried down the trail. The Moors had fought harder and better than the men of Constrasta. My decision not to raid their town was becoming better by the moment. "Get the donkeys to the knarr. Let us see if we can get them aboard."

Rurik said, "And if we cannot?"

"Then kill them and we will have donkey meat to go with the boar!"

I saw that the Franks were on their knees. No doubt they expected to be slain too. I surprised them, "And get these Franks aboard our ship. Take off their chains when they are aboard."

Chapter 7

"I am Alain of Auxerre, lord. I would thank you for saving us from a life of slavery on a galley but I do not know what you intend. Your words suggest you are a Frank but your ship that you are a Viking. Which is it?"

Bertrand snapped, "Having been rescued it behoves you to be a little less demanding in your questions!"

Alain of Auxerre smiled, "Now you are a Frank! From your accent, I would say from the Cotentin! This is a curious mix. To answer you I would say that I have already worked out that you either mean to spare us or sell us in the Dyflin slave market. Can I say that both are preferable to what the Moors intended and so I am happy that I live?"

"Peace Bertrand. You are right, Alain of Auxerre. Before I give you my judgment I would have you tell me your story. We have some time before we reach the sea and then you may have to row." I smiled, "Not as a galley slave but to preserve all of our lives."

He nodded and smiled. "You are the most civilised Viking I have ever met. However, as the rest were trying to either kill me or take my manhood you did not have much to beat. We served Hugo of Lyons. He hired us to be his mounted horsemen. He seemed affable and he said the right things. We followed the Count of Orleans." He shrugged, "We should have left them before we even reached the border. None of them knew that they were doing. Had the Moors had men waiting we would have been slaughtered as we crossed the border. Our lords and masters kept a poor watch on the camp and it was only by luck that we reached the Caliphate intact. Then it became worse. They did not advance and allowed the Moors to bring a great army to meet us."

"But surely you had Frankish horsemen! They could beat the Moors." Bertrand thought his former people were being criticised.

"You would think so but the Moors used archers both mounted and on foot. They made the sky dark. Lord Hugo decided, after half a day of enduring arrows that he would redeem the honour of the Imperial army. He led us and his oathsworn in a charge towards the heart of the enemy."

"He was, at least, brave then?"

Alain of Auxerre and his men laughed. "We wore no mail and so he sent us first saying that we would draw the sting and would travel faster because we had no mail to slow us down. He and those that wore mail would form the second wave."

I shook my head, "Surely he did not believe that?"

"I doubt it. He saw this as a way to get closer to the enemy. We were expendable. He had hired thirty of us. The ones you see here are the only survivors. We were lucky. The Moors hit our horses and took us prisoner." His face darkened. "I watched my young brother as he was gutted like a fish. He lay helpless on the ground. I could not save him. The Moors are butchers. I am glad you slaughtered them but my own people are worse. They withdrew to their camp and then slunk off home. It was as though we did not exist."

I saw my men looking in disbelief at the Frank's words. Leaders did not abandon their men. The silence was broken by Siggi Far Sighted, "Captain, I see the sea!"

"Take to your oars."

I nodded to the Franks. "If you would take an oar. We do not have far to sail. There is a beach north of here and we will feed you well. We will speak, Alain of Auxerre. I have heard your words."

The sea was strong enough to force us to row. I saw '*Kara*' as she struggled to keep up with us. I hung a lighted brand soaked in seal oil from the steerboard rail to help Harold Fast Sailing stay in touch with us. It was almost dark as we anchored off the beach we had used just two nights earlier. Gunnar Stone Face was keen to cook the boar and the two donkeys we had been forced to slaughter. Although we had no wine left we still had two barrels of beer we had not broached. We opened them.

Alain and his Franks busied themselves gathering wood from the beach. I decided that if they ran off I would not pursue them. I felt sorry for them. I had a sneaking suspicion that I knew who their lord was but I said nothing. The food was tasty and all the more welcome for the time we had gone without food. After the beer, we lay on the beach; we were replete.

Alain of Auxerre was speaking with his men. He strode over to me, "Well, lord. Have you made up your mind yet? We have enjoyed your food and your ale but now we wish to know our fate. We are resigned to whatever you decide."

I nodded. I looked around at my men's faces. I had served with them long enough to know their thoughts. They reflected mine. There was only Bertrand who appeared to be a mystery. "No, Alain of Auxerre, we will not be selling you into slavery."

My men erupted and banged dagger handles on stones.

I shook my head. "You are brave men and have been ill served by your leaders that should not happen. I give you two choices. "We are sailing to the Cotentin and I can land you at Ċiriċeburh if you wish. There is a new lord there. However, if you wish I can offer you a place in my warrior hall at our home, Haugr. We have horses and we would welcome Franks who have your courage. It is your choice. If you choose Ċiriċeburh I will not be offended. Many men would choose their own people."

"That is a kind offer, lord and I am surprised. We would speak amongst ourselves for we are of one company."

"Of course."

Bertrand came over to me and said, quietly, "Do we need these mercenaries, lord?"

I took him to one side. "Have they offended you, Bertrand? Their story spoke of honour."

"I know not but…" he shook his head, "I know not."

"They will not replace you, Bertrand. You were the first Frank to join our band and that can never be undone."

He nodded and bowed his head. I think I had shown him why he thought as he did.

Alain stood, "We have spoken, lord. We would join you. However, my men have never fought for a Viking before. Do you pay us as hired swords?"

My men laughed and Rurik One Ear said, "You can swear an oath to the jarl if you wish but we all share in what we can take. If the clan is successful, then we all benefit."

I nodded, "I would make you captain of my horsemen."

"Then we are happy! What is the name of the clan?"

"We are the clan of the horsemen. You join a unique band of warriors."

Now that they were part of us my men treated them differently. They came over to speak with them and to discover more about them. We had taken others into our clan before, Bertrand was one example as were Brigid, Mary and the others. The difference was that these were men grown, and warriors. There was a difference.

Alain came to speak with me. Bertrand and Gilles made to move away. Mindful of Bertrand's attitude I said, "You two stay. You are as close as hearth-weru to me. I would have you listen."

"Do we call you lord or jarl?"

I shrugged, "It matters not to me. Gilles and Bertrand call me lord but my men, jarl. It means the same and there is respect in the title which does me honour."

He nodded, "We are Christians." He said it as a statement. "But I suspect you know that. I do not think that you are Christians."

"Bertrand is and many of our women are. We have a church at home. However, you are the first warriors who are Christians and I would ask you, to get a clear answer, does your religion make you poorer warriors?"

"How do you mean?"

"Your White Christ tells you to love your fellow man and to turn the other cheek. We are Vikings and if you strike us then you had better have somewhere safe to hide for we will find you and kill you."

He laughed, "I like you, lord! You are honest and I have not met that quality in the lords I have served before. When I fight, I aim to win. If you order me to take prisoners, then I will. If not, then they will die. The men we fight will be trying to kill me. I will not let that happen."

I was relieved. I had often wondered at the resolve of Christian warriors. In my experience, they became weaker when they followed the cross. "And your men are the same?"

"More so since we lost so many of our friends."

The next day I had Arne Four Toes rearrange the oars. We spread out the new men to permanent positions. We also taught them a chant. It helped make us one crew. Karl the Singer chose the one about me. We had not used it for some time. Siggi White Hair's death had made his death song our chant of choice. Now he began the one which told my story. It had changed a little since it had first been written. As with all songs and sagas it grew as time went on.

The horseman came through darkest night
He rode towards the dawning light
With fiery steed and thrusting spear
Hrolf the Horseman brought great fear

Slaughtering all he breached their line
Of warriors slain there were nine
Hrolf the Horseman with gleaming blade
Hrolf the Horseman all enemies slayed

With mighty axe Black Teeth stood
Angry and filled with hot blood
Hrolf the Horseman with gleaming blade
Hrolf the Horseman all enemies slayed
Ice cold Hrolf with Heart of Ice
Swung his arm and made it slice
Hrolf the Horseman with gleaming blade
Hrolf the Horseman all enemies slayed

In two strokes the Jarl was felled
Hrolf's sword nobly held
Hrolf the Horseman with gleaming blade
Hrolf the Horseman all enemies slayed

The clan all cheered the horseman's skill
Black Teeth was a jarl whom Hrolf did kill
His place in the clan was now assured
Him, his horse and his powerful sword

Hrolf the Horseman with Heart of Ice
Hrolf the Horseman with Heart of Ice
Hrolf the Horseman with gleaming blade
Hrolf the Horseman all enemies slayed

Hrolf the Horseman with Heart of Ice
Hrolf the Horseman with Heart of Ice
Hrolf the Horseman with gleaming blade
Hrolf the Horseman all enemies slayed

When Sven gave the order to cease rowing I saw the new warriors asking my older crew about the events which had prompted the saga. My actions spoke more than the words of the chant. They told of our resolve. Odds meant nothing to us. It took another day and a night to beat up the coast to our home. The knarr held us up but I knew that it would be worth it for she was heavily laden with many goods. As we passed Ċiriċeburh I stood with Alain at the steerboard side. I pointed to that recently rebuilt stronghold. "You have not yet sworn an oath to me. If you and your men choose not to, then that is the nearest Frank to us. If you choose not to follow me then I will have my men take you there."

He smiled, "I know not what you think of us yet, lord but I can tell you now that once we give our word we do not break it. We are warriors and not fickle Frankish lords who seek power and land." I nodded, "We come to you, however, without weapons and without armour."

"I know. We have mail we took from the Moors. We have been successful and our blacksmith, Bagsecg Bagsecgson, has the helmets and mail we took from our enemies. You are welcome to that." I drew my sword. "This is Heart of Ice and was made by Bagsecg's father. Bagsecg is his father's equal. If the weapon you have is not good enough for you then, for a price, he will make you another."

I handed the blade to the Frank. "This is a good weapon. It is well balanced and the blade looks well made."

"It will not bend and it keeps its edge longer than most. I know not the secret of the steel but our smith does."

Arne Four Toes had joined us. "Jarl I have been thinking of these new warriors. Will they fight in the shield wall?"

It was a good question. "I suspect they will have to. That will be your task Arne to teach them and they can teach you and the others how to be horsemen and fight from the back of a horse as I do."

"You fight from the back of horses?" Alain of Auxerre's voice was filled with surprise.

"Were you not listening to the chant? Why do you think I am called Hrolf the Horseman? We have surprised your countrymen many times when we have done so. We are a new kind of Viking. Your coming was *wyrd*."

"*Wyrd*?"

"It was meant to be. The spirits have decided this."

"Like fate."

I shrugged, "It may be but *wyrd* is the word we use. You will have to learn of our customs and our beliefs. You do not need to believe them but you need to understand them for they make us what we are."

We had just turned south and Rurik had joined us. He had heard the last part of the conversation, "I cannot wait for them to meet Jarl Dragonheart and his Ulfheonar."

"Ulfheonar?"

"Wolf warriors. Many men believe they are men who change into wolves. I fought alongside them and I can tell you that they are men but not normal men. These are the finest warriors I have ever met."

Rurik nodded, "Aye they can appear and disappear in the night. They are the deadliest of killers. If they fight an enemy, they can fight many times their number. Aye, Alain of Auxerre, if you meet Ulfheonar I hope that they are on your side. If not, then you will be a dead man walking."

I was not certain if Alain believed Rurik's words but over the next months he and men heard the story so many times that I think the truth of it sank in.

There was great rejoicing at our return. The booty we brought was most welcome. My men gave the pots, linens, combs, needles, bowls and other such gifts to women who rewarded them with smiles, hugs and kisses. It was only when the knarr and the drekar were emptied that we realised what we had. The donkeys had been carrying the greatest prizes. They contained much treasure taken from the Franks after the battles. We found coins with King Louis and his father, Charlemagne, upon them. We also found spices too. They were more valuable than the gold and we would not trade them. They were shared out amongst all the families. The donkeys which had survived were kept for use in the Haugr and to carry goods from the jetty to the halls of my stronghold.

As soon as we had eaten I gathered the new warriors around me. The rest of the clan formed a circle around them. "Today we have eight new warriors who will be joining us. They are going to swear an oath. This will not be the blood oath of a hearth-weru. It will be an oath to defend me and the clan. When they tire of us," I smiled, "then they can ask to be released from that oath. We hold no prisoners here in the Haugr." I took out my sword. "This sword has the cross of your White Christ within it. I ask you to swear on this sword. It is a symbol of our people."

They each came in turn, knelt, held the sword by the blade and swore their oath. Alain of Auxerre and Theobald the Fair held it so tightly that it cut their palms. That pleased my warriors. The gods had made it a blood oath. Even the two Franks recognised the significance of the blood. It was a warm night and they celebrated by drinking at Brigid's ale house and then sleeping under the stars. I paid for the ale. We had profited greatly from our raid.

That evening as I sat with Mary and my son I could see that she was pleased. "When you said that you were going raiding again, my husband, I thought it unnecessary. This day has proved me wrong. I have never seen the women so happy. The men all returned home and the wounds they suffered will heal. The new men are Christians and that is good. It was a Christian thing you did. I am proud of you my husband."

"You mean Vikings cannot be kind? I thought you, of all people, would have seen the kindness of Vikings."

She smiled, "I will not argue with you husband and spoil the moment. I will say that the clan are happy. When you were away I took it upon myself to visit with the families and to speak with the matriarch in each home. They approve of all that you have done. I know not how you manage to do so for you were low born. Perhaps it is in your nature."

I laughed, "No, I am not insulted, my love. I know you mean no offence." I kissed her. "Tomorrow I will take new men to show them our land."

"Where will they live?"

"They can build their own home. Our slaves will help."

"Good."

The first thing I did was to take my new men and let them choose their own horses. The looked enviously at my three favourites, Dream Strider, Copper and Night Star. They were the only ones I would not let them have. They chose the three we had taken from Jean of Caen's son and the next largest horses. They each picked a helmet with a nasal from those which Bagsecg had not melted down and they wore the mail shirts. Although they picked a sword each they asked Bagsecg the price of a newly made one.

He smiled as he told them the price. "Do not worry about the price. When you raid with the jarl you will make more than enough coin." He swept a hand around the stronghold. "Look at what the warriors wear. They have golden horses about their necks. Their swords are well made and few of the older warriors wear second hand armour. They pay me for mail such as the jarl wears. Be patient."

With Gilles and Bertrand I led the most warriors on horses that I had ever done. There were eleven of us. Gilles asked, "Should I bring your banner, lord?"

"Not this day. We will wait until my new warriors have shields with the clan herkumbl upon it."

"Herkumbl?"

I pointed to the horse on the helmets of Gilles and Bertrand. "It is normally a sign of the clan on the helmet but we use it for the same sign on the shields. Most Vikings use their own emblem on their shield. Many of my men choose the sign of the horse. As you are my first true horsemen I thought it appropriate."

Alain nodded, "That is good." He smiled, "What is the word? It is *wyrd*!"

"We will make a Viking of you yet."

We headed for Rurik's stronghold. His slaves had not been idle and it had been finished while we were away. It would provide a refuge which would hold out until we could reach them. Alain of Auxerre was impressed and said so as we headed towards Valauna.

"We do not know this part of the world. Our home is in Burgundy, far to the east. This looks to be a gentle, fertile land."

"It is. The Frankish castle we visit has an uneasy peace with us. I wounded their Seneschal in single combat and his son, Charles Filjean bears me a grudge."

"It was fair combat, lord?"

"It was, on horseback."

He looked at me with admiration in his eyes, "Then you must have skill. We thought we had skill when we faced the Moors but they were agile. They outran us and used their arrows to great effect."

"My men are skilled archers. I have a bow from the far north which can penetrate mail."

"That sounds like the bows the Moors used; or some of them at least."

We were half way through the woods when Copped neighed and Nipper's hackles went up and he growled. I drew my sword. "There is danger. Keep a close watch."

We did not move but waited. Whatever was coming would be coming down the trail. I saw that it was horsemen with blue kyrtles and shields. The gryphon on their shields told me that it was a patrol from Valauna. I said quietly to Alain of Auxerre, who was now behind me, "You may get a chance now to see the men who seek my death."

The Franks were unaware of our presence until they turned the bend in the trail and saw us waiting. Their hands went to their weapons. I sheathed my sword. I recognised the rider who led them. He now wore mail. It was Charles Filjean. "Unless you would have more blood on your hands keep your weapons sheathed."

"What are you doing in my forest?"

"I thought it was King Louis'?" I saw that I had nonplussed him, "But it matters not. I come and go as I please. Today we do not hunt but, as I told your father, I hunt where I choose."

He had a scowl on his face and he did not move.

"How is your father, by the way?"

"He is a cripple now and it is your fault!"

"If a man fights another he risks death or injury. All warriors know that. If you do not wish the risk, then become a priest."

"I am not afraid of you!"

I smiled, "No, but you would not fight me, would you? The first time we met you fled like a frightened doe and the second time you tried to kill me while I fought your father." I leaned forward and said quietly, "You have no honour."

His face reddened. He had been embarrassed before his men. He had but six with him. He neither could nor would do anything about the insult. He seemed to see Alain and his men. "I see you have hired renegade Franks! Do you not have enough warriors of your own?"

Alain's voice was cold as steel, "Lord let me rid you of this pup."

"Peace Captain." I pointed to the young lord. "Do not insult my men. Now leave or we will make you and if we do then you leave without horses!"

For a moment, I wondered if I had pushed him too far. He jerked his horse's head around but gave a parting shot, "And the Leudes of Rouen has now heard of you. Those men you sent to raid his lands displeased him. You are fortunate that King Louis has him busy dealing with other traitors. When he has time, he will deal with you and I shall be there to see it."

As they rode off Bertrand said, "That is not fair, lord. You did not send Fótr and his men."

"No but I will not explain myself to him. Come the conversation has left a bad taste in my mouth. Let us see where this trail to the west leads." We found it emerged some two miles west and we found the road from Ċiriċeburh to Valauna. We rode north and then headed east. "Tomorrow we will try a journey north to Ċiriċeburh. You will find that lord less unpleasant than the one we met today."

Chapter 8

Alain and his men had already begun to build their hall. They had started as soon as I had given them permission. They had already dug the ditch and made a mound. The eight posts were in their post holes and they had cut the timbers for the roof. It would not look like our buildings but that did not matter. We would learn from each other. They were building it outside the walls. As Alain said, "We will be inside the walls defending it if we are attacked. We can always rebuild and we would like more room."

I approved. It was sensible. This way they could build a bigger hall. When they waited for me, the next morning, I saw that they had donned the mail shirts. "A wise move."

Alain smiled, "In light of yesterday we thought we ought to be prepared." He had adopted the Frank's method of organisation. The Franks used warriors they called sergeants allowing the leader to delegate. We had something similar but we did not bother with titles. My men would take orders from Arne Four Toes and Rurik One Ear in my absence. They were the most experienced. Gudrun Witch Killer gave orders to the four warriors he had brought him as did Knut the Quiet with the five he had brought. My men did not need titles but the Franks seemed to like them. I did not object to the system. When my new warriors rode, they did so in a line of pairs. Alain and his sergeant were at the fore. As he told me it made it easier when they broke formation. The two lines could easily separate and there would be two to give commands.

We headed for the road and then rode north. I was anxious to see Hugo of Ċiriċeburh for I had not seen what he had done to improve his walls. When the Bretons had finished, there was little left of them. Our warm weather continued but I saw, to the west, ominous clouds far out to sea. That normally meant sudden summer storms. They would be laden with thunder and lightning. Hugo of Ċiriċeburh had cleared the trees and shrubs from beside the road. It was a sensible move. I saw, as we approached his walls, that he had added two wooden towers to his gates. Gilles said, "He must have copied us lord."

I nodded, "That is good. It shows that we have done the right thing. Had we not then we would not have been copied."

The gates opened and I saw the lord of Ċiriċeburh head towards us with ten of his warriors. They all have the same gryphon and blue kyrtles but Lord Hugo wore a mail byrnie. He reined in before us, "What is the reason for this visit?"

His tone was both aggressive and insulting. It implied I had to ask permission. I put it down to the fact that he was a young lord. I smiled, "You visited me and, as I have some new men, I thought to visit here and see what improvements you have made."

"You are not welcome here! Your kin have raided the land of the Leudes and he is not happy. Any consideration I might have afforded you is now impossible. Do not come again. If you do, then we will be forced to take action."

I was not worried by his words but rather disappointed. I had hoped for peace and now it seemed I was heading for war. I said, "Very well. We will leave."

As I was about to turn Copper's head Alain of Auxerre said, "Lord, may I speak?"

"Of course."

He nudged his horse next to mine and took off his helmet. "Hugo of Lyons: do you remember us? We are the men you abandoned to the Moors. I see you have been rewarded for your dishonourable act. If my lord asks I will take your head now! We are the last survivors of those men you left. You did not pay us and you did not try to save us. If it was not for my lord here, then we would be galley slaves now." His voice was as impassioned as I had ever heard and his hand went to his sword.

I put my hand on his, "Peace, Alain. This is not the time or the place." I looked at him, "Hugo of Ċiriċeburh, this is your decision. Reflect on it before you act for if you begin a war with me and my clan then make sure you win for so long as one of us remains alive your life will be in danger."

He looked shocked and he blustered, "You threaten me?"

I laughed, "Of course I do! You are a pathetic excuse for a man." I stood in my stiraps, "I warn all of you! Stay close to your home for if you venture close to my land then you will pay for that trespass with your lives."

Suddenly the warrior behind Hugo took his spear and lunged at me. Bertrand and Alain had quick hands. Their swords stabbed from both sides of the errant warrior. He affected a quizzical look and then his corpse slid from his horse. I think Hugo realised that he was outnumbered and outnumbered by better warriors. He turned his horse's head and galloped back to his walls. Alain's men had been waiting for the chance and they hurtled after the other warriors. They were too slow to move and they had spears which hampered their movement. Only three escaped to follow their lord.

"Stay!" My voice brought back Theobald and Stephen who were racing after the three fleeing. "Gather their weapons and horses. We have done enough." As they did so I turned to Alain of Auxerre, "I am sorry. I should have realised."

He gave me a wan smile. "I can see that serving you will be interesting, lord. We have been here but a couple of days and already we have two enemies to fight!" Roger of Dijon threw a handful of coins to Alain. He had found them in the purse of the man Alain had killed, "And already we are in profit!"

As we rode back home I contemplated our predicament. Nothing had changed save that I had thought the Hugo of Ćirićeburh was a possible friend. That was not true. Alain had assessed it correctly. I was not worried about attacks from either Ćirićeburh or Valauna. They could send as many mounted men as they liked. We could hold them off. My worry was that the Leudes would come with an army and war machines. That might defeat us.

When we reached our home, I was greeted with good news. The men who had been digging the well approached me grimy but happy, "Jarl! We have water! The well is dug. All that we need to do is to line it."

"Then we celebrate! The Allfather is good to us." I decided not to give them the bad news that we had two enemies. It would do no good. I wanted them to enjoy the moment. We celebrated and my new warriors fitted in well for they had something to celebrate too. We finished lining the wells and made a roof for it. The well could be a life saver if we were besieged. The hall for my new Frankish horsemen was also finished. They hurried to do so for they anticipated that their swords would soon be needed.

It was Sólmánuður when Fótr and his brother returned. This time they came with two other threttanessa. Both were smaller than the *'Flying Fox'*. Fótr had heeded my warning and they came without shields. When he bounded ashore I saw that he had a brand-new byrnie. It looked to be well made.

"Jarl! It is good to see you!" he waved an expansive hand at the ships. "See, I have a fleet now! I thank the gods each day that I met you.

I went to the Land of the Wolf and bought a suit of mail from the finest smith there is. We sailed to Orkneyjar and Dyflin and found two other captains who wished to follow me. We now go south to do as you did and find a land of our own. Would you join me?"

I smiled, "We are happy here but I am pleased at your success. Where is it that you go?"

He leaned in conspiratorially, "When we last raided we scouted out the river you mentioned, the Orne. It is fertile land and the Franks do not have a stronghold at the mouth of the river. There is a small village only. I could have taken it with one crew. We go there now to capture it and build our walls. While we build them I will take my men to raid the harvests and steal the women. By this time next year, we will be as prosperous as you."

I did not like the way the conversation was going. It sounded to me like he thought it would be easy and I knew it was not. "I urge you to be cautious. It took some time for us to establish the Haugr. We were aided by the Breton attacks. Caen is close to you. That will be well defended."

He laughed, "I plan on having that as my home within a year or two. I went there with two of my men. I have scouted it out and I believe I can take it." He shook his head, "Not yet of course but I have almost trebled the men who will follow me. When I have my new home then I will have even more. If you joined me then we could easily take it."

"I confess that I face dangers here for there are two Frankish lords who wish to sweep me back into the sea. Until I have dealt with them then I cannot offer any aid to anyone."

He nodded, "A shame. The two of us could have cut a swathe through this land."

"You will stay the night?"

"Of course. Your wife's company is always welcome."

After they left, the next morning, I spoke with my men. They had been hospitable towards the three crews. Now I wanted to know what they thought.

"What did you think of their plans?"

They were silent. "Come, I want to know. I have my opinions but I may be wrong."

Arne Four Toes said, "They are doomed to failure, jarl. They look at this and think we walked in and took it over. They ignored our words about the battles we fought and the men we lost."

Alain of Auxerre nodded, "I was not here then but they talk of defeating my people as though it was easy. They will be taking on Franks who have solid walls and horsemen who can control large areas of land. They may be good warriors but are they that good?"

Beorn Beornsson shrugged, "It cannot hurt us. If they fail, then we will still continue. Out life will be no different."

Rurik had said little but he spoke up then, "Do not be too certain. If they are defeated, then it may make the Franks believe that they can beat us. So far, they have not. Could we stand against the whole of the Frankish army?"

"But why would they come against us?"

"We have annoyed them. We pay no taxes and we do not respect their laws. Ask Alain of Auxerre." Einar Asbjornson had spent hours speaking with Alain of Auxerre and respected him and his opinions.

Alain nodded, "The Empire is fragile. The King's sons wish more power and there is insurrection in the air. If the king so commanded, then he could direct all of his forces to quash this little island of rebellion. It would teach his sons a lesson. I think the jarl should be wary and prepare for war."

And so we did. We had no need to raid and we could concentrate on making every man and boy ready to fight. Now that he had seen the land I was able to send Alain's men on patrols to watch our borders. Harold Fast Sailing went to Dyflin to trade and to find warriors who wished to join us. He brought back six. He also spent some of my coin to buy some cloth. I wished my Franks to look the same. It would help them to fight as one. The rest of us improved our defences and became better warriors. Alain of Auxerre and his men had skills we did not and they taught us. They also learned from us. The result was that we had twenty of my warriors who could fight from the backs of horses. I did not think we could match the best of the Franks but we could, at least, hold our own. If either Valauna or Ċiriċeburh sent their horsemen against us they would not have it all their own way. Our small number of horsemen and our shield wall would hold them. Sadly, that was all I thought that we could do; hold them.

My wife, before I had married her, had been a seamstress and I had her sew my Frank's new cloaks. The material was dark blue. I had chosen the colour because it would help us to stay hidden in the dark and yet it was a bold colour which matched the black cloaks my men wore. I forgot to ask her to sew a horse on each tunic and cloak. She could not help sewing a white cross. When I asked why she smiled, innocently, "They are Christians, husband. It will help them to fight."

As Alain and his men did not object then I did not. It looked so smart that Gilles and Bertrand asked for one too. "Are you Christian, Gilles?"

"No, lord but I am a horseman and I see it as the sign of the sword and not the cross!"

At the beginning of Heyannir we had a pair of riders from Fótr. One was Folki, his brother. They brought good news. "We have our new home, jarl. It was not as easy as we thought. The men who lived there fought hard but we slaughtered them and their heads served as a warning for others. We have built walls such as yours and made our home strong. We have granaries full of their grain and we have many slaves. My brother is now jarl and he is building towers and ditches which will be soon as strong as yours."

"Then I am pleased."

"I bring silver to buy swords. We have no smith and yours is a good one."

"You have my permission to ask him to make them for you but I fear it is not a quick process."

"Winter will be upon us soon and we do not expect an enemy until the new grass comes. We have the start of a land of the North men here in Frankia!"

After he had gone I confided in Mary, "I fear this will not end well. Am I being small minded or jealous?"

She kissed me, "No, for he is not doing as you did. You did not take heads. You did not enslave all who faced you. You joined two peoples together and you did not look for war. I am not blind, husband. I know that you have sought, when you could, the peaceful way. I know that we will have to fight to cling on here but this Fótr is trying to be you. That can never be. There is but one Hrolf the Horseman and he is mine!"

Although Alain and the new warriors were good horsemen they were no archers. If you could not use a bow by the time you had fought in your first battle, then you never would. It took years to build up the strength to use the weapon. Well over half of the men in my clan could use a bow well and the rest knew ow to use one. The men of Burgundy, it seemed, did not have that skill. They would have to use the spear and the sword.

As I led my horsemen in their daily patrol I spoke of this to Alain. "When we have to fight, Alain of Auxerre, then you will have to lead my horsemen."

"But you are a good horseman, lord!"

"There are too few of us to determine a battle. It will be the shield wall which decides if we win or lose."

"But there will be just ten of us! How can we make a difference?"

"I have thought of that. There will be some of the younger warriors who can be trained to be horsemen. In time, they will be your warriors. They can dress as you do. However, for the moment, you are our only mounted force. Now that you wear a mail shirt then you can face the enemy Leudes and their oathsworn."

"They will outnumber us."

"Remember I told you of the Ulfheonar? They fight together. If the ten of you rode closely together as we do on foot, in a wedge, then you would have the protection of each other's shields. You should practice riding boot to boot. You could punch your way through them. You said yourself that your lord, Hugo, fled when he was threatened. If the lord goes then his warriors follow."

He nodded, "Perhaps, lord but that would take much practice and we would not be able to ride as quickly."

"Arriving together is more important than speed and we have much time to practice. We will patrol in the mornings and you can practice in the afternoon."

"Will the two enemy lords give you time?"

"Perhaps. We have a horn which can use to summon my farmers to my walls but it is we who will look for signs of an enemy who is preparing to go to war. That is why we ride our borders. Our land is not so big that we cannot cover it all in less than half a day." I pointed to the ground. "We know our own tracks. If there are the tracks of other horses, then our neighbours are scouting our defences."

For seven days we rode and saw nothing. Those seven days gave my men the opportunity to practice. Sometimes I joined in. At other times I was busy with my duties as jarl. We were a peaceful community but disputes inevitably arose and, even though I was young, they were brought to me. I was lucky in that the women were happy for Mary to arbitrate between them. Their rows and disagreements were, potentially more damaging. The Raven Wing Clan had been destroyed because of the arguments between women. The fact that Mary was with child and growing larger by the day seemed to help for it put the women's arguments into perspective. Many of the women were with child. The long winter and the needs of my men had ensured that we would grow. But, each day as I rode, I wondered when that peace and time of growing would be shattered by Frankish horsemen.

As Heyannir approached I began to worry more about our enemies. Would they wait until their own harvest was in before they struck at us or would they wait until they had their grain harvested too?

Ragnvald had grown. Each time I had gone training I had returned to see a different child to the one I had left. He had long been able to both walk and talk. He was a quiet boy but thoughtful. His eyes stared and studied everything around him. When I took him, across my saddle, to visit Rurik, his mother looked as though she was going to object. Then, when a pain in her back made her want to sit down, she relented.

"Come Gilles, we will visit Rurik."

"Do you wish us to come with you, lord?"

"No, Alain. I wish you to continue to train the men to ride in close formation. Bertrand can help." Bertrand had still not accepted the new men. I hoped that by leaving him there he might grow closer to them. I needed all of my men to be as one.

It had been some time since I had ridden alone with Gilles. I missed those days on Raven Wing Island when we rode together without a care in the world. Now I had the clan to worry about. Ragnvald enjoyed riding with me. He giggled and laughed as we rode south. Gilles had something to say and he waited until we were some way from the walls before he said, "Jarl I have something to ask."

"Ask away, Gilles. You know me better than any save my wife. There are no secrets between us."

"How old is Bagsecg's daughter?"

"Baugheiðr?"

"Yes, jarl."

"I think she has seen thirteen of fourteen summers. Why?"

"I think she likes me."

"And?"

"And I thought to take her to my wife."

"She is Bagsecg's eldest child. He may not wish her to be wed. Some men like to hold on to their daughters."

"I spent a long time living among the Franks. I am not certain of all of the customs. What do I do if I wish to marry her? There have been few marriages to the girls of the clan."

"That is because most of them are too young yet for marriage. The custom is simple. You go to Bagsecg and ask him for his daughter's hand. She likes you?"

"I think so. We have spoken. She laughs when she is with me and she is gentle with the foals."

"Make sure it is not the horses which she likes. The winter nights are long. Make sure it is a woman who wishes to be with you."

He nodded, "I am sure. If that is all I have to do, then I will seek her father's permission."

"He is a good man but he will want the best for Baugheiðr. Any father would and she is hard working girl. She worked, with her mother, at her father's forge until the boys were old enough to help." He nodded. I watched him as he put his mind to the words he would use. I smiled. I had not had to do that. I knew that this was a good thing. We had had warriors who had taken Frankish women but this would be the first time it was the other way around. It was *wyrd*.

Rurik's wife was busy with their screaming infant, Hrolf. Rurik laughed, "It is good that I only have one ear! I can always turn by deaf side to his screams but he has a fine set of lungs on him. He will let his enemies know he is on the battlefield."

While Gilles watered our horses, I walked with him to the farm of Finni Jarlson. He had been making stakes and he stopped his work to join us. "Has there been any sign of Franks?"

"We have seen none." Rurik pointed to the sea. "We have seen a couple of their ships. They were not carrying cargo alone for they had men with helmets aboard."

"That may be because of Fótr. If he is raiding the Orne, then they may be putting warriors aboard their ships." I shook my head, "The trouble is that Charles Filjean and Hugo of Ċiriċeburh both present similar problems. They wish to harm us but I do not know if they have either the men or the skills to do so. This waiting is galling."

"We could attack one of them."

"That would be a waste of warriors. If we approached their walls they would hide behind them. We could take them but it would be at a cost. And if we did it might make the Leudes of Rouen take action."

"We have neighbours nearby who can help us."

"Perhaps. If this was a year hence then I might be happier but Fótr has taken much on. I hope his venture succeeds but we know the dangers this land present. For the present we will keep watch but I have a mind to visit with Fótr and see how he fares. From what he said he is not far away."

Rurik nodded, "That would make sense."

"However, if I did then you two would have a great responsibility upon your shoulders. You would have to be our eyes and ears here in the south."

Rurik laughed, "Then I can only do half the job. Do not worry, jarl. We will watch. We both have families. We have dogs who bark at the approach of any who is not of the clan. They are as belligerent as Nipper. But I beg you to be careful. Take men with you. The land between the Orne and here is Frankland!"

I decided, as we rode back, to let the weather determine my decision. If the weather changed and became inclement then I would travel for that would make it unlikely that the Franks would attack. I did warn Mary that I might take the journey. "It is not a short journey husband. My father rode the land for many years. As I recall it is seventy Roman miles or more. Why not take a ship? It will be quicker."

"I have thought of that but Harold Fast Sailing and Sven had planned on taking the knarr to Dorestad. We need new canvas for both the drekar and the knarr. It is better to buy them now before we need them. I will ride. The journey will be two days there and two days back. If we stay one day, then it will just be a five-day absence." I pointed to the clear blue skies. "Besides the weather is so fine that I cannot see me making the visit at all."

"You are all so superstitious!"

"And you are not? You will not have thirteen around the table for that is unlucky!"

She frowned, "Oh be away with you!"

I had won but she had the last word. That was her way.

Two days later we were woken by a storm so fierce that poor Mary and Ragnvald were terrified. There was thunder and there was lightning. I cuddled my son, "Fear not, it is Thor and he is making weapons at his forge. He will not hurt us for we are of his people."

Mary rolled her eyes. Her religion had no answer to the natural world. They just prayed that their god would protect them.

Of course, it meant that we could travel south. I spoke with Alain before I left. "Keep up your patrols. I should be away for no more than five days."

"We could come with you, lord. You are traveling in dangerous lands."

"I will be safe and I need you to keep a good watch. I think that the roads will be too difficult for large numbers of men to travel them but we will be vigilant. I will return."

Chapter 9

The road which headed south from Rurik's farm was well-made but the rains made it less pleasant to travel. The surface was slick. The moss which had sprouted was slippery. I was happy that I had chosen Dream Strider as my horse. He bore the hardships of the road well. Although it was not raining, the skies were heavy with black clouds and there was an unnatural heat to the air. The storms would return. I had planned on making fifty miles a day. I would have to revise that target. I doubted that we would be able to get more than forty miles from my home before we needed to make camp.

To keep up my two companion's spirits I kept up a conversation. "Bertrand, have you travelled these roads before?"

He shook his head. "When we pass Sébeville that will be as far south as I have been."

"And what is there?"

"A couple of farms. I went there with my lord to pick up some horses. They used to breed them there."

"Used to?"

"A lord from further west came and took the horses. He said the farmer owed him money. He did not but he took them anyway. If you have no horses to breed, then you cannot be a horse breeder. Now I do not know who we will find there."

We found no one. We found the buildings, now derelict and decayed, but we saw no sign of people. A few fowl had taken to the trees and were the only living reminder of a people who had once lived here. Even with the covering of mud and the lack of life I saw that this could be a fine place to raise horses. The sea was close by and the land was cleared for farming. We were just ten miles or so from Rurik's farm. If families came looking for land, then this would be a good place to start. As we headed further away from my home I began to plan how we might make it safe. With no natural hills then we would have to make our own hills. Rurik has shown what could be done but it had needed many hands to make it work. Such a construction would mean hard work and much digging but my people did not shy away from such things.

The rain started in the afternoon. There was no thunder with it but it was a relentless rain. When we spied the deserted, crudely built hut on the exposed cliff overlooking the sea we took shelter there. It lay in a small dell and there was a spring nearby. I wondered why on earth anyone would have chosen such a place. The hut looked barely big enough for one man. We discovered why when we entered. There was a body inside. It was long dead. The flesh had almost disappeared. I shuddered as I thought of the animals which have taken the flesh. There was a corona of hair. The body was slumped over a table as though death had come suddenly. There was a wooden drinking vessel nearby. He must have had a drink and then died. Gilles and Bertrand recoiled.

"He is dead and he cannot hurt us for we did him no harm. We will bury him and then his spirit will thank us by guarding our sleep. Go and prepare a shallow grave. There are stones aplenty to cover him with."

I wanted them to have work to do in order to take their mind from the dead body. There was still small areas of flesh and a little hair on the body. From the garments and the hair line I could tell that it was a priest. It looked to be the kind the Christians called a monk. His habit was a rough brown material. Around his neck, he had a wooden cross. His belongings appeared to be a bowl for his food and a wooden spoon. There was no food to be seen and I wondered if he had starved to death. Mary had told me of such men. They lived alone just praying to their god. I could not see the point myself but then I did not understand their religion at all.

Bertrand came back in. "We have scraped a grave. It is shallow for there is stone close to the surface."

"Give me a hand with him. Carry him by his clothes. It will be easier."

We took him out and laid him in the grave. Once his body was covered with the stones I saw relief on the faces of my two young warriors. We piled turf on the top for that was what we did to or dead. "Whoever you were, priest, I hope that your spirit finds sanctuary. Remember that we were the ones who cared for your body and watch over us this night. We mean you no harm." I turned to the two of them. "Come, let us make ourselves comfortable."

"You would sleep here this night?"

"It is dry and there will be rain. Aye I would. And it is big enough for the horses. Bring them in and I will get a fire going. It will be more cheerful with a fire. Gilles, break out the food and the ale. I am hungry."

The rain began to fall not long after we had buried the priest. My people would have said it was the heavens weeping. The rain battered on the roof. The fire we had made it cosy. We ate and we drank from our rations. A day's hard riding made me sleepy and I would have rolled into my cloak immediately and slept but Bertrand asked, "What happened to him, do you think?"

"There is little food here. His habit was old and thin. I am guessing he was old and that he either starved to death or death took him because it was his time." I shrugged, "Few of our people ever get to that stage but I have heard of it happening."

"It must be hard to die alone."

"That is what I do not understand about these priests of the White Christ. They choose not to have women and a family. It means they will die alone." I looked at Gilles, "Did you speak with Bagsecg?"

He smiled, "I did. You were right he was not happy to let his daughter be married. He said if it was any other than me then he would have refused. He asked what you had said and when I told him that you approved then he said he would not go against your wishes. He told me that my dowry would be a fine sword so that I could protect his daughter."

"And no man has ever had a finer dowry. This is good. When will you be wed?"

"Tvímánuður for that is when she will be fifteen summers old."

"And I will have Mary make you a fine suit of clothes so that you can do her honour." As it turned over to sleep I heard the two of them talking about his new bride. I did not think it would be long before Bertrand took a similar leap of faith.

The skies cleared briefly but more storm clouds lay to the north and west of us. I went to the cliff top and looked around. I could see why the priest had chosen this place. There was no access to the beach and the cliffs were steep. He would only have had sea birds for company. The ground meant it could not be farmed. I did not know the reason he had chosen to be alone but this had been as good a place as any to choose. I was happy to leave for it was a sad and lonely place. I preferred to be with my people. I already missed my wife and son. I could never be a priest.

We kept to the road which passed between the sea and the land. It was sandier and therefore drier. We made good time. As we approached the Orne I saw the wooden walls which Fótr had built as we neared his new home. It looked like he had done a good job. He had chosen a piece of high ground above what looked like both the sea and the river. I could just make out the masts of his drekar beyond the walls. Perhaps he would make a success of this venture.

We were spied as we approached. Although we did not have my banner my armour and helmet were distinctive; not to mention the horse I rode. Few Vikings rode such a magnificent horse. The gates were opened and Folki was there to greet us. His arm was in a sling. He grinned when we dismounted, "Good to see you, jarl. My brother will be back this evening. He has taken most of the men raiding the land to the south and east. The sheep need shearing."

As he led us to the hall I asked, "What happened to you?"

"A Frank with a long spear managed to penetrate my defence. He paid for the wound with his life but it is slow to heal. That is why I stay here at home. What brings you her? Have you brought news of our swords?"

"They will be ready by the end of Tvímánuður. As for why I came, it was to see how you fared. I feel responsible for your being here and I would not sleep if anything unpleasant happened to you."

"Do not worry about us. The Franks we have fought do not even possess mail. They ride horses but they cannot breach our shield wall. We have scoured the land close by of all the Franks. As far as you can see is the land of the fox. Already we have sent a drekar back to Dyflin. My brother wants more men. He plans on attacking Caen after the winter. Soon he will have the land which is now owned by the Leudes!"

I forced myself to bite back on the words which threatened to spill out. I did not want to upset the young brothers but Fótr was over reaching himself. The trouble was that there was no one to question what he was doing. I had Mary. Always supportive, she made me question my own decisions. It was a good way to be. I smiled, "Good, then may I beg the hospitality of beds for the night. I am anxious to speak with your brother. I think our two clans can help each other."

"Come we will make you comfortable. All of our warriors know that if we had not met you then we would have nothing. My brother may make light of it but we know that it was your advice which directed us here."

I liked Folki. He was not as brash as his brother and he seemed, somehow, more genuine. "Thank you. We will shed our mail and join you in the hall."

While Gilles took the horses to the stable we went to the warrior hall and took off our mail. The hall was unfinished. It had a roof and a floor.

It had a fire but the things which would make it a home for the warriors were missing. They would come. I found a bowl of water and I washed. I took my comb and combed my hair and beard. Mary had instilled in me the need to be clean and to be presentable. I did my best.

We had enjoyed three goblets of wine by the time Fótr returned. As Folki told me, they had no ale wives and it was easier to steal wine from the Franks. The wine was pleasant. "Our men grow used to it but you need to drink less of if than ale."

I nodded, "Aye, our old men prefer it for it means they have to pee less in the night!"

The door to the hall opened as the raiders returned. Fótr saw us and rushed to embrace me. "Jarl it is good that you are here! What success we have had this day! We have many slaves and grain! We will eat well this winter! When my new men arrive, who knows what we might not do!"

"I am pleased. When you have time, I would speak with you."

"Of course. We will eat well this night for we killed some of the sheep. It was easier than herding them. We will feast and sing songs of our victory this night." I heard screams and squeals from the far side of the hall. I guessed that his warriors just took their women. It was not the way of my clan but who was I to judge?

The young warriors whom Fótr led were full of their recent success. I did not blame them. They had done well and they celebrated. They reminded me of many who were in my clan. I remembered when we had been a young clan on Raven Wing Island. That seemed a lifetime ago. I sat next to Fótr. He recounted, many times, the events of his raid. He was becoming more garrulous as the wine took hold. I did not mind. He had done well and was entitled to be proud of what he had done. As the rest of his warriors fell into a drunken stupor he and Folki took me to one side where we could speak. Gilles and Bertrand stayed close by us.

"Well jarl, what do you wish to ask us?"

"Our clans, it seems, have annoyed the Franks. I fear there will be retribution."

"We are not afraid of the Franks."

Folki had had less to drink and he shook his head, "Brother, listen to the jarl. He has survived here longer than we have."

"I know but so far I have seen nothing which might worry me."

"What I wish, Fótr, is for us to be able to go to the aid of the other if danger threatens."

"Jarl, I have plans already which will make that unnecessary! When the new grass comes, I will attack Caen! If we can capture that stronghold, then the whole of the Orne valley will be ours!"

"It is a stronghold which would defy many more men than we have."

"We have made much coin. I have sent a drekar to Dyflin for more warriors. We will spend the winter gathering tribute, grain and weapons. When the new grass comes then we will attack Caen. Are you with me?"

"There are enemies closer to my home. The garrison at Valauna would devastate my home if I left to join you at Caen. First, I will reduce Valauna and then I will join you. I hoped that you would take Valauna with me."

"Aim higher jarl! You once did. Your Valauna is a hovel compared with Caen. If we took Caen, then Valauna would fall anyway! Do not doubt yourself." He closed his eyes. "This may suit my plans. Reduce Valauna for it will draw the men of Caen to aid the garrison there. Then we can go together to defeat the men of Caen."

I saw the doubt in his brother's eyes but he said nothing. I smiled. Fótr was drunk and his ideas were dreams. We had nowhere near enough men to take Caen. That would take a concerted effort. It would need more drekar crews than we could muster. We would first have to weaken it by laying waste to the lands around it.

Folki and I carried his brother to bed. "He has good ideas, jarl and the men follow him. We have a chance."

"I saw it in your eyes Folki. You do not truly believe that you can succeed."

He shrugged, "I have seen the walls and they look like they would bleed an army to death but who knows. Last year we were picking up crumbs from the coast of the Angles. Now we have our own land and a stronghold which will defy our enemies. Many men now wear mail and we have good swords. Perhaps Fótr is right. The Dragonheart took land from the Saxons with fewer men."

I did not believe that was true but I could not gainsay it. "Perhaps but Jarl Dragonheart had the Ulfheonar. I wish you well."

After promising to send the swords by knarr we left the next morning. I had hoped for an alliance which would allow us to fight with allies. I saw now that was not going to happen. We would have to rely upon ourselves. I would have to rethink my strategy.

I could tell that Bertrand and Gilles were unhappy about passing by the hut of the dead monk again and so we headed inland, travelling a longer route but one which would show us more of our land. I found that parts of it were boggier and less fertile. We saw fewer farms the further we went from the coast. We sheltered, that night, in a wood. We cut small branches and bushes to make a shelter for the sky still threatened rain. We were, however, spared a dousing. In fact, it was a warm muggy night which made us rise earlier than expected. We left before dawn. We rode quickly and the cool air helped.

When we reached Rurik's farm it was early afternoon. As we had ridden our mounts hard we rested them while I told the two of them what we had learned.

"So, we get no help from Fótr?"

"No but I have travelled the road. Fótr is further from us than I had thought. We will just have to be wary and do as I originally planned."

"Wait?"

"Aye Finni. And I believe that they will be waiting for us to attack them too. This will be a test of nerves of both of our people."

"Alain of Auxerre has visited each day. He has ventured not the woods to look for signs of the Franks."

"He is a good man. I am pleased he joined us."

Even as we had headed home the skies had begun to clear. The breeze came from the north and was cooler, clearing away the heavy air which had oppressed us for most of our journey. Perhaps it was a sign; I knew not.

Alain was still on patrol and our knarr had not returned from its voyage. After greeting Mary I went to speak with Bagsecg. "How go the weapons for the clan of the Flying Fox?"

"They are ready. I finished the last of them today." He gestured at the pile of polished weapons. "They are good swords but Fótr paid well. Will they be used well?"

"He is an honest warrior. He has enthusiasm and he has ambition. He has listened to what we have told him and he now seems better placed to hold on to his new home. I believe that they will be used well."

Bagsecg laughed, "I think I know you well enough now, jarl, to hear the but in your words."

I nodded, "You are right. The but is that he has ambitions which are a little too high. He would take on a Frankish stronghold. Rather than wait until he is stronger he thinks to take it now. It would be like casting grain onto a field while the pigeons are roosting. Most would be wasted."

"Then perhaps my swords might keep more of his men alive. These will not bend."

I nodded, "And you Bagsecg Bagsecgson, are you happy about young Gilles' offer of marriage?"

His head bowed, "I confess that I was a little hasty in my response. I answered with less civility than he deserved. When I told Anya, she made my ears burn for days. She said that Gilles is a fine young man and that my little one has chosen him. She is right. It is just that if she marries she leaves and she is my only daughter."

"It is not as though she will be travelling far. Gilles has not spoken to me of it but I am certain he will build a home close to mine and the stables. That will make her as close to you as she is now."

He smiled, "You are right!" He went to the rear of his workshop. He unwrapped a hessian sack, "And here is the new helmet you ordered. I would have had it finished long ago but I needed to make the herkumbl on front. I used some of the gold you gave me to pick out the detail on the horse."

I took the helmet. It was well made and the horse on the nasal would give added protection whilst telling the world who I was. "Thank you, Bagsecg. I think my old helmet has seen better days. There was a time when I thought it was the equal of my sword."

"Aye time passes. Your sword will never age. My father made two swords of which he was truly proud. One is Ragnar's Spirit and the other is heart of Ice. I am still learning. One day I will make a sword of which I am proud. Perhaps by the time your son is grown I will have the skills my father has."

As I left him I wondered if I would change when Ragnvald became older. I knew how I was now but what would happen when I was older? I had been denied a father for almost my whole life and my mother for half of my life. I had no experience of the problems my son might have growing up in a home. I had grown up a slave. Would I cling on to my son?

Alain rode in after dusk. He and his men were weary. He threw himself from his horse. "Lord, it is good that you come. The men of Valauna have stirred. We rode close to their walls this day. There was much coming and going through the gates. We heard the sound of metal being beaten."

"You think war?"

"I think that something is going on."

"Then tomorrow I will ride with you."

When we rode we rode mailed. I rode Night Star. I tried to ride my three best horses equally. Dream Strider had had a hard five days' riding and Night Star was a good horse should this come to combat. I wore my new helmet which had a more open face and a nasal. If we were scouting it would be better. My other was the one I would use when I was behind a shield wall. This was my horseman helmet. Riding a horse and seeking an enemy needed something which gave me a better vision. As we rode I noticed that Alain and the Franks had finally finished their shields. They all had the sign of the horse upon them but they had varied the colouring of each one. It was well done. With their dark blue cloaks and white crosses they looked like a bodyguard now.

"Did you get close to the walls?"

"We found a copse some fifty paces from the gates. I left my horse in the main wood and crawled closer."

"Then I will join you today. If we can I would take a prisoner."

Leaving our horses with the others the two of us made our way to the copse. The road looked to be empty and we reached the handful of trees without having to crawl too far. The gate was open and there looked to be just two men on guard at the gates. No one entered and no one left. I knew we had to be patient and we waited until the late afternoon. When people did emerge, it was in larger numbers than I had expected. More than that there were some well-dressed men with their women amongst the party. The pale blue coated horsemen formed the rear-guard as they left. I stiffened when I recognised the banner and the tunics of the column of men who rode through the gates last. It was Hugo of Ċiriċeburh. I saw Alain's knuckles whiten as he gripped the branch which lay before him. His former lord headed north. Smaller groups of riders came from the gates and headed south. After a short time, the gates closed.

We rose and headed back to our horses. We did not speak until we reached an anxious Gilles and Bertrand, waiting with the rest of the men. "We thought something had happened, lord."

"Something has but I know not what."

"Perhaps it was a council of war, lord?"

"I do not think it was. Some of those who left were not warriors. Only half of those we saw leave had horses and there were women amongst the numbers. We need to find a prisoner to question."

My captain of horse pointed north, "If we rode hard we could catch Hugo of Ċiriċeburh. We know where he goes. He had just a dozen or so men with him. He will run."

I knew that vengeance was in Alain's heart when he spoke but he was right. "Very well. We try to catch one of them." I turned to the men, "We need a prisoner to question!"

Alain's patrols had allowed him to become very familiar with the land. There were ancient greenways and trails and we took them. The result was that we caught up with the Frankish horsemen ten miles from his home. I was riding a horse which was better than any. I began to extend my lead. Only Gilles, riding Freya, could keep up with me. The distance between ourselves and the last warriors in the column shortened. I saw the two rearmost riders glance over their shoulders. Terror filled their faces. A column of mailed warriors whom you know are killers will make you panic and the last two riders were panicking. A horse responds to a rider. These two were not concentrating on the horses. They shouted the alarm and the rest of the column began to gallop even faster. The mounts of the last two slowed as they turned to see how close we were and we caught them even faster. I guessed that they were either young or inexperienced or both.

I did not draw my sword for I needed a prisoner. I urged Night Star to race even faster. The warrior at the rear made the mistake of trying to draw his sword as he rode. It must have snagged on his belt or his saddle for his horses suddenly slowed as his grip on the reins loosened. In two strides I was next to him and I grabbed his left arm and jerked him from the saddle. He fell, heavily and awkwardly to the ground. I rode after the other rider who lagged behind. He had managed to get his sword out. The problem he had was that I could choose which side I approached him. I chose his left. He could still swing his sword around but he would not find it easy to hit me. I drew my seax. It was a shorter weapon but easier to use on horseback.

I drew inexorably closer to the rear of his horse and his head swivelled as he tried to work out from which direction I would come. I dug my heels into Night Star and he leapt forward. As I came abreast of the Frank he swung his sword at my head. I easily blocked it with my seax and, as he drew back his hand for another blow, I slashed my seax down his left arm. It tore it open and ripped into the tendons. His hand dropped the reins and his swing with the sword made him fall to the other side. I grabbed the trailing reins and brought both of our horses to a halt. The other Franks were now a hundred paces away. There was little point in exhausting horses. We had done what I intended. We had two prisoners.

When I reached the warrior whose arm I had cut I saw a pool of blood already. I jumped down and handed the reins of both horses to Gilles. I tore part of his tunic and tied it tightly above the wound to stem the bleeding. I said, "What were you doing in Valauna?"

He looked at me as though I had spoken Greek. "What?"

"You and Hugo of Čiriċeburh were in Valauna. Others were too. What was the reason."

He winced as pain course through his body, "A funeral. The Seneschal is dead and his son is the new Seneschal. We were there to bury him."

I was both relieved and anxious. There was no immediate danger but the son now had no one to curb his belligerence. There would be retribution. He would blame me for his father's death.

Alain rode up leading the horse of the other rider. He shook his head. "He is dead, lord. The fall killed him. What do we do with this one? Should I slit his throat?"

I saw that the Frank was younger than even Gilles. I shook my head, "Bring him back with us."

"But he will be of no use as a slave! Better to end his life now."

"No, Alain, we will take him back with us."

I still do not know why I made that decision. All that I knew was that I could not see his life ended because we did not know what to do with him. We took him to the priest who lived in the church on our island. I did not think the Frank would be happy to have the women who were our healers treating his wound. A Frankish priest would be more acceptable. Leaving Gilles and Bertrand to watch him I rode to my hall. "Alain, send a rider to warn Rurik that there is a new Seneschal and he may well attack without warning."

"Aye lord."

I changed from my mail and went to take out the map I had of my land. It was not a detailed map, as yet, but I could add to it. I was busily adding the details when Mary appeared at my shoulder. "Your son wonders what you are doing?"

I smiled at him. He was still shy of me. I knew not the reason but I just spoke to him gently when I did speak, "I make a map for I fear our enemies come again soon."

Mary looked alarmed, "How do you know?"

"Jean of Caen died and his son now commands. I fear that he is reckless. We will prepare."

A short while later one of the slaves said, "Jarl, Master Gilles waits without."

I went to the door. I saw that they had the Frank I had wounded on a litter. "The priest says he must lose the arm at the elbow or he will die. The flesh is dead."

Alain of Auxerre said, "I told you we should have ended his life."

Mary and Ragnvald were at the door and she scowled at Alain. "And you call yourself a Christian! These pagans have more Christianity than you do!" He quailed before her ire. She knelt and looked at the arm. The Frank was either asleep or unconscious and unaware of the debate about his fate. Mary looked at the wound. "I think the priest may be right."

I nodded, "Then we must take his arm. Fetch him to Bagsecg's forge. The fire there is hot and he has the sharpest of weapons."

Gilles said, "The priest gave him a draught to make him sleep and to dull the pain."

"Then we have a chance." A crowd followed us as we carried the wounded man to the forge. "Bagsecg, we need to take this man's arm above the elbow. It must be a single blow and then we must seal the wound with fire. Have you an axe sharp enough to take it in one blow?"

"You insult me, jarl! Of course I have." He turned to his son, "Put more air into the fire. I want it white hot." He took an axe and put an edge on it. When he was happy he placed the blade in the fire. "Hopefully this will help to seal the wound when I strike. Gilles, hold the limb out away from the litter. Jarl, if you take a brand then when the arm is gone you can seal it."

I took a piece of half burned wood from the fire which burned next to the forge and blew upon it. It flared. Bagsecg seemed satisfied that the axe was hot enough. "May Thor guide my hand." He was a strong man and when he brought the axe head down it was with such force that would have taken a head from a bull. This was a hiss as it sliced through the flesh. I held the brand against the wound for a count of four and pulled it away. There was the smell of burning hair and flesh but, apart from an involuntary convulsing of the Frank's body, there was little sign of the effect it had had on him. There was no blood.

"Take him to our hall!"

I saw Gilles look at me and I shrugged, "Do as my lady commands."

They did so and then she said to us, "That was well done. You may have saved his life. Now let us see if we can make him a man again."

Chapter 10

Now that Heyannir was almost over we would have to think about gathering in our crops again. We had done well the previous year. Would this crop be as good? We now had many more mouths to feed. Our successful raids meant more slaves. Next year they would begin to pay for themselves but, for the present, we would have to make sure there was enough food for the winter. That afternoon, as I spoke with Arne Four Toes, Beorn Beornsson and Einar Asbjornson I told them of my worries. "We should raid again but if we do then the Franks will fall upon our farms."

"Then wait until the Franks have been. From what we know of this Filjean he will not wait long. Your attack on Hugo of Ċiriċeburh will have worried him. I would expect him soon." Einar was a thoughtful warrior and I agreed with his assessment.

"I hope that our knarr returns soon. I would have the drekar ready to raid."

Arne laughed, "You are assuming that we will be able to defeat the Franks."

"If I did not then I would take our people and return to Raven Wing Island. I am confident in the abilities of our men. From what I have seen the Franks of Valauna and Ċiriċeburh do not pose as much of a threat as other Franks we have met. Of course, if they both arrive at the same time then it might cause a problem."

"How many men do we have who live within these walls? I mean men who can ride and fight. Which of our men have skills with a bow."

Beorn said, "Perhaps twenty. If you count Rurik and Finni, then twenty-two."

"Tomorrow we ride to Rurik. I want the twenty-two how can ride mounted, armoured and with their bows. I plan to forestall this attack and try to discourage them. I will leave Bagsecg and Erik One Arm in charge of the walls. Have a beacon built so that we can light it and summon in all of those who live in the outlying farms. If we do not discourage them then we will enrage them and they will attack us like hornets whose nest has been disturbed."

When they went to tell the men, I sought Alain, Gilles and Bertrand. I told them what I had planned. "I would have us tempt the Franks into an attack on us. We will fall back and our men can ambush them in the woods. If we kill enough of their best warriors, then even the headstrong Filjean might reconsider."

"Would you have us use your new tactic and charge together to break their resolve?"

"No, we will save that surprise. I want them to think that we are not very good horsemen. Your helmets and shields mark you as Vikings. Do not wear your blue cloaks. I am the one they will fear. I want them to think we are cowards who run away. This is a ruse we can only use once so play your part well. Today you are not Franks who can ride well you are Vikings who have just been shown a horse and cling on for dear life!"

We left before dawn to ride to Rurik. We sent their families back to the Haugr and then headed into the forest. I had taken Nipper with us and I led. We encountered no one. I took that as a sign of the inexperience of the new young lord. If I had thought that enemies were close I would have had the forest filled with scouts. When we reached the place I had chosen as an ambush site I had my men line the trail. They placed themselves twenty paces from the path but each had a clear view of the path. When the arrows began to fly, the Franks would not see their attackers. Of course, if they chose not to attack then this would all be for nothing. I took out my seax and marked a cross in each of the two trees at the side of the path. The white, oozing wound would be seen easily when I came back.

I led my horsemen towards the gates of Valauna. The ambush was a thousand paces inside the wood. The Franks had cleared the woods which lay close to their lands. They would see an enemy coming. I had my Saami bow with me. We stopped in the eaves of the wood and I took an arrow. It was never easy using a bow from the back of a horse but the Saami bow was easier than most. The range was less than a hundred and fifty paces and I was confident that I could hit my target. The arrow flew straight and true. The guard was pitched from the wall and the others looked around for the assailant. I sent another one. It clattered from the helmet of a second guard. I slipped my bow into the sheath I had beneath my saddle and I led my men out.

The alarm bell in the church sounded and the walls were filled with warriors. I arrayed my men in a single line. I took out my sword and pointed it to the gate, "Charles Filjean, your father has died and for that I am sorry. I know it was only your father's command which kept your hand from your sword. He is dead. I would not have uncertainty between us. Come and fight with me. Let us decide this by combat. Your father was an honourable man and took the challenge. Willyou do the same? What say you?"

In answer a flurry of arrows came my way. They were poorly made and the archers had no skill. I held up my shield and most bounced off. Two struck the mail covering my legs and fell to the ground. I laughed, "Is that the best you can do? Come, show me that you are a man. Your father was such a warrior and he had honour. Do you have none?"

I hoped that he would accept my challenge but I knew that he would not. However, my words would spur him into action. He had the men of his town listening to him. How could they follow someone who was afraid to fight?

We had to be patient. More arrows came at my men and they were dealt with in the same way. Alain of Auxerre shouted, "Why do you allow your women to use bows? This insults us!"

His men jeered at the walls. I saw that only half of the men who had first stood on the walls were still there. He had taken the bait. He was mounting his men and hoping to catch us unawares. I knew that he had four gates. He would use all four to try to encircle us. I felt the vibration of hooves on the ground. They were coming from our left and right. "Be ready to run." I had told my men precisely what I wanted them to do. It went against their nature but they promised to do as I had ordered.

The gates of the stronghold opened and mailed warriors spilled out. Alain and his men took flight. They did so badly, affecting the manner of Vikings who were unaccustomed to riding. I shouted, "Come back you cowards! Do not leave me here alone!"

When Gilles and Bertrand joined them, I heard a derisory cheer from those charging towards me. I whipped Dream Strider's head around when they were less than thirty paces from me. As I did so I saw a second column of men coming from the west gate. They had taken the bait. Dream Strider opened his legs and I soon began to catch Gilles and Bertrand. I glanced over my shoulder as though I was nervous. I saw that just one column follow us. The other two charged towards the eaves on either side; they were seeking the archers they thought I had brought with me. I was at the rear of the line for a reason. I wanted them to think they could catch me and I slowed Dream Strider down as though I did not know the trail. I heard their hooves thundering behind me. When I glanced behind I saw that they were less than twenty paces and catching me. They had formed one long column. The nature of the woods meant it was difficult for me to estimate numbers but there was enough to make it worth our while. They had taken the bait. Could we now hurt them?

I had marked the tree where the ambush would begin. I had to draw them to the last tree where Rurik and Finni Jarlson waited. They were the last men in the ambush. Alain of Auxerre was already leading half of his warriors back into the woods but taking them around in a long loop to catch the Franks when they returned home.

As soon as I passed the Rurik and Finni I turned around and drew my sword. Even as the leading warrior saw me arrows thudded into them. Unlike the arrows the Franks had loosed at me, these were well made arrows with heads which could pierce mail. They were also less than thirty paces away from my archers. My men had both a horse and a rider to hit. Even so the first Frank managed to evade most of the arrows. One struck him in the leg but he hurtled towards me. He leaned forward with his spear, a triumphant look in his face. I kicked Dream Strider in the flanks and took him to the left of the rider. His spear struck fresh air. I brought my sword around in a long, powerful swing and it bit into his jaw and face. He fell backwards over his horse's hindquarters. I carried on up the path with Gilles and Bertrand in close attendance. I heard the shouts and cries from those who had been hit by the arrows. A pair of Franks held their shields before them. Their horses danced skittishly showing the nervousness of their riders. Three of their companions lay dead or wounded. Another was afoot, his mount having been killed. The three of us rode between them. I stood in my stiraps and brought my sword down across the shoulder of one while Gilles despatched the second.

I heard a Frankish voice shout, "Fall back! Fall back!"

The damage had already been done. At least twelve warriors lay dead. I could see that some of those who fled before us also had arrows sticking from shields, saddles, arms and horse's rumps. Many would not make the edge of the wood alive. They were clinging to life as their worst nightmare dawned. We were Vikings and we had caught them. As we approached the end of the woods I heard a cheer as Alain and his men fell upon those who thought they had reached the sanctuary of their stronghold. It did not matter that there were only eight of my men. They appeared from nowhere and me who were already shaken became totally demoralised.

When I reached the gates, I shouted, "You have seen what we can do, Charles Filjean! Stay within these walls where you are safe!" There was silence from the walls.

I turned and rode back into the forest. My men cheered. It had been an easy victory. The numbers we had slain were immaterial. It was the manner of our victory which would have the longest lasting effect. We were also ten horses better off as well as having more mail and swords. We could now consider a raid. I would decide where after I had spoken with Sven and Harold.

It was dark when we reached our home. Nervous wives watched from the walls as we trooped triumphantly through the gates.

"Gilles, see to the horses."

The new horses we had acquired were good horses. The Franks knew their horseflesh. We now had a good herd. The days when I had just two stallions and two mares were long gone. Gilles and I could begin to breed bigger horses and we would be able to wear more mail. As I walked past his forge Bagsecg shouted, "A good victory, jarl?"

"Any victory where I bring back all of my men is a good victory!"

When I entered my hall, I saw that the wounded Frank was seated at the table and Mary was feeding him. When he saw me, he tried to push himself backwards. My wife restrained him and said, "No, Pepin, you are quite safe. This is my husband the jarl of this land. You will not be harmed."

"It was he who wounded me! I lost my arm because of him!"

"And he saved your life by bringing you here and removing the arm which might have killed you. Be thankful that you have life. You can never be a warrior again. Let us see what you can become. Now eat. You need your strength."

I was not happy with the Frank's words, "He has one good arm. Why cannot he feed himself? Erik One Arm does!"

She scowled at me, "Just take off your mail and wash yourself. You reek of blood and sweat. This is not a stable it is our home! Leave this to me!" Her eyes told me to heed her words. I did.

When I returned, the Frank was no longer there. I sat at the table, "Where is he?"

She shook her head, "That was not kindly done! Just when I think well of you then you have to do something like that. I fed him because he saw no reason to live with one arm. He thought to take his own life and that is a mortal sin. It was my Christian duty to give him hope. Do not take it away!"

I felt ashamed of myself. My wife's words had been gentle. "I am sorry. I will try to be a better husband."

"You are a good husband. I would have you be a better man!"

"I will try." I sat at the table and a slave brought me some wine and a bowl of food. "You say his name is Pepin?"

She nodded, "He is called Pepin of Senonche. He is the same ages as Gilles. He had only recently joined Hugo of Ciriceburh. He has barely had time to be a warrior and your blow ended that."

"What will he do now then?"

"I do not know but I will try to find something that he can do. If we abandon him then he will die. Erik One Arm manages."

"He is a Viking."

"Then perhaps you need to make him into a Viking."

I laughed, "Easier said than done. I think the best we can do is make him fit into the clan although how we do that I do not know. He appears to resent me."

"That will change." She sipped her wine, "You attacked the men of Valauna today?"

"We made them attack us. There is a difference. We have dampened their ardour for battle against the clan of the horse." I hesitated, "I will take the drekar and raid when the knarr returns."

"Why? Will that not make us vulnerable?"

"No for I will leave Bertrand, Alain and Alain's men here. They are no sailors."

"And why do you need to raid?"

"It is the new slaves and the new men. They need feeding. Until we clear more fields to grow more crops we will not have enough from our harvest. Last year we were lucky. We had a good harvest. We will go to the land of the Saxons. They harvest their grain earlier than we do. We would only be away for three or four days. I do not think that any will attack in that time. However, even if an attack is made I believe the Haugr could hold out for four or five days at least."

She nodded, "You are right. We have too many people now and we would not wish any to starve. There are more babies and young children to feed." She patted her belly. "This little one will be here by the end of the month. If you go then go soon. I would you here when your daughter comes."

'*Kara*' arrived in the middle of the next afternoon. Sven pointed to the skies, "It was the weather which delayed us. We had some bad storms on the way there and we had to repair some strakes. We bought all that we needed. We have spare sails and even a spare mast for the knarr. We bought as much rope as we could. We are happy."

I took them both with me to my hall and I explained what had gone on in their absence and what I planned. They did not seem unhappy. "You are right, jarl. We can reach the south coast quickly. Where would you raid?"

"The land around Haestingaceaster. When we took shelter in that bay it was in my mind that we could use it to raid. We have never taken from that shore. They might not expect us. We just need more grain to augment our crop. Anything else we could take would be a gift from the gods. I thought to sail to the bay and then slip around to Haestingaceaster after dark. We were lucky last time we raided. Let us keep '*Dragon's Breath*' close by this time."

"Then we will prepare the drekar."

Alain and Bertrand were happy to be my eyes and ears while I was away. Perhaps it was the blue cloaks but whatever the reason Bertrand seemed happier about my captain of horse and his men. They divided the men so that they could keep watch on both of our enemies. Bagsecg and Erik One Arm took charge of the Haugr. I did not take all of my warriors. I took just forty. I did not think we would need more and that left twenty to protect my walls. With the other men in the Haugr that would be enough. Poor Mary was suffering as we left. Her back was aching. I secretly blamed Pepin for she had done too much for him. I considered taking him with me as a sort of punishment but Mary would have none of it.

"I had a bad back with Ragnvald. It will pass. It is a good thing that it is women who have babies. If it were left to men, then we would have none!"

We left and headed north. The wind was our friend. It billowed the sails and took us into the dark waters of the deep ocean. Our recent success had buoyed us all. If we could get enough food for the winter, then when the Franks came after the grass had begun to grow then we could meet them in battle and defeat them. As we sailed we spoke of their shortcomings.

"The bows they use are hunting bows and their arrows are as dangerous as a summer midge."

"Their shields are too small."

Rurik shook his head, "You are missing their greatest weakness. They have no leaders. The two we have seen are even worse than Ketil Eriksson was. We thought he was bad but at least he had courage and some idea how to fight. If all the Franks are as bad as this Hugo and Charles, then we can conquer the whole land with just ten boat crews."

"I think you are wrong Rurik. We are lucky that the two lords who are so close to us are so poor. Charlemagne had a great empire. It still is. You do not get that with poor leaders. It is just that we have not met their good warriors yet. I, for one, am happy, that is so. Do not let our little successes go to your heads. We are growing in number and I am pleased with what we have. This is just the beginning."

Arne Four Toes said, "Aye you are right. Let us enjoy what we do! We are Vikings and we go to raid! Talk not of Franks for we go to fleece the Saxon sheep!"

The wind took us north and we saw the coast appear in the late afternoon. Sven adjusted the course we were taking. We would head for the bay we had found on our last visit. Knowing it would be empty made us bold and we did not wait until dark. Once we were in the deserted bay we donned our mail and put on our war faces. I had my old helmet with the face mask for I wanted to inspire terror. The wind from the south meant that we would not have to row the last few miles to Haestingaceaster.

Although we had had not scouted out the port we had passed it before now. It had a wooden quay while the wooden town wall was barely forty paces from the water. We would rely upon surprise to enter the burgh. We hoisted the sail and headed west. The sun had almost set when we left. It meant we could see, by the glow from the western sky, what lay ahead while we were sailing from the dark. We did not chant and we kept silent. The only sounds we could hear were the cries of sea birds, the slap of the canvas and the rush of water beneath our dragon prow. Siggi Far Sighted was at the mast head and he used whistles and waves to direct Sven. Death was stalking the Saxons silently.

As we passed the end of the cliff which marked the start of the bay, the last light from the west went out as though someone had snuffed out a candle. Siggi whistled and Sven put the steering board over. My men were already lined up on the deck. Our shields were around our backs. It made disembarkation easier. As we turned I saw the glow from the fires which warmed the sentries. There was one at each end of the quay. All that we could see were shadows. When we were seen, we would know for there would be a shout. The longer they took to spy us then the more chance we had of success. We knew the sentries would not be mailed. Warriors who could afford mail spent their nights in warm beds and not huddled around fires watching the sea. But we also knew that they would see us.

We were less than a hundred paces from shore when the alarm was raised. As the cry went up Sven shouted, "Down sail!" He put the steerboard over and the wooden jetty which had been racing up to meet us was suddenly on our steerboard side. Two ship's boys were ready to leap ashore. The jetty was not empty. There were ships tied there, end to end. Sven bumped us, none too gently, against them.

I stood on the sheerstrake holding the stay. Raising my sword, I shouted, "Clan of the Horse!" I leapt down onto the deck of the ship. A sleepy sailor stood. I punched him in the face with the hilt of my sword and in two strides was across the boat and leaping down on to the wooden jetty. Two sentries stood facing me while I saw another two running for the gate. I did not have enough time to pull my shield around and so I drew my seax and ran at the two sentries who stood before me. Their spears wavered. I knew what a terrifying aspect lay before them. In the glow of their fire all that they saw was a mask behind which burned two fierce eyes. Encased in mail I would appear bigger than I actually was.

I brushed aside the two spears with my seax and my sword and kept running. Behind me Arne Four Toes and Beorn Beornsson ended the lives of the two sentries with two sword strokes. I kept running. The two sentries who had fled were just a short way ahead and they had almost reached the gates. I heard men shouting from the walls and, inside Haestingaceaster was the sound of chaos and confusion ringing with shouts and cries. They might never have seen a Viking but they had all heard of us.

I heard someone, from the fighting platform shout, "Close the gate!" It should not have been open. It showed their inexperience. Perhaps the two sentries who ran had friends on the walls who wished to save them. I know not but the gates were closing too slowly as those within tried to give their two sentries the chance of life. Spears and stones were hurled at us. We were in the dark and they were badly aimed. The last of the sentries had just managed to squeeze through the gates and they were about to close shut when I hurled myself bodily at them. Alone I would not have had an effect but Arne and Beorn were behind me and their bodies crashed into the back of mine a heartbeat after my shoulder struck the gate. It burst open. Three mailed Vikings are a powerful force.

As I stepped through a spear was rammed towards my head. Had it been my middle I might have struggled to stop it but my seax flicked up with enough force to deflect it above my head and Heart of Ice rammed into the Saxon's middle. I pushed his body from my sword and slipped my seax into my belt. I pulled my shield around. Arne and Beorn flanked me. Their shields were already out and they protected me.

Rurik's voice, behind me, told me that my men were there. "Ready jarl!"

"Then let us take them!"

Saxon burghs were all similar. The main path in the burgh would be wide and would lead directly to the main hall where the warriors and the thegn would live. We ran up it. It was wide enough for seven men and we formed an impromptu wedge. I was in the centre and flanked by six mailed men. Arrows were being loosed at us but our shields and our mail protected us. Distance is harder to estimate in the dark. A spear caught the top of my mail but the clasp which held my cloak deflected it. We were not in a solid wedge but moving quickly together to tray to strike the Saxons before they had time to organise themselves.

Some brave Saxons hurled themselves at our advancing line. Without armour and without support they were not difficult to deal with. I took the spear on my shield and I lunged forward with my sword. Although the Saxon's shield moved across to protect himself he was not quick enough and my sword slid deep into his body. I saw a thegn organising his bodyguard. There were five of them in mail. Around him other warriors clustered to form a rough shield wall. It was just two lines deep.

I shouted, "Shields!" The seven of us locked our shields. It meant we slowed down but we were just five paces from the Saxons.

Behind me I heard Gudrun Witch Killer shout, "Lock shields and help the jarl!"

I felt the reassuring presence of a pair of shields pushed into my back and a couple of spears jabbed over our heads.

"For Siggi White Hair!"

We stepped forward with three quick steps and we thrust at the same time. The enemy spears smashed into our shields or clanked off helmets. I heard a grunt from Arne Four Toes as a spear laid open his cheek. Then we were so close that spears would not help. We were face to face with the Saxons. I had kept my sword down and now I stabbed forward blindly with it. There was a solid line of Saxons before us and the odds were that I would strike something. I felt it sink into something soft and then grate along bone. The Saxon next to the thegn I faced gave a shout and his shield dropped a little. Beorn Beornsson had quick hands and the Saxon fell with a sword to the throat.

Beorn became the tip of the wedge as he broke their front line and stabbed a surprised Saxon who stood behind him. The thegn dropped his, now useless, spear and tried to pull his sword. The press of our bodies against theirs made it hard and his right hand became trapped behind his shield. I brought my head back and butted him as he tried to free his sword. He was a strong warrior but he took a half step back. It was enough and I stabbed across his shield. My sword went into the side of the warrior fighting Arne Four Toes. Arne pushed the body out of the way and stepped through the gap to slay the next Saxon. The thegn was now isolated. Beorn and Arne had started to work their way down the second rank of Saxons.

The thegn drew his sword and swung it at me. He now had space to do so. My shield came up and his blade clanged off my boss. "Pagan pirate! God will punish you!"

I did not try to swing. Instead my hand darted forward. It slid over the rim of his shield. His helmet was open faced and my sword slid inside it slicing through his cheek and then his ear. I twisted it as I tore it backwards and, before he could react stabbed again. This time my blade entered his mouth, already screaming a curse at me, and the life went from his eyes.

The thegn was the last of those who stood before the warrior hall.

"Seal off the gates. Stop them leaving!" If there were any warriors left they would be isolated and without mail. I was confident that my men could deal with them. I turned to Arne. His face was a bloody mask. Kneeling down I tore a piece of material from the dead thegn's tunic. "Here, press this against the wound to stop the bleeding then go down and find the warehouses. Collect the grain. Beorn go with him."

"Aye jarl."

Rurik, Einar, come with me. We will search the hall. The rest of you, begin gathering weapons, mail and slaves!"

When we entered, I saw a priest standing with a cross protecting two women and a child. He was chanting in Latin. I said, "Priest if you try to fight us then you will die! I promise you that you will not be harmed. We do not kill priests and women."

He hesitated and Rurik took two strides, tore the cross from the priest's hand and shouted, "You heard the jarl now sit!"

The priest said, "This is King Egbert's niece! He will not rest until you are slain! This will not go unpunished!"

I smiled, "Thank you for that information. Einar, take the women and the child to the drekar. We have just increased our profits. Rurik, hold the priest."

"No!" The priest tried to put his body between Rurik and the woman.

Rurik silence the priest with a back hand to the face. He fell, stunned.

I said, "You will not be harmed, ladies. You will be ransomed. If your uncle values your lives, then he will pay to get you back."

The woman who was obviously the king's niece glared at me, "You are savages!"

"Perhaps but you are our prisoner and life will be easier if you do not annoy us!" I gestured to the stunned priest.

As Einar led them away I said, "Knut the Quiet. If this is the home of the niece of King Egbert, then we can expect jewels as well as the books of the White Christ. Search everywhere. Asbjorn and Audun, help him."

I sheathed my sword and headed out. The streets were remarkably quiet. Bodies littered the square before the hall. I saw that my men had already stripped them of mail, weapons and anything valuable. Harold Haroldsson and Gunnar Stone face came from behind me. "Jarl some twenty or thirty escaped out of the north gate."

"Then they will seek help. Have the men hurry to load the drekar. Tell Sven we leave as soon as I arrive."

When I re-entered the hall, I saw that my men had found some small chests, a couple of holy books and some fine linens and dresses. "Good, take them to the ship. Some escaped. We can expect enemies soon."

"Aye jarl." Laden, they left.

I saw that the priest was coming to. His face would bear a large bruise the next day. "Rurik, help him to his feet." He roughly pulled the priest upright. "You will live, priest, and you will be free." I saw incredulity on his face. "In return you will tell the king that we have his niece. If he wants her, the other woman and the child then he must send one hundred gold pieces to Dorestad. He has until All Saints Day. I choose a Christian date so that you will remember it. We have Samhain and that will remind us. His family will be returned unharmed. I will wait there for two days only. If the ransom is not paid by then I will sell them as slaves."

"That is barbaric!"

"I do not debate. Do you understand or shall I keep you as a prisoner and find another to be a messenger?"

Shaking his head, he said, "I will do as you ask. And what is your name so that I may tell King Egbert?"

"I and Jarl Hrolf of the clan of the horse."

He nodded, "I will remember and I am certain that the king will too!"

I laughed, "And if you think I fear his enmity then you do not know me! Now go!"

He scurried out like a frightened doe.

Rurik asked, "Was that wise, giving him your name?"

"Do you fear the Saxons? The day we fear them is the day we just farm and do not raid."

He laughed, "You seem to gather enemies like a squirrel gathers nuts!"

"Then let us make a few more. Set fire to this hall and I will do the same to the others. It will slow down pursuit."

I went to the large fire and picked up a log. Half was already on fire. I left the hall and went into the darkness. Next door was the church. My men had already cleared it. I threw the burning log beneath the altar. Made of wood it soon began to burn. The next two huts had fires within and it was easy to spread the fire and set them alight. Eventually, as I emerged from the fourth hut, the settlement was ablaze and thick smoke filled the air. I hurried down to the quay. Rurik and I were the last two to arrive.

Sven shook his head, "We thought you were going to stay!"

"No but I wanted to leave our mark. Let us go!"

"Man the oars!"

With the wind against we would need to row home. My men took off their helmets placed their shields on the sheerstrake and took up their oars. After Siggi used an oar to push us from the land we began to head south. Our chant was a joyous one for we had done well. The two dead men we had suffered now lay by the mast and we would mourn them when we were home but for now we were happy.

Siggi was the son of a warrior brave
Mothered by a Hibernian slave
In the Northern sun where life is short
Is back was strong and his arm was taut
Siggi White Hair warrior true
Siggi White Hair warrior true
When the Danes they came to take his home
He bit the shield and spat white foam
With berserk fury he killed them dead
When their captain fell the others fled
Siggi White Hair warrior true
Siggi White Hair warrior true
After they had gone and he stood alone
He was a rock, a mighty stone
Alone and bloodied after the fight
His hair had changed from black to white
His name was made and his courage sung
Hair of white and a body young
Siggi White Hair warrior true
Siggi White Hair warrior true
Siggi White Hair warrior true
Siggi White Hair warrior true

he journey home was slower than the outgoing one. The slaves wept and moaned all the way back. The exception was the thegn's wife who glared at us. Had she been Viking then I would have sworn she was lying a curse or a spell upon us. If she thought to intimidate us she was wrong. We had six other women we had taken and four children. It soon emerged that the woman with the thegn's wife was her servant and the child her daughter. I was no certain if I had asked too much or too little. It did not matter over much. There were men in Dorestad who would pay more for a slave who had been a lady. I would prefer to sell them back to Egbert but that all depended on how he viewed them.

We arrived back after dark and Sven had the difficult task of negotiating the rocks around the causeway. It meant that we had many hands to help us unload. I saw that Bertrand and Gilles were there. "Escort these two women and this child to my hall. Guard them well for they are to be ransomed."

The other slaves were taken to our slave pen. They would be yoked; at least for a while. Once they realised that there was no way that they could return home they accepted their life. I had. We would have to be their hosts for two months. My home would not be the pleasant place it had been. Alain strode over to me. "It looks like you had a good raid, lord. We had no trouble here. We saw no signs of our enemies. I did not expect any."

"Why not?" I was curious. If the situation had been reversed, then we would have wreaked revenge quickly and decisively.

"The Leudes. Both lords will have to tell their liege lord of the attacks. He will decide what they ought to do. He is the embodiment of King Louis in this part of the world."

I nodded, "Thank you, I am relieved."

"Do not be for if the Leudes of Rouen comes it will be with a mighty army and Philippe of Rouen would not have been given such a responsibility if he was not a good general."

"Thank you for the warning. We have more weapons, helmets and mail. Some of the swords will be better than the ones we have. Give them to the men who have good skills."

Eventually I went to my hall. I had put it off as long as I could but I could delay no longer. When I entered, I saw that my wife had managed to deal with the situation well. Even though she had had no warning she had managed to use screens to make a sleeping are for the three Saxons. It was a small thing but I saw that the Thegns wife was happy.

Mary smiled, "I have told the Lady Aethelflaed that she will be treated as a lady here. She was not impressed by your men. She thought them barbarians." She was speaking openly and I guessed that the Saxons could not speak our languages. I could speak at least three.

"Good. And how is our other guest?"

"Pepin is in better spirits. I have had him watching over Ragnvald. He seems to like our son." She winced, "And I fear that my time is almost here."

"And I am home. All will be well."

She laughed, "You have done what you always do. You have triumphed!"

Chapter 11

Our daughter was born in the middle of Tvímánuður. We named her Matilde after the Frankish lady who had held her people together for so long. The lady Aethelflaed and her woman, surprisingly, helped with the birthing. I suspect it was something to do with a common understanding of birth. My people celebrated. The jarl had a son and it was right that he should have daughter too.

Just after she was born I sent Sven and Harold, along with Bertrand, to Dorestad. I wanted news of Egbert and we needed to sell the holy books and spend some of the treasure we had taken. We had captured great quantities of grain. We were now well supplied with food but the women of the Haugr all wished for more and better pots. The ones we had found in Haestingaceaster had been of poor quality. We used them for the slaves. We also needed wine for I wished the upcoming marriage to be a great celebration for our people. It would double as a feast of the harvest. Since we had hostile relations with the Franks we would have to go further afield.

I resumed my horseback excursions around my land. We had stretched out a little further. More trees had been cleared. They were used for building and for timber. The ground was used by pigs and sheep. When the new grass came, we would plough it and plant crops but the animals could graze and fertilize it at the same time. Each month saw me having a longer journey to meet all of the clan. I did not mind.

When my knarr did return, Sven brought a message. King Egbert has sent word to Dorestad that he would pay the Vikings on All Saints Day as we had asked. He would send a ship there with his representative on board. I told the lady Aethelflaed. She was pleased. She and my wife got on well. If it were not for the situation it might have been a pleasant experience.

We now had a well-armed body of men. Everyone had a helmet and a shield. Everyone had a spear and almost all of them had a sword. The ones who did not preferred an axe. More than half had mail of some description. None of it matched. It was that which we had taken form those we defeated. Others made their own armour. They used hide and metal plates or pieces of discarded mail. We knew that this time of peace was but a respite. King Louis and his Leudes would not have forgotten us. They would be plotting and planning our demise.

The birth of my daughter was not the only celebration. Gilles and Baugheiðr's marriage was welcomed by all. Both were popular. Baugheiðr was considered the most beautiful maiden in the Haugr. Brigid made a special ale and that, along with our specially purchased wine ensured a convivial atmosphere at the wedding feast. Gilles had no parents and so I decided that the expense would be borne by me. Mary approved. She said that, as the leaders of the Haugr we had a duty. They were like children to us.

We invited our Saxon hostages. The Lady Aethelflaed was softening. She glared and glowered less. She smiled more; especially when she held my daughter, Matildhe, for Mary. The harvest had been a good one and all were happy. Matildhe had not been the only baby born and our clan had grown by twenty. Life was good.

When Folki arrived in the '*Flying Fox*' I half expected bad news but there was none. He brought only good news. As he stepped ashore he said, "We have conquered a large part of the land along the Orne. We have colonised part of the coast north of where we live. Soon my brother thinks we will have a mutual border."

"Good. Is that the main reason for your visit?"

"No jarl. We sail to Dyflin. My brother needs more men."

"You have lost some?"

He shrugged, "My brother says that losses are inevitable. We slay more of the enemy than they do of us. They fear us now. Their horses are not the threat they thought they would be." He smiled, "I called here in case you wished anything buying from the market in Dyflin."

I nodded. I handed him a purse of coins, "If you can purchase any Saami bows then do so. I know not what the going rate is these days but whatever it is, the price is worth it."

"I will buy all that I can. My brother does not value the bow. I think it is a good weapon. I will see you in a month or two."

"May the Allfather be with you."

"And with you."

Folki was as good as his word. He arrived back in the third week of Haustmánuður. We were preparing the drekar for our visit to Dorestad. The crops were in and the stubble burned. The animals had been brought to their pens for the winter and the haugr and outlying farms were a hive of activity as meat was preserved and fruit sorted and stored. The leather workers were busy tanning and the charcoal burners making as much charcoal as they could. Bagsecg now had three forges. He seemed to eat

120

both iron and charcoal. Folki beamed when he landed. He had managed to buy two bows. He shook his head, "They are worth a king's ransom! I cannot see their value."

"We do and I thank you for your efforts. Did you hire the men you needed?"

He nodded, "The Jarl Dragonheart has scoured his land of Danes. There were many who had fled to Dyflin for safety. They were keen to get as far away from the Land of the Wolf as they could."

I frowned, "The enemies of the Dragonheart would not be my choice of warriors."

"My brother will make them swear a blood oath. Any that do not we let go. We managed to secure thirty. They are battle hardened."

After he had gone I spoke with Arne Four Toes and Einar Asbjornson. Neither of them approved of Fótr's actions. Arne, in particular, had strong views. "I do not say that there are no Danes with whom I would fight but I have yet to meet large numbers that I would trust. Many of those who came to Raven Wing Island were Danes. I hope the young jarl knows what he is doing."

"He appears to be successful. I wish him well. He has already helped us for I believe this is one reason my the Leudes has not reacted to our handling of his men."

Once again, I left Alain to train more horsemen. We now had enough horses to mount over twenty-five riders. Gilles and Bertrand would help him. Nor did I need a large crew. We used one man at an oar. We would not be going to war. We would be handing over three prisoners. We left the day before Samhain. I wanted to be there a day before the exchange took place. We rowed north and then found some south easterly winds which meant we did not have to.

The Lady Aethelflaed had been speaking to me since my daughter had been born. It was as though the birth made me a civilised person. She gazed north to the smudge of land that was the kingdom of Cent. "You know that my uncle will make you pay for my kidnap?"

"I know he will try. But as his first wife ran away with the Dragonheart's daughter and he did not manage to wreak vengeance until many years later I will not worry. When you see him then tell him where my home is. If he thinks he can take it then he is welcome to try. If he does the bones of his warriors will lie bleached on my beaches!"

"But he has vast armies! he has conquered Cent, Corn Walum and Mercia. The East Angles acknowledge him as Bretwalda and as soon as Northumbria bows its knee then he will be."

"That matters not. If the Saxons do not wish us to raid, then make your homes stronger. Do you think my home could be taken easily?"

She shook her head, "No, it came as a surprise to me. Are you not afraid that I will tell my uncle how he can capture it?"

I laughed, "And you know how to capture it?"

"I know where the gates lie and the ditches."

"Good then tell him that. I like overconfident enemies."

She seemed nonplussed that I appeared unconcerned. I knew that any ships coming to my land risked the rocks. Once they landed they would have the sea and my men to fight. My walls were cleverly constructed using what nature had provided and my guile could construct. The double ditches and bridges we could draw up had been copied from those in the land of the wolf. I was confident that we would not be an easy conquest.

"He is an ally of King Louis you know."

"I know."

"I have heard that King Louis hates all Vikings."

"He probably does. I have lived in his land for almost three years. So far he has not taken back enough land to bury a man."

"Are all Vikings as confident as you?"

I shrugged, "We are all independent. We do not recognise a king and value family and clan above all else. It is what makes us who we are."

She shook her head and looked aft. "You are lucky to have such a good wife. She is a real lady."

"And now you are a widow."

"That will not be for long. My uncle will marry me off again to make a political alliance."

"That does not sound very civilised."

"It is our way. I will marry some lord and my uncle will have more allies to help him become Bretwalda."

For the first time, I felt sorry for her. Her ordeal had been as nothing compared with her normal life. In my home, she had been treated well and enjoyed more freedoms than she would in the land of the Saxon. It was strange.

It was late in the day when we reached the port of Dorestad. I did not wish to try to find rooms and so we slept on board. The next morning I

122

went with six of my men to the inn we had used and where we had met Fótr and Folki. The owner remembered me and we were able to hire a room for the lady and her family. Six of my men stayed with them. It was not to guard them but to protect them. Dorestad was a wild town. I went, with Einar Asbjornson and Harald Fast Sailing to collect information.

We went first along the quay to speak with other sailors and captains. We took a jug of wine we had bought and it loosened tongues. We were also aided by my reputation and that of Fótr and his clan. They knew we were warriors and had coin to spend. We were worth cultivating. We learned that the civil unrest in the Empire was worsening. Brother vied with brother for power and King Louis had no control over his family. In the land of the Saxons King Egbert was now moving to take control of Northumbria and soon he would have complete power in the whole of that land: from the land of the wild men in Pictland to the borders with the Cymri. No one knew anything new about the Dragonheart save that he had defeated Danes and then disappeared. I knew, in my heart, that he was not dead for Folki had brought news that men of the wolf had traded with Dyflin. Jarl Gunnstein Berserk Killer would have known if the Dragonheart had perished. There was just one ship which did not give us any news. It was a Frank and the sour faced guard at the gangplank told me to go away. It was a little annoying as it was moored next to us. We had unpleasant neighbours.

After we had plied the sailors with drink and learned all that we could we went in some of the low taverns. There we heard more about Neustria. The Leudes, Philippe of Rouen, had been buying weapons and horses. I found that ominous. He had hired the men of Brabant who used the crossbows. He had sought Germans who knew of siege weapons. Was he coming to get me? My visit to Dorestad now seemed *wyrd*. Had I not captured the lady then I would not have come and I would be blithely unaware of the plans Philippe of Rouen was making.

The three of us made our way back to our ship. As we neared it I saw that the next ship along was Saxon. It had the standard of Wessex flying from its mast. King Egbert had sent the ransom. Fearing an attack, we kept double guards watching the quay. I suspected treachery. When I awoke and there had been no attack I felt foolish. It was five ships from ours and if they tried anything then we would have warning.

We went aboard our ship. "I want a keen watch kept. The Saxons may try something."

I watched, half the night, with my men but nothing untoward occurred. I rose the next morning bright and early. I armed myself and turned to Sven, "Sven and Harold, prepare the ship for sea. I will speak with these Saxons and then fetch the Lady Aethelflaed."

"Aye jarl. The wind has turned overnight and now is from the land and we can leave the port quickly. The gods favour us this day. We know that it could change again by the afternoon. It is that time of year when winter storms begin.

Rurik asked, "Do you need warriors?"

"No, they will try nothing so long as we have the prisoners and when they hand her over they will sail and we can leave." I strode down to the Saxon ship.

Two mailed warriors walked towards us and clambered over the side. "You are the pirate who kidnapped Lady Aethelflaed?" The taller of the two warriors spoke.

I ignored the insult and smiled, "We have King Egbert's niece and she has enjoyed the hospitality of my home."

He looked over to my drekar, "Well bring her. She has endured your company long enough. We are keen to sail."

"You have the coins?"

The second warrior reached down and opened a box. He kept hold of the box. I saw that it was fill with coins. Jut to be certain I reached in and took one from the bottom. It was gold. I smiled, "Just checking. I will fetch them."

I strode down to the tavern. I did not think they would try anything until they had Lady Aethelflaed on their ship and so I did not take guards with me. My men and the hostages were waiting for me when I arrived, "Your saviours are here my lady. The ship awaits. Your ordeal is over."

She smiled, "It could have been worse. I thank you for your hospitality. I wish we had not been kidnapped but I am aware that we could now be slaves or dead."

When we reached the Saxon ship, we stood to one side to allow the three of them on board. I think the boy, Athelstan, was disappointed to be going home. My men had made a fuss of him and he had played with the boys in the Haugr while he had stayed with us. Perhaps that was what his mother meant.

I took the chest which was accompanied by a surly grin, "Make the most of this barbarian. Your days are numbered. Your dragon will roam the sea no more! You will die badly. Your bones will lie at the bottom of the ocean!"

I nodded, "They may be but it will not be by your hand!"

He turned and shouted, "Hoist the sail! There is a foul stench around here! Let us get to sea, quickly."

I shook my head. It was a childish insult. We walked back to my ship which was moored four ships down. I wondered if we had the opportunity to spend some of the money. Then I decided it would be better to take it home and spend it on something we needed. We had already bought that which we needed.

We were almost at our ship when the Frankish ship which was next to ours suddenly spilled out warriors who ran down the quay towards me. They did not make a noise. They just ran as though they were heading for a tavern but I saw their weapons. This was an ambush and I had walked into it. My crew were busy preparing for sea. The warriors had passed my drekar and were just forty paces from us. I saw that they were not all Franks there were more Saxons among them. This was a trap. I had six men with me. We could not reach our ship in time and so I laid the chest behind me and shouted, "Clan of the Horse!"

My crew had been busy organizing the drekar for sea and were slow to react. It was Siggi Far Sighted who yelled, "Treachery!"

I drew my sword and seax. It was Knut the Quiet and his five men who were with me. They were hard men and could handle themselves in a fight. That is what this would be. The men who came at us were pirates themselves. They wore helmets and some had mail but the wicked looking daggers and hatchets showed their true vocation. Luckily none had shields. We waited for them. It allowed the leading attackers to reach us before their fellows. I flicked up the sword which lunged at my unprotected middle and, stepping in close, tore my seax across the Saxon's throat. I had no time for self-congratulation. There were two more men running at me. I heard a cry as Finni Jarlson threw a Saxon between the quay and the Frisian ship. He was crushed as the ship rolled on the tide. I blocked one sword with my own and the second with a seax. One of the Saxons had a seax and he tried to rip it across my throat. I would have been dead but he struck my golden horse first. Even so the blade ripped across my chest opening up a wound.

I brought my right knee up into his groin and, as he bent double, brought the pommel of my sword into the back of his head. I jammed the cross piece into the eye of the other. As he screamed I gutted him with my seax and then brought Heart of Ice into the neck of the kneeling warrior. My men had joined the fray and the Saxons were overmatched. The sight of my bloody face made my men furious. The dead were slaughtered.

Sven shouted from the steering board, "The Frank! She is fleeing!"

I saw that the Frankish ship, having seen that their plot had failed was leaving harbour. "Grab their weapons and search their purses. These are brigands paid to kill me."

"But the Frank is escaping!"

"Einar do not let Sven hear you. Do you honestly think that a tubby little merchant ship can out run *'Dragon's Breath'*? We have time."

Rurik handed me a piece of tunic. "Here, jarl, hold this to your chest and stem the bleeding."

By the time we reached the ship the Frank was two hundred paces from us. Sven had a black look on his face, "I am sorry, jarl. We should have been more alert! If aught had happened to you..."

"It did not. You can catch him, can't you?"

"Before he has got a mile offshore." He cupped his hands and shouted, "Get the oars ready. Cast off and loose the sail. Let us show these Franks how to sail!"

Karl the Singer brought over some vinegar and honey. He took off the cloth and said, "This will sting, jarl." I nodded. I knew that it would. Taking a clean piece of linen, he wiped it across the wound. It came away red and the pain was excruciating. It was worse than the pain of the cut. Then he smeared it, liberally, with honey. That brought some relief and then he wrapped and tied a bandage around it.

"Thank you, Karl."

"I had better get to my oar. We have to pay back this Frank!"

I went to my chest and took out my helmet. Harold Fast Sailing shook his head, "You will not need that, jarl. He has but fifteen crew and they are no match for our warriors. You are wounded. Our men wish to avenge this act."

"I am the jarl, Harold. I will be going aboard her." It was not just bravado. I wanted to look for the evidence on the ship. I knew that there would be something to lead me to whoever planned this. Ultimately it would be Egbert but this had been planned by someone else. This ship was from Neustria. Who was it that had provided the vessel?

My men chanted and their song was an angry one. It was one from our days as Raven Wing Clan.

A song of death to all its foes
The power of the raven grows and grows.
The power of the raven grows and grows.
The power of the raven grows and grows.
A song of death to all its foes
The power of the raven grows and grows.
The power of the raven grows and grows.
The power of the raven grows and grows.
A song of death to all its foes
The power of the raven grows and grows.
The power of the raven grows and grows.
The power of the raven grows and grows.
Through the waves the oathsworn come
Riding through white tipped foam
Feared by all raven's wing
Like a lark it does sing
A song of death to all its foes
The power of the raven grows and grows.
Through the waves the oathsworn come
Riding through white tipped foam
Feared by all raven's wing
Like a lark it does sing
A song of death to all its foes
The power of the raven grows and grows.
The power of the raven grows and grow

ith each stroke, we grew closer and closer. We had our sail billowing and there was no way the Frank could outrun us. He had little alternative. You do not ambush Vikings and expect to live. You either succeed or find somewhere to hide where they will not follow. I did not think he would try to sail off the edge of the world.

The end came when he panicked. With our dragon prow almost touching his steering board he made a sudden turn to larboard and his sails flattened as he turned into the wind. Sven shouted, "In oars! Down sail!"

The wind took us to bump gently into his steering board. The master and his crew ran towards the bow. After Siggi Far Sighted had thrown a rope with a hook to secure us together Arne Four Toes led my men aboard the ship. Normally I would have been first but my warriors all stood before me so that I could not. When I finally clambered aboard my warriors had scurried down the deck. They did not need me.

I stood at the steering board. The chest which was there obviously belonged to the captain. I opened it. As I expected it was clothes which were at the top. The sealskin coat was there to be grabbed when rain came and to protect the contents. Beneath it lay a woollen garment to keep him warm. Below that was what I sought. There was a sealskin pouch. I took it and opened it. I could not read the words for although I could speak Frank I could not read it. What I did recognise was the seal. It was the gryphon. This had come from the Leudes of Rouen. I guessed it was some sort of warrant which the captain could use. Beneath that was a small cask with coins within. They were all imperial. Egbert might have ordered the assassination attempt but it had been carried out through Philippe of Rouen. I now knew why he had not tried military action. This was an easier way to rid himself of me and my crew.

Arne came back. There were four terrified Franks with him. "The captain and the rest threw themselves into the sea. They are dead."

The ship was now pitching as the wind twisted around the flapping sail. "Get back aboard Dream Strider. Leave two men with me and send Harold Fast Sailing over to sail this ship. We will return to Dorestad."

He looked at the four men. "And these?"

"They did not jump and they will wish to live. I think I can handle them. Now go. This delays our departure home and I can see a web of the Norns in this."

"Aye, jarl."

He left Sven Siggison and Rurik One Ear with me. While we waited, I said to the nearest sailor, "Where is your home port?"

He swallowed and said, "Rouen."

I held up the letter, "What is this?"

"The master was given the trade route to Lundenwic. He would be rich in a year."

"And now he is dead. The men who came with us, where were they from?"

"Lundenwic and Rouen."

Harold Fast Sailing boarded, "Jarl?"

"Take us back to Dorestad. We will sell this ship after we have stripped it of anything of value." I looked at the four men. They were ordinary sailors. "Obey my helmsman's orders and you shall go free when we land."

They nodded gratefully.

It took some time to turn and to tack back and forth. '*Dragon's Breath*' rowed back and forth behind us protecting us from further attack.

"We were lucky, jarl. Had they slain you then who knows."

"I know Sven. I think they thought to kill me quickly while I was carrying the chest. They hired not warriors but bandits and brigands. It was false economy. Mailed warriors might have defeated us. Siggi Far Sighted's quick reactions and eyes saved us."

Rurik shook his head, "If they thought they could end us with that band of brigands then they were wrong."

"Those men were expendable. It is another reason why I returned here. The Saxon thegn who made the exchange knew what was going on. They thought to kill me and enough of the crew to make us vulnerable to attack." I pointed astern. "King Egbert will have Saxon ships waiting to take us when we leave. They will be close by the narrow part of the sea. I am guessing that the Saxon will sail to Dwfr and join other Saxon ships. This is not over."

Harold had heard all, "That makes sense, jarl. The Saxon ship was well handled. I was watching her as we chased the Frank. They were almost below the horizon by the time we managed to catch the Frank."

"Can you arrange the sale of this ship? I am unconcerned what we get for it but if there is profit to be made from this then it should go to us."

"Aye and you can have your chest seen to by a healer. Knut did a good job but I can see the blood coming through your bandage already."

When we reached the quay the two berths were still empty. The harbour master and his guards were examining the bodies. After we had tied up Harold said, "I will go and speak with Günter, the harbour master. I know him."

I turned to the four sailors. "I want everything of value brought from below decks. Rurik go with them. When that is done then you may go but if you ever cross my path again then I would choose a watery death for I will not forgive you twice."

"Thank you lord! Our days at sea are ended!"

Perhaps Harold had been right about my wound. I began to feel light headed. As I left the ship the ships' masts began to spin and I found that my legs could not hold my weight. The sky went black and I fell.

Chapter 12

When I awoke, I was lying on my deck. "How long was I asleep?"

Sven shook his head, "You were almost dead! Your bandage was soaked with blood. We found a sailmaker. He stitched your chest. Harold gave him a gold coin from the Frank's captain's chest to make sure he made small stitches. None of us would risk the wrath of your wife if they were large ones."

I held my hand out. Rurik said, "You should rest."

I waved it. "Help me up!" He did so. "And the ship?"

Harold Fast Sailing said, "Günter, was annoyed with the Franks for bringing such disorder into his port. He has bought it from us." He shook his head, "He will profit from the sale for we were not given its true worth."

"Whatever it is we have more than we would have. It is weregeld for my wound. Can we sail?"

"Aye. We have the cargo from the Frank. It was fine pots and linens."

"Good." I turned to Sven, "We will be attacked. They will think that their attack hurt us and that we will be undermanned. Let us continue with that illusion. Do not line the strakes with the shields and have the crew stay hidden. Let them think they have an empty drekar."

"You have a plan, jarl?"

Arne Four Toes laughed, "That is like asking an eagle does it know what it has planned for its prey."

"I have a plan."

I explained the plan as Sven took us out to sea. We would not need to use the oars anyway as the wind was with us. It took us until early afternoon to reach the narrow straits between Dwfr and the coast of the land of the Franks. As we approached them I waved Einar Asbjornson over, "You are the best archer we have on the drekar. Here, take my Saami bow." I handed him my weapon.

"What do I do with jarl. I cannot slay a whole boat crew."

"When I give the word, I want you to send as many arrows over to the steering board of the closes Saxon ship. It does not matter if you hit any, just so long as you make them think they can be hit. I would do it myself but the wound in my chest would make it a waste of arrows."

"I will do it jarl but I know not what good it will do."

"Sail to steerboard!"

Siggi's voice made us all look.

"Now it begins, Sven. There will be another ship to the landward side too. Where the third will be, I know not."

My men took their places at the benches. We would only be using six oars each side to give the illusion that we had lost men in the ambush. Each oar would be manned by a single oarsman until I gave the word and then they would be double oared. I hoped to give them a surprise.

Erik Half Grown shouted from the bow, "Ship to landward!"

A moment later we discovered where the third ship was. Siggi shouted, "Ship astern." There was a pause. "It is the one which left Dorestad."

I nodded, "Now we have his plan we can deal with it. Sven, they will converge knowing that if we turn either way they will have us. Steer straight. Have the oars run out. They will expect it."

Harold said, "It is the one astern I worry about. I saw her when she left Dorestad. She is faster than most Saxon ships and she has two sails. With the wind astern, she will close with us until we have the oars fully manned."

"I know. Do not worry, Harold Fast Sailing. I do not think the Norns have finished with us yet."

The wind had whipped up the waves. It was stronger now than it had been. Sven had been right. The wind at this time of year was unpredictable. If the gods really favoured us, then they would make it swing around and halt the Saxons. I did not think that would happen. The two Saxons were being cautious. They were using the wind from their quarters to converge slowly. I had no doubt that the thegn who followed us had devised this plan. This way would take more time but they would catch us.

As the oars began to bite we moved quicker. I turned and saw that the Saxon astern had rigged another piece of canvas. It the wind changed they risked broaching for they had so much canvas that their gunwales would be temptingly close to the sea. But the extra canvas on the prow was edging them closer. I had to time this right or I would exhaust my men and for no good reason. The twelve men who rowed were the strongest warriors I had.

The two Saxon ships were close enough for me to see that their decks swarmed with men. I saw helmets but no mail. The Saxons feared the sea and would risk mail. They were both closing with us. They were less than one hundred paces from our bow. Einar, try an arrow at the ship to landward."

"Jarl he is two hundred paces from us."

"And that bow is powerful. Just try. The first arrow will allow you to gauge the range." Those who were not rowing watched as the arrow arced into the air. Its converging course necessitated skill from Einar but he was a good archer. The arrow sailed over the drekar and cleared the steering board by forty paces.

"You were right jarl."

"Good now send three arrows in that direction and then three at the other. Sven ready the other oarsmen."

I did not look at the two nearest Saxons. I looked astern. The third ship was now two hundred paces from us and closing rapidly. I heard a cheer and looked to landward. The Saxon ship had suddenly changed course. Siggi shouted, "Einar has hit the helmsman! The sail=or next to him has an arrow in his arm too!"

Einar changed to the other ship, because of our sail, had not seen the fate of its consort. This one was even closer and I watch Einar's three arrows as they plummeted to the steering deck. A warrior fell transfixed. The helmsman was hit and a third wounded. This time the helmsman took matters into his own hands and pushed the steering board over to take it away from us.

"Sven, the rowers!"

The rest of our men joined the oars and we almost leapt forward as the extra power took us further from the nearest Saxons. The third one had changed course slightly to come down our steerboard side. They were now a hundred and fifty paces from us. Soon we would extend our lead but the angle of their approach gave them more wind.

"Einar, the last ship. Use as many arrows as it takes."

He had the range and he was not tired yet. When he had emptied the quiver then he would be tired but he had just warmed up. The Saxon had aided him. If he had stayed on our stern, then the sails would have hidden the steering board. This way Einar could see it. He would have to send them over the sails but the angle was such that he could. His first arrow fell slightly sort but managed to hit the ship's boy who was at the masthead. We heard the crash of his body hitting the deck over the sound of the wind and the waves. His second arrow hit the helmsman but I saw that the thegn was ready for that. He held the steering board and another man was pushed towards it. The third arrow did it. Before the next helmsman could take over Einar's arrow pitched the Saxon thegn over the stern of the ship. The new helmsman put the steering board over and they moved away from us. Their last chance had gone. I had thrown the bones and we had won. The men cheered as we began to extend our lead. The ones who had not rowed joined the oars and, with a song in the air, we escaped.

The horseman came through darkest night
He rode towards the dawning light
With fiery steed and thrusting spear
Hrolf the Horseman brought great fear

Slaughtering all he breached their line
Of warriors slain there were nine
Hrolf the Horseman with gleaming blade
Hrolf the Horseman all enemies slayed

With mighty axe Black Teeth stood
Angry and filled with hot blood
Hrolf the Horseman with gleaming blade
Hrolf the Horseman all enemies slayed
Ice cold Hrolf with Heart of Ice
Swung his arm and made it slice
Hrolf the Horseman with gleaming blade
Hrolf the Horseman all enemies slayed

In two strokes the Jarl was felled
Hrolf's sword nobly held
Hrolf the Horseman with gleaming blade
Hrolf the Horseman all enemies slayed

We stopped rowing as night fell. Sven changed course slightly in case they were still following. I doubted it. We had killed the man who would have pursued us. No one in his right mind follows a wolf to its lair. They hunt them in the open.

I began to feel light headed again. Harold Fast Sailing saw it and shouted, "Jarl, lie down! We do not want you falling. You have done all that you could. Sleep. We will take the drekar home."

He was right and, wrapping myself in my fur, I lay down. Soon I was asleep.

"Jarl, we are here."

I opened my eyes and saw sky. It was daylight. As Sven and Harold helped me to my feet they said, "We sailed through the night, jarl. The wind was with us until the last part and the men only had to row for a short time."

I stepped ashore it felt strange. I had rarely slept for so long on my ship. I turned and said, "Have the cargo unloaded. You all did very well. Einar, keep the bow. You have earned it."

Gilles and Bertrand hurried towards me. "Did it go well, lord?"

"It did Gilles. We have coin and we have booty. The Saxons tried treachery but we outwitted them."

They turned to walk with me. They were both sharp. Gilles especially had followed me for years. "Lord, what ails you?"

"I have a wound. It is nothing. Do not make much of it. My wife will worry."

"Aye lord." Gilles turned to Bertrand, "I told you we should have been with our lord."

"And I wanted you here. The land is safe? No Franks came while we were away?"

"Everything was quiet lord but…"

"But is what we fill with water or ale. Leave it at quiet and I am happy. Nothing untoward happened to me and it was a lesson learned. I shall go mailed, even where I think I am safe. My wife may prefer me in silks and fine tunics but not I. I would live to a ripe old age. My mail does that for me!"

In the end, it was the mouths of my crew which alerted my wife. They could not help themselves. They told all of our escape and ow their jarl had outwitted three Saxon ships even though he had a bad wound. Once alone, Mary had me strip off my clothes so that she could examine the sail maker's handiwork. "But is the wound clean?"

"It was cleaned with vinegar and honey. It was fresh gut which was used to stitch it. It does not smell bad."

"But it looks so red and angry!"

"It does not bother me." That, of course, was a lie but Odin never minds when a man lies to his wife. It is often out of necessity.

When she was satisfied, I dressed and she waited on me hand and foot. It was only when Matildhe demanded milk that she stopped. Then Ragnvald came to me. "Could I see the wound?"

"Ragnvald!"

"It is fine, wife. He will be a warrior. He should know of such things." I opened my tunic and showed him. He was young and he was curious. He ran his fingers over the stitches. He was gentle. "It will not affect me. In a month or so I will be as good as new. Perhaps even better for the scar will be tougher than my skin!"

He reached up and rubbed my beard, "Your beard is rougher now than when I was little."

"That is because I do not trim it. I used to. Your mother found it rough."

"It makes you look different."

"How?"

"It makes you look older!"

"I am son. All men age and all men die. That is what the Allfather wills."

"Mother said that when we die we go to heaven if we are good."

I looked at my wife and then back to my son. "If you are a warrior and die with a sword in your hand then you go to Valhalla, which is a warrior's heaven."

I saw now why the Norns had spun their web. Because of my wound my wife did not argue and that was the day my so began to become a Viking. He disappointed his mother for he never followed the White Christ. He followed the way of the sword and became a warrior.

She would not, of course, let me ride for the next few days. That was just as well as it began to rain with that biting rain which comes just before Yule. If we had been in the land of the wolf, then it would have been made of rain. We shared out our booty and our coins. The clan had half of the ransom and I kept half. That was the decision of my warriors. My men spent a day putting the drekar in her winter cradle and preparing it for winter. The Seven and Harold made sure that '*Kara*' was ready for sea. We might not raid but we would trade.

I spoke with Alain and told him of the treachery of the Leudes of Rouen, "I knew that he would not allow us to get away with this insult. I am not surprised he used assassins. You Vikings have a different code to that of the Frank. To them you are a barbarian and do not count as a person."

I was interested. "This Leudes will think us wild men?"

"Everything you do would lead him to that conclusion. You fight odds which are too great. You fight beyond hope and you are fearless. A Frank fears the wild. You are wild."

"Then if he fought us he would expect me to be wild and irrational?"

"Aye he would. What is on you mind, lord?"

"Some time, I know not when, then he will come to punish me and he will bring an army. If I can make him think I am reckless then I might be able to trick him."

"How, lord?"

I laughed, "I do not know, yet but I have the short days and long nights to devise a way. If he has not attacked yet, then he will not do so until after the winter."

Just then a sudden squally descended upon us like the wrath of Odin. We hurried into the shelter of the stables. "I cannot get used to this weather, lord. Where I come from, we are far from the sea. We have cold and we have snow but we do not have this constantly damp and wet weather."

"It makes for good grass and that makes fine horses." I stroked Dream Strider's mane. "I do not think we need ride out each day. Let us cosset our mounts for I fear we will need them in the spring."

"The men we have trained are improving each day. I would not like them to face the Franks yet but that will come."

"For the present so long as they look like horsemen that will do. They have met eleven of us who have bested them each time we have fought. If we go to war with treble that number they may believe we all have the same skills. If there is doubt in an enemy's mind, then that is half the battle."

He nodded, "I heard how you deceived three Saxon ships. It may be harder to do that on a battle field."

"What do we have which the Franks do not?"

He looked confused and then said, "Archers."

"Aye. And we now have three Saami bows. When Harold fast Sailing next sails to Dyflin I will use my share of the ransom to buy more. Mounted Vikings and good archers allied to a sound shield wall will surprise these warriors of Charlemagne."

PART TWO

Revenge of the Franks

Chapter 13

The winter was a hard one. It was the coldest we had had in our new home. We even had snow. It did not last long but it made us worry that it might. My wound healed well. The scar was vivid and red at first but gradually it softened to a white line. It was a reminder to me of how close I had come to death. We had also spent the winter practising, when we could. It exercised our horses without taxing them. We rode on the beach. I had finally given in and changed my helmet. Alain and Bertrand had persuaded me that the helmet with the nasal would give me as much protection as my helmet with the face mask but I would have better vision and it would not be as heavy. They were right. I added more protection by having a mail coif underneath it. It covered my neck below my fuller beard. Now that I had finally stopped trimming it for Mary it was thick and lustrous. Unlike many of the other warriors I did not plait it.

We had made changes, too, for our riders. The shields we used on foot were too large to be used on a horse. We made new ones which were slightly smaller. It meant we were able to use them on both sides of the saddle. Some of Alain's men adopted the spike boss. I retained my round one for it felt more familiar. Being smaller it was easier to fit a metal rim around it and we could stud it with more metal. Finally, I added metal to my cloak, especially around the neck. The wound to my chest had made me warier of such blow. Bagsecg beat some metal so thin that it hardly weighed anything and my wife sewed around the edge of my cloak. It made it look more attractive and, with the thick material of the cloak would make it harder for an edged weapon to hurt me. I was still vulnerable to a mace or a hammer.

Sven and Harold bought us four more Saami bows and the sailed to the clan of the fox. They took gifts from our clan. When they returned, it was with the disturbing news that Fótr was contemplating attacking Caen. I wanted to go to him and dissuade him. It was Mary who argued that I should not. She was backed by Alain and Bertrand. They sat with me and Gilles, around my table as we discussed our young neighbour.

"If you do try to dissuade him he will think it jealously, lord. He will say that because you do not wish to go to war he should not."

"No, for I will tell him that I am happy to go to war with him but not yet."

Mary had shaken her head, "He will resent you. He has had success which was nothing to do with you. He admires you for what you did. If you try to tell him it is like a big brother telling a younger one what he should and should not do. He will rebel and do it anyway. If you say we are not ready for war, then it is right that you wait. I agree with you. I do not think that you have the men to defeat a Leudes like Philippe of Rouen."

"You know him?"

"No but I knew men like him. I grew up with lords like that around my father's table. My father might not have been able to withstand a sudden attack by Vikings but he and his friends knew how to plan a campaign and use strategy to defeat an enemy before a battle. The Leudes will know that Fótr comes for him. He will be prepared."

Gilles suggested, "Perhaps this is a good thing. If he has a bloody nose, then he might listen to you."

They convinced me. I wish they had not but they did and I would have to live with my decision. We did not look out, we looked in. We planted crops. We began to train young boys. We cleared more fields and we patrolled our land. When we met the men of Valauna or Ċiriċeburh they fled before we could come to grips with them. I knew that they were under orders but so long as we were safe then it did not seem to be a problem. My son was given his first dagger and we began to plait his hair. Gilles told us he would be a father and our world seemed perfect.

The first news of problems came at the start of Einmánuður. It was a busy time of year for us. Gilles and Alain were busy with the mares who were foaling and my farmers were just finishing sowing their summer crops. My sailors had repaired, cleaned and readied my drekar. They were now fitting the new sail. I was with Mary and Bertrand and we were dealing with the Haugr and the business of administering justice. With more people than ever living in close proximity there were disputes. On Raven Wing Island the jarl had ignored them and it had led to deaths and civil unrest. We had decided that would not happen to us and we had a court in the spring and at harvest time where I settled disputes.

The three of us were just going through the cases I would hear when Finni Jarlson burst in, "Sorry to bother you, jarl but there are armed men in the woods. I think they are Vikings."

We dropped everything. Anyone close to our settlements was a danger. I donned my mail and sent Finni to tell my men to mount. By the time Gilles and I were ready Alain had brought his men around along with our horses. The elven of us rode, with Finni, south.

"Did you not ask who they were?"

"It was not us. It was two of Rurik's slaves. They were in the woods gathering blackberries and they rushed back to say they heard the sound of fighting and they had seen a dead warrior. They recognised him as a Viking but as he had no clan markings and no head they knew not who he was."

Rurik had brought both families behind his walls and he was ready for war. Leaving Finni there we rode into the woods with drawn weapons and cocked ears. We found the Viking. I recognised him from his arm rings. "This is Audun. He is one of Folki's men. What is he doing here? Spread out and move through the woods."

Once I was away from the others I could hear, in the distance, the sound of metal on metal. Men were fighting. I whistled and my men joined me. I pointed my sword in the direction of the fighting. Soon it became much louder. There were cries and shouts and the clash of swords. We were almost at the place where we had ambushed the men of Valauna when I spied the first horse. They were Franks. I did not shout nor did I give orders. I waved my sword and kicked Copper in the flanks.

The Franks were not on their horses. As Copper crashed through the woods a Frank turned. He was just tin time to see Hart of Ice come towards him had lay his chest open. I wheeled to the left and brought my sword down across the neck of another warrior. My handful of men had caused mayhem amongst the enemy. When they heard horses, they thought they were friends. Now they saw that they were foes. They melted back south, away from our flashing blades.

I reined in, "Come, they will reorganise! If you wish to live, then come north with us!"

There were less than eight of the Vikings left and four of them were wounded. One turned around and I recognised him as Folki Kikisson. "Jarl? Is that you?"

"It is now hurry. We do not have enough time. Alain, have four of your men ride double with the wounded. Hurry!"

It would not take long for the Franks to find their horses and come after us. They would rapidly realise that we were a handful. I waited until Folki and his men had passed and then shouted, "Back but keep your ears open." The Franks were never stealthy in the woods. They tended to lumber around them like a wild bull. We would hear their horses. It was

Theobald the Fair who had led the wounded Vikings from the woods. He would keep Folki and his people safe. It was now up to me to give them time to reach Rurik.

We were a thousand paces from the end of the woods when we heard the hooves of the enemy horses. It was Bertrand who heard them, "Lord, they come."

There were just seven of us. "Come to the trail and we will ambush them." As they joined me I placed them on either side. I had Bertrand and Gilles with me. The trail was the fastest way through the woods. The alternative was a twisting, turning and potentially hazardous route over tree roots and wickedly positioned branches. If you wished speed, then you used the trail. You kept your eyes ahead. By keeping our horses just three paces from the trail I hoped to surprise them.

When the first Frank passed, I kicked Copper and leapt forward. My sword hacked into the arm of the third Frank in the line. I heard shouts and orders from further down the column. Alain and I turned our horses together and rode at the next Frank. Alain favoured the spear and his spear took him in the chest. I lunged at the next warrior while holding my shield before me. His spear smashed into my shield and I lunged at his leg. My sword went deep into his thigh.

"We have done enough. Ride!" My new helmet saved my life. Even as I turned a Frank had left the path to attack my shield side. In my old helmet, I would not have seen him but I chah the movement from the corner of my eye. Pulling Copper's head around I was able to swing at him as his spear came towards me. He went for my face but his spear head caught on the clasp which held my cloak. The metal on the edge stopped penetration and I brought my scything sword around to lay open his stomach.

I continued the turn and headed through the forest. I knew I had less than a thousand paces to reach the edge of the wood and I rode as skilfully as I ever had before. I twisted and turned; I leapt fallen trees. I laid low over the saddle to avoid low branches and I used hands, knees and eyes as never before. It was when I heard the cries of those following who fell from their horses that I knew I had a superb horse and that I was now, truly, a horseman.

As I burst from the woods I saw my men waiting anxiously, twenty paces to my left. "I am safe. Where are the others?"

Alain pointed to the north. "They will be close to Rurik now. We should go!"

"Aye, we have used all the luck we have."

Now that we were in the open we made much better time. Our ambush and my hazardous escape had divided the Franks and they were five hundred paces behind us as we hurried north through freshly cleared land and across a greenway which had been compacted over the year by our hooves. We began to catch Folki and his men. I saw, just four hundred paces away, the sanctuary that was Rurik's. It was only a small place but we could defend it.

"We will keep our horses outside to threaten them. I think our attack in the woods was effective."

Theobald the Fair and his men entered the gates. They were followed by Folki and his men. Alain shouted, "Theobald rejoin us!"

I saw that Rurik and Finni were already on the walls with their slaves. Folki and his men joined them. They soon filled the walls. Theobald brought the others to line up behind me. The Franks hurtled up the greenway in a disorganised line. Rurik and Finni both had bows and they loosed arrows as soon as the Franks were in range. They did not cause wounds but the arrows falling amongst them made them stop and form a line. Even as they began to do so Finni sent an arrow into the shoulder of one of the Franks. I saw that there were thirty of them. They began to debate what they ought to do. Folki and his men must have been give bows by Rurik's people for there was a flurry of arrows which descended upon the Franks. They were not as well aimed as those of Rurik and Finni but it did not matter as it was the numbers which disconcerted the Franks. They wore no mail.

They withdrew. "Alain, follow them at a discreet distance and make sure they return whence they came. We will wait within these walls for you. See if you can capture any of the spare horses."

"Aye lord." He smiled, "That was as skilful a piece of horsemanship as I have witnessed. You are truly named."

"I was lucky."

I went with my two men into the stronghold. Agnathia and Finni's wife were tending to the women. "Water the horses, Gilles. I will see Folki."

I hung my shield from my saddle and climbed the ladder to the fighting platform. Rurik was speaking with Folki. Folki turned. I saw that he had been wounded too. He had a wound which ran from his eye to his chin. He was lucky not to have lost the eye. He held a piece of cloth to it. "We owe you our lives, jarl."

"What happened?"

His head dropped, "It is hard to tell."

"We have time. I would wait until the Franks have gone. Where they from Valauna?"

"No, they are the men of Caen. They have chased us for the last three days." Rurik handed him a horn of ale. He drank it and nodded. My brother decided to attack Caen. Men had begun to desert us for we just sat behind our walls and they had joined us for profit. We thought we had enough men and he thought to use an attack from the river and from the land. The Leudes anticipated our move. He was waiting for us. Our scouts had counted the men in the stronghold but they had not seen those who were hidden by the woods and on the far side of the river. He had machines which threw fire and stones. The three drekar were all destroyed. One burned and the other two were beached. When they were lying helpless on the shore, then the Franks fell upon them. The men were slain."

He emptied the horn of ale.

"My brother led the attack in the walls. I was with twenty men and we attacked the gate. The Franks and their horses attacked when we were committed." He shook his head. Some of those who had recently joined us, the Danes, they fled. It was a waste for they were cut down. My brother saw that we were trapped and so he descended and we made a shield wall. We began to head back to the drekar. The crews had been slain but two were beached by the river."

"We had a hundred men in the shield wall when we started to fall back. Twenty died before we reached the drekar. Even as we reached it they fired one. Their horseman attacked again and again. We beat them off but, after every attack there were fewer of us. We fought our way aboard the drekar and the fifty of us who remained boarded and we took to the oars. My brother said we would sail back to our stronghold. It seemed a good idea. Even as we sailed their machines hurled stones at us. The weakened the hull and we rode lower in the water as we headed north to our walls."

"We barely made it. The forty-four who had escaped the slaughter had to run the last thousand paces but it was in vain. The Franks had sent men to fire our home. It burned along with all of the treasure we had collected. My brother decided that we would head here and join you."

I nodded, "That is a long journey. I have done it on a horse."

"We had to fight our way past the men who had fired the walls and we kept fighting until the sun went down and then the thirty-five who were still alive found shelter in a forest. Fótr thought we had lost them. We spent the next day moving through the woods. He was confident that we would have lost them."

"But you had not." I now knew that this Leudes was a clever man. He had not sought them out for he knew where they were going. They would be heading for me. "They were waiting for you close to the woods where we found you."

Folki looked at me as though I was a galdramenn. "Aye, how did you know?"

"It is what I would have done. The only place you would find a sanctuary was here."

"We woke the next morning and headed north along the greenway. When we were not attacked then Fótr took heart. He sent me and fifteen men ahead to spy out the road ahead. We had just found the woods when they attacked. They fell upon Fótr and his men. We tried to get to them but there was a wall of horses between us. We slew many horses. Fótr was the last to die. A lord with a dragon on his shield took his head. When I saw that they were dead then I fled, with those who survived into the woods. After we had slain some of their horses they dismounted and then you found us."

"He had a good death."

"Aye he had a good death."

"Jarl, Alain returns."

I looked up and saw Alain and my men riding easily towards us. They were leading five horses. This skirmish was over but the war was about to begin.

Chapter 14

Leaving Rurik and Finni to guard their home I took the rest of my men and Folki's warriors north. The wounded were on the horses. One of them would never fight again. Fótr had paid a heavy price for his ambitions.

"These war machines which threw stones, what did they look like?"

"They had four wheels and had a basket. The men pulled back on them and then released them."

"How far did they throw their stones and fire?"

"Perhaps a hundred and fifty paces. They had three but when one of the pots they used set fire to one they just had the one."

"Was that how they sent fire at you?"

He nodded, "They had clay pots and there must have been fire within them."

"Have they used them against you, jarl?"

"Not yet. I think, Folki, that your brother had ambitions and spoke loudly of them. You have Franks who lived with you?"

"Aye slaves. We used their women."

"Did any escape?"

"Some. Others tried and we captured them. Fótr took the toes from one foot to stop them doing so again."

"Then that is how the Leudes knew you would attack. He waited for you. He knows how Vikings fight. Or, at least, he believes he does. He expected you to use your ships and your men. He was ready."

"Will he wait for you to attack him?"

I shook my head, "I have irritated him long enough. Rescuing you and slaying his own men will be the last straw. He will come."

He nodded, "Wyrd."

"And what of you and your men? I can have my knarr take you to Dorestad or Dyflin if you have had enough of Frankia."

"No, jarl. With your permission, we would join the clan of the horse. All the advice you gave my brother was good but he chose to ignore it. I am no jarl. I will follow you as will my men. There are few of us but we have vengeance to extract. If we are to perish then it will be under the banner of the horse."

"Good. We will be proud to have you in the clan."

"Do you expect your warriors to ride?"

"Many do but many do not. Let us see if you have the skill. If not, then you will fight in the shield wall."

"That we can do."

Our arrival was the cause for both concern and consternation. There were many who had seen the clan of the fox and thought that they would survive. They had more warriors than we had and yet they had been slaughtered. My warriors, however, knew better.

Arne Four Toes said, "This is the clan of the horse. We do not break as easily."

Einar nodded, "Aye and we do not take warriors we do not know. You are welcome Folki Kikisson but your brother took any who would follow his banner. We do not have great numbers because we only accept those who are of good heart. You will see Franks and Swabians, Norse and Frisian but they have one thing in common. Our jarl's eyes sought their hearts and they were good. He has done the same with you."

My wife also welcomed them. "It is good that they had no women to lose. It is the difference in you, my husband. Your vision stretches to the end of the world and beyond. Others can see no further than the end of their sword." She turned, "Pepin, you had better arrange beds for the new men."

"Aye my lady."

My wife had wreaked a great change in the maimed Frank. She had healed his body and then nursed his mind. She had given him ore tasks each day and more responsibility. He was Ragnvald's unofficial bodyguard as well as a sort of Steward who did tasks my wife gave him. He seemed happy and even carried a sword. It made him feel more like a man. I had been lucky in my choice of wife.

I sent for my warriors over the next day to convene a council of war. I sent Sven and haro9ld in the knarr to Dyflin to buy more bows and to tell jarl Gunnstein Berserk Killer of the infidelity of the warriors who had deserted Fótr. The jarl was an honourable man. He would make sure that others who wished to join us were made of sterner material.

It was cool but pleasant and so we met under the skies which were filled with scudding clouds. "I think our respite is now over. So long as Folki and his brother held the land to the south of us then we only had the two local Frankish lords to worry about. I am now certain that Philippe of Rouen will come to not only punish us, but also wipe us from the face of the earth."

There were rumblings from my men and Rurik One Ear spoke for them all when he said, "Let them come! I relish the prospect!"

"Do not expect an easy victory such as we had over the men from Valauna. This is a cunning lord. He has war machines. He has a mind and will devise strategies to trick and trap us."

Einar Asbjornson said, "But you have a plan, do you not?"

"I do. We now have sixteen warriors who do not farm. Most of you will need to sow your crops and tend to your animals. You cannot watch for our foes. Alain of Auxerre and his horsemen will stay with Rurik and Finni. They will watch for signs of the enemy heading from the south. Folki and his warriors will live with Erik Green Eye and Rolf Arneson who live a short way to the north. When Sven returns, we will use the knarr to watch the coast. I have no doubt that this Leudes will try to stop us going about our daily lives. He will see that as a way to weaken us. We saw his patience with Fótr."

"Will he not try to exploit his victory and attack sooner?"

"No, Folki. He lost men. Your brother and your clan killed many. We took and slew horses. He cannot just follow us. It will take time. He has no slaves who will be deserting us to tell him what we plan and so he will send scouts. If we cut off his information, then he will be the one who will become worried."

"When will he come jarl?"

"If I knew that then I would be a galdramenn like Aiden but I am just a warrior who knows how to use his mind. Bagsecg and his family will make arrows and spear heads. We will be ready." I pointed beyond the walls. "We will mark the range of our arrows with disguised stones. They will not be ready for our bows. We have a number of Saami bows. I have sent for more. Our best archers will all have a weapon which the Franks do not know. We have a greater range than their war machines. They will not find us such an easy target for it is we who will watch their coming and we will be the ones with surprises."

There was, as there always is, much discussion and refinement of my plan but everyone was happy with it and the clan was united. The part which I had not told them involved me and my two warriors. We would go to annoy and irritate the two lords who lived close by in an attempt to draw them out. I counted on their hatred for me to override the orders given by their Leudes. I had more hope with Charles Filjean but I was confident that we could weaken the young Hugo of Ċiriċeburh.

It did not take long to position our stones and then my two sets of warriors left. I went with Alain of Auxerre. I told him what I had planned. He smiled, "That may work. If you wish to annoy Hugo of Ciriceburh then mention his brother. Guiscard was a noble warrior who died bravely fighting the men of Cordoba. He and his oathsworn died to the last man."

"Thank you, I will. Be wary in the woods. They know we have skill and they will try all sorts of tricks. Do not believe any message which comes from them."

"I know my own people, lord. I am not easily fooled."

Instead of riding through the forest we rode to the road and thence to Valauna. I had my bow with me as well as a spear. Gilles and Bertrand both knew what we were doing. I had explained in detail what I would do and what they should do also. We fought well together. The two of them almost anticipated my moves and actions. It saved time. We were about a mile from Valauna when we came upon two messengers. I heard the sound of their hooves approaching and had an arrow ready in my hand. As the two riders emerged around a bend I sent an arrow at no more than one hundred paces range to pitch one rider from his saddle. They were not expecting trouble and our attack took the survivor by surprise. As Bertrand and I kicked our horses in the flanks he whipped his horse's head around and sped back to the town. Gilles galloped after the horse. They were too valuable to allow to wander in the countryside.

We were gaining. The rider's head turned in terror as our horses drew closer. I heard his shout as we approached the gates, "Northmen! It is the devils from the north!"

I almost laughed at the panic which ensued. The warriors at the gate moved so quickly that the harbinger of their doom was almost cut off outside their walls. I could hear a bell tolling within and warriors appeared on the fighting platform in great numbers. We reined in two hundred paces from the walls.

Bertrand chuckled, "We nearly had him, lord."

"Aye we did. Let us wait here and see what they do." We both leaned forward to stroke the manes of our horses. I heard hooves behind and turned to see Gilles with the messenger's horse. He reined in next to me and I saw a leather tube hanging from the saddle. "What is that?"

"I know not. I took his sword but I did not examine the saddle." He took it and opened the end. Inside was a document. I could see the seal hanging from it. He held it out to me. I unrolled it. The writing was in Frankish. The seal, however, I recognised. It was the gryphon.

"Bertrand, it is in your language. Can you read it?"

He took it, "Aye, lord. It is from the Leudes of Rouen. It orders Hugo of Ċiriċeburh to raise the levy and await orders. He is also ordered to discover the defences of the stronghold of the barbarian." He laughed, "The last part is interesting, lord. It says that under no circumstances is he to engage in military activities against the barbarians."

I nodded, "Replace it in the tube. I will have my wife read it too. There may be hidden meanings in the words." He did so. "I am guessing that Charles Filjean also had the same message. I cannot see him venturing forth. A pity; still at least we know that what I deduced is what will happen. We might as well ride to Ċiriċeburh. He has not received this message and he may decide to react. I hope so. I woke up this morning ready for a fight."

We were seen a half a mile from the walls and the gates slammed shut. I rose close enough to shout but far enough away to be safe from arrows or slings. I would speak with Hugo of Ċiriċeburh. Is he within?"

A moment later a head, encased in a full mask helmet appeared over the top. "I am Hugo, lord of this burh. What do you wish, barbarian?"

"I one offered you the hand of friendship and you spurned it. For a warrior like me there are only two kinds of people: friends and enemies. Having said you are not my friend then you must be my enemy and as my enemy I am here to fight you."

"Three of you would fight us?"

"That would not be a problem, but I had in mind a combat between you and I."

2Like the one which maimed and ultimately killed Jean of Caen? Do you think me a fool?"

"No, I think you a coward. You abandoned the men who fought for you. When I attacked your men, you fled and left them to be captured and killed. One of them now serves me. Pepin of Senonche may only have one arm but he has more courage than you. Perhaps all the courage in your family lay in the blood of Guiscard, your brother. It is a pity that he died and not you. Your family might not have to live with the shame of a cowardly son."

I heard him roar, "Kill him! Kill him now!"

I turned and winked at Bertrand, "So it works eh?"

I waited until the gates opened and twenty horsemen galloped out. When they were a hundred paces from us I turned and we cantered down the road. They came hard and I heard their hooves thundering. We urged our horses to go a little faster. I knew that we had good horses. I realised that some of those who were following would also have good horses but others would not. Glancing over my shoulder I saw that they were already strung out and we had covered barely half a mile. I let the leading riders get to within twenty paces of us and then I had Dream Strider open his legs. The leading riders kept pace with us and, from their faces, I saw glee that they thought they were catching us.

I kept the speed so that they remained twenty to thirty paces from the rumps of our horses. I wanted them to follow me. I needed them to chase us to Erik Green Eye's home. I said, "Now Bertrand, abandon us. You know what to do."

"Aye lord!"

Gradually Bertrand opened a gap between him and us. I heard a shout of triumph from behind. They had the illusion that they were catching us. They were not! The twenty men were now spread out in a long line. They covered almost six hundred paces from the eager leading riders and the laggards at the rear. We knew our land well and they did not. Our patrols had kept them from our borders. When the leading riders began to drop back I slowed Dream Strider so that they kept contact. We still had some miles to lead them. Our two strongholds were less than eighteen miles apart and Erik Green Eye's walls were just fifteen miles from Ćiriĉeburh. When we passed the burned-out farm from the Breton attack, I knew that we had just a mile to go.

"Are you ready, Gilles?"

"Aye lord."

"Then when I give the word slap the spare on the rump and turn. We will give these leading riders a shock." I slowed down Dream Strider. It would give me more control when I turned. "Now!"

I turned to my left and, after sending the spare horse down the road Gilles turned right. My sword was out already. The leading Frank had his shield hung over his saddle as I did and his sword was in its scabbard. I swung my sword hard and it hacked deep into his arm. I wheeled my horse to the left and rode across the front of the third Frank in the line. His horse baulked when my mount passed before him and the rider found himself thrust forward. My sword hit him on the side of his helmet and he fell to the ground. Gilles had slain the second Frank and I yelled, "Enough, Gilles. He wheeled too.

As we resumed our ride I saw that our attack had bunched up the franks which was what I wanted. One lay dead, two others were wound, one looked to be serious. I wondered if they would decide to retreat and flee for their stronghold but when I looked back they did not. Now they rode in a column of twos. Whoever had taken over from the man I had wounded had more sense than he did. We were catching the spare horse and I saw the spiral of smoke which told me we were close to Erik's hall. There ten warriors and Bertrand awaited them. There would be four boys with slings. I was confident.

As we crested the rise I saw that Erik and Folki had formed a shield wall. It was less than thirty paces from the rise. Bertrand waited on one side. Gilles and I wheeled our horses to the other. As they came over the top they were galloping. They had two choices, try to stop or try to wheel out of the way. They tried to stop. They did not manage it. A wall of spears jabbed and poked at them. I saw two horses rear as spears plunged into their chests. Stones clattered from the helmets of the warriors as four boys enjoyed themselves hurling lead balls at them. The three of us who were mounted urged our horses forward. We had a perfect killing platform. With the spears preventing the warriors from advancing we pressed into their sides. I brought my sword over and smashed into the shield of a Frank. It hurt him. I swing again at head height. Although he ducked beneath his shield my sword knocked his helmet from his head. Gilles lunged forward and his sword found flesh. As Bertrand slew another a third was felled by lead balls and the ones at the rear turned and fled.

There was little point in exhausting our animals and I shouted, "Halt! We have done enough!"

Gilles and Bertrand dismounted to calm the four horses who remained alive. I dismounted and, taking my seax, ended the misery of the two wounded horses, "Go to the Allfather. You died as warriors. He will welcome you."

Folki led the rest of my men to despatch the wounded. None would have lived above an hour anyway. There were five dead Franks. I knew that others had been wounded. We had accounted for eight Franks and I was satisfied. Now that I knew the plans of our enemies I could act accordingly.

Folki had a cruel smile on his face as he wiped his sword on the tunic of dead Franks. "It felt good to be able to fight these Franks on our terms. I can see now, jarl, why you are successful. You know how to fight and you adapt to your enemies. We did not do so. My brother paid with his life."

"I think that your tactics might work. I have fought that way before. This Philippe of Rouen, though, he is clever. If we do things the same way with him then we will get the same result. When we fight, he will see our shield wall and think that is all we have. He will find that he is mistaken."

The three of us led our five horses home. The day had not ended as I had planned but it had gone well. I held the leather pouch in my hand. Had the Norns spun again? Were they responsible for putting this important letter in my hand? Who knew?

Chapter 15

When my wife read the letter, she frowned. "Bertrand misread a couple of the words. Hugo of Ċiriċeburh is supposed to send men to get into our stronghold rather than just discover our defences."

"That does make a difference. He had the franks who fled Fótr to tell him what their plans were. As Hugo as not received this news then we must expect something similar from Valauna."

"It does not change the fact that we will be attacked and, from the sound of this letter, before summer is out."

"My warriors and I knew that."

"But Rouen has many soldiers. This is the representative of King Louis. He can call up the levy for the whole of this land."

"Yet I do not think he will."

Matildhe had finished feeding and my wife waved over the servant, "Take Matildhe to bed. I will be along later." She then turned to me, "Why not?"

"It would take too many men from the fields. It would also expose them to fierce Vikings for they fight on foot. He will use just local levies. If he fails, then his farms will not suffer."

"That sounds a little cynical."

"His opinion of his two lords is obvious. He has no confidence in them. If he had, then he would have told them to be more aggressive. They are both expendable. He will have others he can appoint. This is not the Viking world where the clan elects the best warrior to be leader. This is a Frankish world where politics and intrigue rule."

"So, that makes you the best warrior?"

"It makes me the leader they wish to follow. I would never call myself the best of anything."

She smiled, rose and kissed me, gently on the lips, "But you are. I will let you know when you make mistakes. So far you have not."

I rode, the next day, to appraise Alain and Rurik of what I had learned. I also took two of the horses. They would enable my old friend and his family to flee faster when the Franks came. "I know it goes against our ways but if any Frank comes here; no matter what the story then they go no further. Rurik, you and Finni will let them stay with you and watch them. Tell them nothing. If we find they are spies, then they will die. If they are genuine refugees then, when all of this is over, we may let join our clan."

"I believe you are right, jarl. This Leudes is clever. We should not underestimate him. I know how to question men and to get answers."

"I would not have you hurt any until they are proved to be enemies. That is why they stay here. They cannot hurt us here." I turned to Rurik and Finni. "And I do not want you two to be heroes. As soon as the enemy comes use the horses I have brought and get your families within my walls."

"We will."

Our crops were in but my clan still had much work to do. The summer meant we could begin to harvest the salt from the sea. Women and children went each day to the pools we had created and collected the salt which appeared when the water evaporated in the heat of the summer sun. Sigurd and Skutal and their families took advantage of the longer days to collect as much fish as we could. The process of drying and smoking began. We had not smoked fish in the island but here, with the sea so close, it was easier and safer. The smoke hut lay to the north of the causeway where it could not set fire to houses or ships.

This year our hunts were even more important. We went, once every six days to the woods which lay to the south of Rurik and we hunted. With the threat of a Frankish attack we could also look for signs. Along with my two warriors I did not hunt but, when my men did hunt, I joined Alain as a thin screen to the Valauna side of my hunters. It meant we did not kill as many animals but my men were safe and we could look for signs of the enemy.

It was the hunt at the start of Skerpla where we found our first sign of others in the woods. We were well off the trail, walking through the dense undergrowth when I spotted the broken branches. They were too high to have been made by animals. Animals tended to move slowly through the woods and brushed the branches aside. A poor scout would break them. Once I saw the broken branches I began to look for the signs on the ground. Harpa had been a wet month and the ground had been soft. If you had been trained by Ulf Big Nose, then you learned to see that which others could not and I saw the print of a foot.

"What do you see, lord?"

"A print in the ground, Gilles. You and Bertrand take the trees further south and imitate my route. Look for signs on the ground and broken branches."

When we emerged close by the sea I knew that we had at least one scout or spy in my land. Gilles and Bertrand had seen nothing and I could only find evidence of one man. It was disturbing. I was not worried for whoever it was had not arrived in the Haugr. We had been especially vigilant since we had read the letter and no one new had arrived. When I rejoined Alain I told him my news.

"I am sorry, lord, we have not been as watchful as we might."

"Do not be so hard on yourself. It was one man and the forest is large. Had I not been trained by the best of scouts then I would have missed it." I pointed north. "We three will watch to the north. There are few places where a spy can hide."

The meat from the hunted animals was invaluable but everything else from the animal could be used. The hides were cured and the leather used for a whole range of things. The usable bones were used to make tools, needles and jewellery. The rest were used to make stock and then burned to make a fertiliser for our fields. We lived in harmony with the land.

Despite the threat of an attack we still had those who wished to farm and that meant using the land which was further away from the Haugr. Rurik was still the only one who lived far enough away to make me worried but we had farms in a circle around the Haugr. Each farm reflected the warrior who farmed there. The ones who used the bottom lands and grew crops had smaller farms while those who raised animals on the upland areas had more land and needed to use their families to herd the sheep and cattle.

Beorn Tryggsson was unusual for he farmed close by the sea. Low sand dunes had formed a barrier to the sea and he had salt pools behind them. Winter storms sent waves over the dunes and watered he grass which grew there. He had cattle, pigs and sheep. My wife thought him wise for the salt fed animals made the best of meat. It tasted of the sea. He also grew crops. But he was the only one who farmed so close to the sea. He would be in danger of inundation if we had a bad winter storm. Consequently, those warriors who fought with him in the shield wall had dug a deep ditch around his farm. This was not for defence from man but from the sea. It worked and Beorn prospered.

Six days after we had found the tracks of the scout my knarr returned with much needed weapons and supplies. I sent the knarr to patrol down to the deserted stronghold of Fótr and back. As we rested at

Beorn Tryggsson's farm I waved to Sven as the knarr headed south. "Have you seen any evidence of Franks, Beorn?"

"I know not what I have seen, jarl, but one of my slaves said that he saw lights dancing on the water."

"Have you seen them?"

"Aye. Once."

He hesitated and I said, "Well, what did you think it was?"

"My slave was afeard for he thought it was spirits. He comes from Hibernia and they believe in all sorts of spirits. For myself? If I was to take a guess I would have said it was a candle floating to see. It danced because the sea rises and falls." He saw Gilles look of incredulity and he shrugged, "It is what I would say."

I looked at Gilles, "And how would you explain it?"

"I have not seen it so how can I, lord?"

"Then do not dismiss Beorn's idea. Come Beorn show me where you spied the light."

He had a horse of his own. It was a small working horse and not a horse for war. He rode with us towards the dunes. His cattle complained as they moved away from the lush grass. The rains of Harpa had not flooded but fed Beorn's land and the cattle were fattening nicely. As our horses sank in the sand of the dunes I realised that this would be a perfect place for a spy to hide. The dunes shifted with the wind and the tides. They would hide the tracks of a spy.

"Here, jarl. My slave saw the lights on the sea here. He came to check on the cattle and used the top of the dune to make his task easier."

I looked and saw that the slave had word a barely visible track to the top of the dune. "Spread out and look for any signs of someone other than a slave."

If Gilles and Bertrand were confused they said nothing. This was how they would learn. It was me who spotted the evidence. "Beorn!" I dismounted and dropped Copper's reins. I knelt and examined the ground.

Beorn rode up and dismounted, "What is it, jarl?"

I pointed to the blackened piece of sand. "Someone has had a fire here. Would you or your slaves have lit a fire?"

"Not here, jarl. There would be no point. But this cannot be the fire which danced on the water."

"No but this could be the fire that signalled the ship which was the fire on the water."

"Signal?"

"I am guessing that they have s ship which comes here so that the spy can report. Keep your eyes open during the day. I will come back in a day or two to help you look. I need to see Alain of Auxerre."

I told Alain what I had discovered. "Then I will cover the land between Beorn's farm and the Haugr."

"Is there any sign in the forest?"

"None."

It was as I was riding to Rurik's that I saw Finni speaking with a man. It was a Viking, by his dress, and he looked thin. It proved to be the Leudes' first mistake. Finni smiled as I rode up, "Jarl, this is Thord the Grim. He was taken by the Franks after the battle with Fótr and he has escaped."

I smiled, "You were lucky. Did the Franks not slay all of Fótr's men?"

"No jarl. When Folki and Fótr were slain, our jarl led us in an attempt to break out. We failed. We were surrounded and he was killed. I was knocked out and when I awoke I was taken. There were twelve of us who were taken as slaves. Two tried to escape and they were executed. Three more died in the winter for they did not feed us well. When two of my clan fell ill with the coughing sickness I decided to take my chances and I fled."

"What clan are you?"

"The clan of the otter. We came from Eoforwic to seek our fortune with Fótr. It was not meant to be."

"Look after him, Finni."

"Can I not come with you to the Haugr? I would not want the Franks to find me here."

"Do not worry. Finni and Rurik will watch over you. You will be as safe here as at the Haugr." I smiled, "Besides Agnathia can fatten you up. She is a fine cook."

"But, jarl, I came from Caen. The enemy will follow the same route as I did. This place is not safe. We should go to your stronghold."

"Finni, care for him. I will speak with Rurik."

Rurik was at the hedge which marked the end of his land. He had trimmed the wild brambles to forma wind brake and a barrier to men. He was using his scythe to prune it. "Finni has found a survivor from the battle."

"Here? That seems odd."

"It is more than odd, Rurik. It makes the hairs on the back of my neck prickle and Ulf told me not to ignore such things. Watch him and tell him nothing. I ride to speak with Fótr."

It was as we headed directly back to the Haugr that we saw the Frank. It was the sudden movement in the distance which alerted me. I realised later on that it was his head I had spied. I kicked Copper in the flanks and waved my hand to the right. Giles and Bertrand knew what I intended. Beorn's farm was to our right. If this was the Frankish spy, then he would be returning to his lair. He had to follow the shallow beck which ran to the sea. The rest were cleared fields. The only place he could hide would be there and we would find him.

I entered the beck and heard a cry from my right, "Lord, I have him." Then there was another shout from Bertrand and I saw his horse rear.

I galloped down the beck. I saw that the Frank had unhorsed Bertrand and was standing over him with a raised sword. As much as I wanted to question the Frank I needed my warrior safe. I kicked Copper in the flanks as I took out my seax and hurled it. A seax is a poor throwing weapon but the movement to his right made him turn. Bertrand rolled away from the descending sword. Giles' spear struck the Frank in the middle and he fell backwards.

When I reached them, Bertrand had taken the Frank's sword and was standing over him. "I am sorry lord. I was careless. I took my eyes from him when I shouted."

"Do not worry. You are safe and we have him."

Gilles dismounted, "But I have killed him and you cannot question him."

"He is not dead yet. And look, he is dressed as a Frank but what is around his neck?"

Bertrand reached down. The warrior opened his eyes and tried to grab it. The movement proved too much and he sighed as he died. "It is Thor's hammer. This man is Viking!"

I rolled up the arm of his tunic, "He is a Dane. Look at the warrior bands." I recognised the clan markings. "You two take his body and cast it into the sea. The tide will take it out. I will go and find Alain of Auxerre."

I had planned on riding home but this new news made me return. I reached Rurik's stronghold as Alain and his men were dismounting. Even as I approached I saw Alain speaking with Rurik. They both approached me as I dismounted. "We have caught and killed the spy." I saw relief on both their faces. "He was a Dane."

Alain shook his head, "I should have realised." He pointed to the stronghold of Rurik. "I know not how this man slipped past us. Am I slipping?"

"No Alain. Do not concern yourself. This is wyrd. We continue to watch but I think that our actions this day will make Philippe of Rouen act sooner rather than later."

When Gilles and Bertrand returned, we rode back to my hall. I had intended speaking with Folki but that would have to wait until the morning. I was also accosted by Sven and Harold. They too had concern on their faces. "Jarl we saw a Saxon ship. We are fast but she was faster and she fled before we could approach her."

"Where was she?"

"She was lying offshore, close to Rurik's stronghold."

I was beginning to see the picture now. "Tomorrow prepare the drekar. We will sail her the day after when I have summoned a crew. I can now see through the mist and fog of this Frankish plot."

"Then I pray you tell me for I am lost."

"I need to speak with Folki first."

The next day we rode to find Folki. I took a spare horse with me. "Come with us, Folki. I have need of your mind. Erik will command your men but I do not think any Frank will come this day."

As we rode I told him of my news. His face darkened, "Jarl, it was the clan of the otter who deserted us before the battle. They were Danes and we thought they had gone to raid on their own. They were not at the battle."

"I did not think so for they said that you were slain. I think that the Frank has Danes he has hired. One of the spies we killed was also a Dane. I found warrior bands and they, too, were of the sign of the otter. We will question this so-called survivor. Let us see if he changes his story when he sees you."

When we reached Rurik's home the survivor was inside. I shouted, "Come forth, Thord the Grim. I have someone you should meet."

He emerged from the hut and, seeing Folki, tried to flee. It was pointless. Folki galloped after him and kicked him hard in the back. He fell to the ground and lay still. Folki was off in a moment and had rolled the spy over. "Folki, I need what he knows and not his death."

Just then Theobald the Fair rode in. "Jarl, there are Franks in the woods. They are in numbers."

"Folki, question him. Rurik get Finni and bring your people behind your walls."

We followed Theobald. He turned, "There were twelve of them. The captain worried that they might be the advance guard of an attack."

"No, the attack is some days off. This is to test our defences. I wondered how long it would take the Leudes to realise that I had read his letter."

I heard the sounds of combat. With just seven men Alain was outnumbered but they were better armed and mailed that the Franks they would be fighting. As we galloped into the clearing where they fought I saw that I was mistaken. These Franks also had mail. They had learned from their errors. I saw Stephen of Andecavis lying with his back to a tree.

I yelled, "Heart of Ice!" as I drew my sword, swung around my shield and galloped into the fray. Gilles and Bertrand automatically flanked me and the three of us bundled into the two Franks who were attacking Günter of Swabia. One fell from his saddle as three horses barged into him. Gilles' sword sliced across the arm of the other. As Theobald slew a third the rest fled. Alain was going to pursue them but I shouted, "Let them go! There is nothing to be gained. See to Stephen!"

I dismounted and went to the Frank who had been knocked from his horse. He was not moving but he was alive. "I beg you end my life. My back is broken."

I could see, from the angle of his body that this was likely to be true. "First, information. The I will give you a clean death."

"I know nothing."

"Let me be the judge of that. Where is Philippe of Rouen?"

"He is in Caen."

"What is the purpose of the ship?"

He winced, "What ship?"

"What were your orders?"

"We were to capture one of your men and take him back for questioning."

"When does the Leudes attack?"

"I know not, I swear."

His eyes told me the truth of it. I took out my seax and said, "Go to your god," as I drew it across his throat.

Stephen had a wound to his leg. While Gilles and Bertrand gathered the horses, mail and weapons I said to Alain. "We can now stop the patrols in the woods. Stay close to Rurik's home. Have one of your men take Stephen back to the Haugr. I leave Gilles and Bertrand with you. They can take the horses and escort Stephen of Andecavis to safety. Our warriors are too valuable to risk. I will speak with this Danish spy."

When I returned to Rurik's I saw that my mission was a wasted one. The Thord the grim was dead. His bloody body was testament to Folki's torture. "I am sorry jarl, I was too heavy handed but I have learned that the clan of the otter have joined Philippe of Rouen. They fight for his pay. It is they who crew the ship which has been sailing along the coast. He and the one you slew were landed from the ship. They passed information back." He looked at me. "They needed to know where you were."

I nodded, "Next time do not be so hasty. There might have been more information we could have gathered. "Take the body to the sea and let the tide take it. Then we return to the Haugr. We have a drekar to prepare." Before we left I spoke with Rurik and Finni and gave them thei instructions.

Chapter 16

We waited until dark before we sailed. I had told Sven that we would not use the mast. I wanted us to just use oars. We rowed out to sea and then down the coast. I had a fully crewed drekar although my men did not wear mail. Only the four of us who would board wore mail. I gambled that the ship would come to the same place each night and receive the messages from the shore. Finni would light alight to hold the attention of the ship and I hoped that we would be able to stop it leaving. We rowed in silence. The sea was a little lively. There were white caps on the waves but Sven now knew these waters well. When Sven estimated that we were close to Rurik's farm he had us turned to face the shore and the oars just kept us in the same place. Siggi Far Sighted was under strict orders not to shout. He was leaning over the dragon. I stood at the prow with Gilles, Bertrand and Folki. I had already decided that we would be the first aboard the ship.

Sven had said that it was not a Saxon ship. At least it was not a Saxon ship we recognised. It had oars and was narrower and longer than the ones they normally used. It explained why they were able to evade Sven.

Siggi hissed. I looked up and saw that he pointed ahead. I saw the flash of light from the dunes. Finni had done as I asked. Alain and his men would be with him on the beach in case they tried to land anyone else. What we now needed was to spot the ship but none of us could. If they had not signalled with the light, then they would have remained invisible. Siggi pointed. There were just off the larboard bow. I said, quietly, "Go and tell Sven. We will keep watch."

Once we saw the light I could make out the dark shadow that was the ship. We had been right to leave the mast down for that was the marker we used as a target. The oars slid through the water and we started to turn. I slid my sword out as did the other three. I did not need my shield for I had my seax. Siggi raced back down to join us and he used his bare arms to direct Sven. Arne Four Toes was keeping a steady pace. We did not need to go too fast. My aim was to board her and, perhaps, capture her.

We were seen when we were just sixty paces from her. They reacted quickly and I heard a Danish voice shout, "Down sail!"

We could not throw caution to the wind, "Arne, full speed! They are moving!" They were facing south and would escape.

Siggi shouted, "Larboard a touch, captain!"

They were not going to escape but I knew that we would hit. Whatever damage *'Dragon's Breath'* suffered would have to be endured. I could not allow this ship to escape. I wanted the Leudes in the dark. He had been making all the moves and this was our one chance to make him wonder what we were doing. The ship was moving but it would not escape. I saw the crew as they ran out oars to try to evade us. There were confused shouts as the crew tried to bring order to a confused situation. We would strike them just aft of the mast.

"Brace yourselves!" I turned and shouted, "Up oars!" I grabbed the stay and pulled myself up on to the bow. I gripped the dragon with my sword hand. Folki stood on the other side. The sound of splintering oars told us that we had struck theirs. Men would be hurt. A shattered oar could be as deadly as a spear. Then our bows struck their sheerstrake. There was a crunch and then a crack as we broke it and the strakes below. It had doomed the ship. I was almost shaken forward, into the ship but I kept my balance. I leapt down into the well of the ship. I landed on a Dane who had a broken oar sticking from his chest. I slashed my sword at the two Danes who ran at me. My blade tore the bicep of one. The other hit me in the middle with his sword. My mail held but it knocked the wind form me. Folki's sword ended the Dane's life and then Gilles and Bertrand were next to me.

Water was already puddling around my feet. Some Danes were throwing themselves over the side while others were intent on taking us with them. Had we not had mail then it would have gone badly for us but their blows hurt without wounding. I pulled my seax and rammed it into the eye of a Dane who tried to get under my swinging sword. Then I heard Siggi shout, "Jarl! Come back! Their ship is about to sink!"

He was right. The water was up to my knees. "Back to the drekar!" I swung my sword before me although there were just two men left alive and both had wounds. I sheathed my weapons and grabbed the rope which snaked down towards me. As the ship sank below the waves my men pulled me and the others aboard.

Arne Four Toes shook his head, "You had no need to risk your life jarl. When we struck the ship, she was doomed."

"I know but when I jumped we did not know that."

We rowed slowly back to the Haugr. Sven did not want to take any chances with the drekar until he had examined the bow. I had been close to the impact and I was not worried. We had struck the Dane perfectly and hit just pine strakes. Our oak prow and keep were far stronger. As I tried to move down the boat I felt a pain in my foot.

"What is it, jarl?"

"I must have twisted my ankle, Gilles, when I landed on the Dane. It will pass."

They insisted that I sit down. I know now that I should have put my foot in cold water. My wife told me when I returned to my hall but I did not. We arrived back shortly before dawn. We were barely able to take off my seal skin boot and I would not let them cut it. They were expensive. I suffered the pain. My wife sent for a pail of sea water and she wrapped me in my furs and sat me on my chair. "You can sleep there!" She sounded cross but it was concern that I heard. The salt water helped and I slept.

When I awoke, it was mid-morning and the swelling had gone down although the ache was still there. Mary had the servants take away the water and then bound my foot. "You will sit there until I say that you can move. There is naught for you to do. You warriors can deal with any problems which arise. You are jarl. You should be able to sit for one day."

She busied herself with Matildhe and the hall. Ragnvald came and sat by me. He was a curious boy and this was his chance to ask me questions. He threw question after question at. Often a question would come as a result of my answer. My head began to spin. I had not had the chance to do this with my father and so I endured the questions.

Pepin and a slave came with our food at noon. I was hungry. There was smoked fish, fresh bread and a nettle cheese I was partial to. With a freshly brewed ale I was happy. Ragnvald tucked into bread and cheese. Pepin however nearby after the slave had gone. "I will stay in case you need anything else, lord."

I had not had much opportunity to speak with him. During the day I would normally be riding and at night I would be too tired to talk. After I had finished and while Ragnvald still played with his food I spoke with him.

"How is the arm now, Pepin?"

"I still think I have the hand there but I am used to it. I am just grateful that it was my left hand."

164

I nodded. I would not apologise for the wound was as a result of war. When you went to battle then such things could occur. What is your story, Pepin?"

"My story, lord?"

"Yes, how did you get from Senonche to Ċiriċeburh?"

"I was the youngest son of a cloth merchant. There was no chance for me to be involved in the family business and my eldest brother had been given the chance to serve the Count of Burgundy. My father made it clear that I had to find a position for myself."

"How old are you, Pepin?"

"I have seen eighteen summers, I think."

"How did you get here. Senonches, it a long way from here."

"Aye, lord. It is on the way from the royal palace and the lord, Philippe of Rouen passed through our town on his way back from visiting the king and being given the governorship of this land. He stayed with us. My father said that I was looking for a position. The Leudes said he might know of something. My father gave him a bolt of cloth to ensure that I was taken care of."

I nodded. "At least he did something for you."

"I suppose but I was unwelcome. I knew that. I was not the son of a warrior. Everyone made me feel like a fraud as we rode west. I had a sword, a horse and nothing else. When we reached Rouen, I was forgotten until Lord Hugo came. He had a letter from the Count of Orleans and the Leudes saw a chance to kill two birds with one stone. Lord Hugo had been given Ċiriċeburh and he needed men. I was given to him."

"Then things must have changed when you reached Ċiriċeburh?"

"No, lord. Lord Hugo left us in the charge of a sergeant who had little patience with me and the others who were novices. That was why I was at the rear of the line when you attacked us. Michel and I were always at the rear. I suppose I was luckier than he was. I survived my first battle. He did not."

I suddenly felt guilty. I had killed a novice and maimed another. It had not been fair. "What do you know of the Leudes?"

He frowned. "I am not sure what you mean, lord?"

"You travelled a long way with him. Describe him to me,"

He nodded began to clean up Ragnvald as he did so. "He is young and was with the Count of Orleans and Hugo of Tours on the Cordoban campaign. He has studied in Constantinopolis. He knows of the campaigns of Alexander the Great, Pompey the Great, Julies Caesar, Emperor Vespasian and Justinian. Many men think he will be a general as great as Charlemagne."

"How did he fare in the Cordoban campaign?"

Although Pepin had seen Alain of Auxerre and his men around the Haugr he had not spoken to him. He did not know that he had been in that campaign. "He commanded my lord, Hugo of Ćiriċeburh."

I now understood. The young general had not done as well as he had been expected. He was no more cautious. One disaster might be excused but not two. The Count of Orleans and Hugo of Tours had been held responsible. Philippe of Rouen would show King Louis that, left along, he could rid the land of this new pestilence, the Vikings.

I nodded, "Thank you for being so frank. I would like to apologise to you for your wound."

"It was war, lord, I understand."

"But you were inexperienced. You should not have been in that position."

He smiled, "That shows that you have true nobility, lord. It takes a great man to see his own failings and to admit to them. I am happy here. This is not a Viking land it is something new. I have seen frank and Norse working together. I am pleased that I am here." He took the wooden platters and knives. "It is, what do your people say, *wyrd*."

I was up and about the next day. One day lying on my back was more than enough for me. And I had plans. I saw now that the Norns had meant me to sprain my ankle so that I could talk with Pepin. My enemy was being cautious for he feared failure. I could use that fear. Even now he would be wondering where his ship was. Where were his spies? What did I know? His original plan had failed. He had not weakened us. My men had not been waiting for an attack which had not come. He did not know of my Franks nor, I suspect, did he know that Folki had joined me. In terms of numbers I now had more men than my clan had ever had. It was more than when Jarl Gunnar Thorfinnson and his brother had taken two drekar to raid Andecavis. We might only have one drekar but we could field a large warband.

I threw myself into improving the defences of the Haugr. If the Leudes did not come, then it would not matter but if he did then we would be prepared. I had sand brought from the beach to pack around the base of the wooden palisade. It would make it harder for the enemy to damage it. We added more traps to the ditches and deepened them. The metal chains on the bridge across the ditch were now in place so that we could draw up the bridge and have a double gate. I had barrels of sea water brought up and the wooden walls soaked. If they tried to use war machines and fire, then our walls would be slow to burn. The barrels were then refilled. We could not drink it but we would not waster precious drinking water to fight flames. The only weakness now was the pen for the horses. We had a ditch around it and a wooden fence but we could not defend it. There was no fighting platform.

It was Alain and Bertrand who came up with the solution. "We have ten riders who will not be needed inside the walls. We can take most of the horses outside the walls and move away from danger."

Gilles said, "And there are boys who work with the horses. They can ride. If we have your horses and Freja inside the walls, then when danger threatens we take the herd to where the enemy cannot get at them. They cannot have enough men to surround the haugr completely."

And so that problem was solved. Gilles and Bertrand moved outside of the Haugr and set up their home close to the horses. They were happy and I was contented. Alain and his men now rode the borders. Half of his men would sleep at Rurik's and the other half in their hall at the Haugr. I wondered why until, one evening as I went to visit my horses, I saw two of the Franks with two of the new slaves we had taken from Haestingaceaster. I had no doubt that there would soon be two new huts. I realised that we would have to work out some way to expand our home without damaging its defences.

I summoned Pepin of Senonche. Since our talk, I realised that he had skills which could be used. The lack of an arm would not hinder him. He could give orders. "Pepin I want you to have some slaves build another bridge for the ditch. It needs only be as wide as one man must it must bridge it. You do not need to attack it."

He nodded, "You wish another way out of the haugr." I nodded. "Thank you for letting me do this, lord. I do not mind helping the Lady Mary organize the home but I am part of this clan now and I should help to defend it."

The clan, I now realised, was more than just the Norse who had followed me from Raven Wing Island. It was everyone who chose our way of life.

Einar Asbjornson also had a son who was a year older than Ragnvald. After his day's work was done he had taken to showing his son how to use a slingshot. He took him down to the beach and they would hurl stones at the seabirds. It was good practice. When other fathers sent their sons of a similar age it became almost a ritual. It was good that they did so. They began to form the bonds that would help them to fight in the shield wall when they were older. Ragnvald asked to go. He was, perhaps, a little young but it would do no harm and so he joined the other boys on the beach. There was healthy competition and when they began to bring home dead gulls to put in the pot we knew that they were becoming more skilful. When they manned my walls, and used Bagsecg's lead balls, they would be even more accurate. The Franks would be in for a shock.

Sven and Harold had one more voyage to make and that was to the land of the Cymri on the Sabrina. There they mined iron ore. We now had goods that we could trade with them. Our successful raids meant we had a surplus of fine linen as well as much sought-after pots and cooking vessels. We could always get more by raiding. If the local Franks did not want peace, then they could would have to endure raids. Bagsecg needed good quality iron ore to augment the re-used metal from capture mail and swords.

While they were away I devised a plan to weaken our enemies. I sent for Alain and his men. I had twenty of my men who were good riders and I sent for them also.

"We have sat on our backsides long enough. I intend to raid our neighbours. If they shun our friendship, then they can suffer the consequences."

"We take the drekar?"

"No Einar. We ride to war. We have over thirty good horses. We ride down to the village south of Valauna. Bertrand things it is the stad of Edmons. We raid it."

"What is there?"

I nodded to Bertrand who said, "They breed horses and raise cattle. It is just thirteen miles from here."

I nodded, "And the horses are the bigger ones the Franks breed. If we can get a couple of good stallions, then it will improve our stock and our herds."

My men knew the right questions to ask. "And does it have a wall?"

I smiled, "They raise horses and cattle. The one thing which is hard to do is to keep such animals within the walls of a town. I do not think that there is a wall but it does not matter in any case. I have no intention of bleeding on my enemy's walls. We ride boldly south and if there is no wall we take the village. If there are defences that we cannot secure, then we take their horses and cattle and drive them home."

The men were happy although my Norse were not as happy about riding to war and, possibly, fighting from horseback. They were getting better but they still preferred having the ground beneath their feet.

We left before dawn. I led. I was still the best scout in the clan. Bertrand rode next to me. Rurik and Finni were awake as we passed their farms. Instead of riding through the forest we rode down the beach way. Sven's voyages up and down the coast had made us familiar with it and it was an easier route. As dawn broke we cut inland to head directly for the village. The land was flat with barely anything higher than a barrow. We passed farms and fields dotted with horses and cattle.

We rode in pairs as the Franks did. With Alain and his men at the fore we looked like Franks. We had swept around to approach from the sea. Perhaps they thought we were from Rouen for they waved at us.

"We could take them now! They suspect nothing."

"We need not slaves, Sven Siggison. We are here for cattle and horses." Bertrand had told us that there was a lord who lived in the village. He was a warrior but the others were not. It was as we approached the village that the alarm was given. There must have been someone with sharp eyes who saw my men at the rear who still looked like Vikings. The bell in the small church sounded and men grabbed weapons to face this foe. We were a hundred paces from the village when I saw a man mount a horse and wave for the people to head south. This was horse country and I saw two and three people clamber on to the backs of horses and head south.

"Do we chase them jarl?"

"No Captain Alain. Take your men and collect the horses and cattle from the farms we have just passed. They will now be warned. I will take the rest and we will secure the village. Bring the horses you capture here."

The lord who sat on his horse with a single retainer was a brave man. He waited until he was certain that the village was empty before he raised his sword in defiance then turned and the two of them galloped after the rest. As we entered the village I said, "Gilles and Bertrand, search the church. Rolf Arneson and Harold Haroldsson, ride to the end of the village and keep watch in case they return."

"Aye jarl."

"Erik Long Hair, see if you can find a cart."

I wondered if the sound of the bell had reached Valauna. It was only eight miles or so away. I did not know if the refugees would flee there. It did not matter. We had not lost a man. I would gamble that my thirty could defeat any number from Valauna. I dismounted and tied Night Star close to the stone water trough. The trough was a sign that this was horse country.

Erik Long Hair and Sigtrygg Rolfsson manhandled the large wagon from the yard behind the lord's hall. My men began to pile the booty on board. There were sacks of grain as well as candlesticks and linens from the church. They also brought out unexpected treasure: saddles, reins, halters and bridles. In the forge, they found the tools of the smith and they were brought. Gunnar Stone Face and Gudrun Witch Killer managed to life the anvil on to the back of the wagon which creaked alarmingly.

"Take off the bags of grain. They can be tied to the backs of horses. Just use the wagon for the rest."

Pots, vessels and furs were brought out of the hall. The lord had been well off. Olaf Head Breaker had also found a chest with coins in it. The lord must have taken the rest but the chest was welcome.

David the Quiet and Jean son of Jean rode in with eight horses. "The captain is still collecting animals. Theobald guards the cattle."

"Good. Hitch four horses to the wagon. Load the rest with the grain. You two will wait with me."

Rolf Arneson and Harold rode in. "Lord we have seen riders in the distance."

"Valauna?"

"It looks like it. They were a couple of miles away."

"You two tie your horses to the wagon and drive it back. Gilles, Bertrand, David and Jean we will stay here. The rest head back to the Haugr. We will catch up with you. When you meet the captain then ask him to join me with his men."

We rode to the end of the village and I drew my sword. I took my shield and, after removing my cloak hung it from my back. I then replaced my cloak. Gilles did the same but the other three kept their shields hung from their saddle. I had had my life saved more than once by a shield which protected my back. We each chose our own method of fighting.

I saw the column of horsemen approaching. The blue banner with the gryphon told me that it was the garrison from Valauna. I doubted that it would be Charles Filjean. He would wait for the battle fought by his Leudes. That would be his opportunity for revenge. I now knew that it had been his father who had been the better warrior. The son knew that. If his father could not defeat me then he stood no chance.

The Franks halted two hundred paces from us. I saw that the leader, wearing mail, peered around suspiciously. We had ambushed them with archers before and he was not going to ride towards five warriors who were a potential trap. He waved left and right. Four men detached themselves and, in two pairs, began to circle the village.

"Do we retreat lord?"

"No, Jean son of Jean. I am not afraid of four men. This buys time for our men to get further up the road. We will move when the main column advances."

The two pairs of men circled the village. I could see what they intended. They were looking for signs of archers and warriors hiding in the buildings. There were none, of course. They waved to the main column and it continued to move towards us. The sergeant who led them was cautious. We were not moving and he was trying to work out why. I waited until they were fifty paces from us and then said, "Draw your swords and let us go. Watch out for the four flanking riders. They will attempt to attack us."

We wheeled around. Our horses had been patient long enough and they leapt through the heart of the village. The two pairs of Franks raced after us to try to cut us off. David the Quiet veered to his right and, as the Frank closed with him David whipped his horse's head around and slashed at the Frank's head. The warrior tried to jerk back and pull his horse around at the same time. All that he succeeded on doing was pulling his horse to the ground. His companion almost suffered the same fate but he stopped his horse. The two on the other side decided that discretion was the better part of valour and they reined in.

The Frankish column was now gaining with us. Ahead I saw Alain leading the other six warriors. He had adopted a wedge formation. He was the tip of the arrow.

"When we get close, go left and right. The Franks will have a shock when the captain and his men strike them." The road dipped ahead of us and I knew that my warriors would be hidden. "Now!"

I wheeled to the left with Gilles and Bertrand. Jean and David went to the right. Alain ploughed into the sergeant. He might have been a cautious warrior. He might have been experienced but Alain had become a killer. He deftly deflected the sergeant's spear and lunged at the warrior's neck. When two more warriors fell, the rest turned and fled. Their leader and his deputy were dead and they had lost five warriors.

We watched them leave and took the two horses which had not bolted. The sergeant had good mail and we took that with their swords, helmets and their purses. We turned and followed our wagon. We caught up with it at Rurik's farm. I wondered how the Leudes would react to our bold attack.

Chapter 17

It took a week for us to discover his reaction. Sólmánuður was upon us and the crops were all beginning to ripen in the summer sun. Folki sent one of his men with a message. "Jarl, the Franks are gathering close to the farm of Erik Green Eye."

The news came as a surprise. I nodded, "Go and tell him that I will bring some men." I waved over Gilles who, along with Bertrand was giving some of my warriors, horsemanship lessons. "I want ten mounted warriors. The Franks, it seems, are approaching Erik Green Eye's farm."

As they left I waved Arne Four Toes over. "Arne ride to Alain at Rurik's farm. Tell him to see if there is any movement from the south."

"But the attack is from the north."

"I think this may be a trick. I wonder of this Franks is trying to deceive us. We will see."

Gilles brought over my horse and I mounted. We headed north. I turned to Bergil Bjornson who had brought the news. "How many men were there?"

"They were mounted, jarl, and it was hard to get true numbers."

I nodded. It was easier to estimate men on foot for you could count the spears but horsemen, in a line, were harder. Erik's farm was closer to the haugr than was Rurik's and we soon reached it. Although he only had a palisade and ditch around it they had closed the gate and all were within when we reached them. I waved my men inside. "I will take Bertrand and Gilles to spy out the numbers." I did not need to ask where they were for I saw a banner and spear heads on the edge of the wood four hundred paces to the north. The three of us rode across the field of beans. Erik's slaves had left two paths for them to ten the crops and we rode up those. I saw that the beans were ripening. The summer had been a good one thus far.

At the edge of the field we stopped. There was a natural hedge of wild blackberries and nettles. If we had to then we could leap it but I was content to sit there and count. Gilles said, "It looks like a large army."

"Does it Gilles?"

"Aye lord, look they cover the whole of the front of the wood."

"Then count the horses for me, you too, Bertrand."

"There are sixty horsemen that we can see."

"And you think there are more behind the ones who sit astride horses?"

"There must be, lord."

"I think not. I think that there are just the sixty we see there." I pulled Copper's head around and began to ride back to the farm. "It is a large number of men but not enough to attack the Haugr. They are there to draw our main force north. Out enemy can then attack from the south."

They opened the gate and we entered. With the ten men I had brought and Folki's Erik had twenty warriors in his farm. That was more than enough to defend the palisade against sixty horsemen. The ditch which surrounded the farm was wide and deep.

I dismounted, "There are sixty men in the woods. I am guessing that they will not approach any closer. If they had greater numbers, then they would have surrounded your farm, Erik. This way they tempt me to bring my horsemen and try to chase them away. If I do, then they will flee back to Ċiriċeburh."

"It is the trick we have played on them."

"It is. We will ride back to the Haugr. If they attack, then light a beacon and I will come to your aid. Be prepared to evacuate the farm and bring your people into the Haugr. When the Leudes and his army attack us, we shall need every warrior behind my walls."

Riding back Gilles asked, "If you are wrong and this is the main attack, lord, what then?"

"Then I will have been guilty of over thinking this but everything I have learned about this Franks tells me that he is both careful and clever. He did not attack us as soon as Fótr and his men were defeated. He has bided his name preparing for an attack. I have thwarted his earlier plans and disrupted his attempts to subvert us. He must now attack and this," I waved a hand behind me, "is his last trick. He will be coming from the south."

Arne was waiting for me when I arrived back, "The Captain took his men into the woods to scout. He said it had been quiet."

"That is an illusion." I handed my reins to Gilles and my shield and helmet to Bertrand. "I will go to speak with Sven and Harold."

When I reached my ships, they were both working on the drekar. She was in her cradle and they were finishing caulking her with horsehair and seal oil. "I think the Franks may be about to attack. I would have the ships moored beyond the causeway and the church."

Sven nodded, "The weather looks set fair but if we get a summer storm…"

"Then we will know that this is part of the Norns' web."

Sven touched his hammer of Thor. "Aye. Will the attack come today? We have still some work to do."

"You have time to finish but be prepared to move quickly if I send word." I went to Sigurd and Skutal and gave them the same information. They would moor their fishing boats astern of the knarr and then join my men the walls.

That evening I picked at my food. I had done all that I could but I was still unhappy. I was gambling with the lives and the livelihood of the whole clan. Warriors like Folki, Alain, Gudrun and Knut had joined me because they believed I was a good leader. The clan had moved here because I had persuaded them. What if I was wrong? What if the Norns were tricking me?

Mary's hand began to stroke my hair, "What troubles you, my husband?"

"What?"

She smiled, "Ragnvald has been talking to you and you have just been staring at your ale. What is on your mind?"

"I do not know if I have read this enemy aright. Perhaps I have given him too much credit."

She sat next to me. "Let me tell you of my home when I was growing up. My father's friends would come over each week and go to church. After church, they would sit around the table, drink and talk of old wars and wars yet to come. They would move knives, salt pots and goblets around on the table to represent armies and men. This Philippe of Rouen will be the same. I am afraid that your people like to fight and to war. My people like to plan and to plot. You are not Fótr. You will not fall into his trap as easily. Now eat and speak with your son!"

I nodded, "Well Ragnvald, what is it you were saying?"

"When our enemies come, father, will I be on the wall with the other boys?"

I looked at Mary. The slightest of frowns crossed her face and then she shrugged. I drank some of the ale and then stroked my beard, "Let me think on this. You have trained with the other boys."

"I nearly brought down a gull!"

"I know, I was told. It would be right that you joined them. If you are tall enough for your head to be above the palisade on the fighting platform, then you can."

"Thank you!" He jumped down from his chair and ran off. Going, no doubt, to collect his sling and stone.

Mary smiled, "Clever my husband, you know he is not tall enough yet."

"It is practical. He cannot throw his stones if he cannot see the enemy."

Alain of Auxerre rode in during the afternoon. "Lord the enemy comes. We went last night and spied out Valauna. He has a mighty host gathered there. He waits."

"He waits for me to attack the men he has sent to the north. Ride back and fetch Rurik, Finni and their people. I will send for those in the other farms which lie to the south of us. Then have your men drive the horse herd north to the farm of Bárekr. His farm should be safe for it is close to the sea. We prepare for a siege."

"Aye lord."

I knew that the farmers would be unhappy. There was a risk that the Franks would destroy their carefully tended fields. There were eight farms to the south which would have to be abandoned. The warriors who farmed them would understand but it would still be hard to see the work of a year undone.

After I had told Mary I donned my mail and sent for Bertrand and Gilles. "Come, it is time we made the Leudes think he has fooled us. We will attack his horsemen."

"The three of us?"

"No, Gilles. It will be a large number who attack."

Arne Four Toes and my other warriors who lived by the Haugr had seen the preparations and joined me. "It begins. I go north but I will return. Rurik and Finni will be joining us and the other southern farmers. Watch for tricks from now on. We have enough water?"

"The earlier rains were harvested in barrels and the well is high. We have enough dried and smoked fish and meat. It is only the bread we will lack."

"That cannot be helped." Our bread oven was outside our wooden walls. The risk of a fire was too great to have it within. It would be a sacrifice we would have to make.

The three of us rode to the horses. We tied halters to them so that we would lead them to safety. Gilles said, "What of the mares in foal, lord?"

"Take those to the Haugr. We will care for them there."

He led the six mares to the Haugr. I saw my men returning form Rurik's farm. Alain of Auxerre and his men peeled off to join us. "Take the horses to Bárekr. He can watch them. When they are secure then bring your men to Erik Green Eye's farm. Have all of our people's animals take to Bárekr's farm. He can watch them there. We go to war."

There was relief on the faces of my men at Erik's farm. I smiled, "This is where we ride to battle. Folki mount your men. Today I would have them look like Franks. When Alain comes, we will attack Hugo of Ċiriċeburh and his men."

"But it will soon be evening."

"I know Folki and that will aid us for they will not be able to see out numbers. We have less than thirty warriors but I would have them think that there are twice that. I want all of you here to tie a second spear to your left leg."

"That will make fighting difficult, jarl. My men find it hard enough fighting with just one spear."

I shook my head, "Only the captain and his men and we three will fight. In the dark he will see horses and spears. If he counts the spears he will think I have committed my men to an attack and send word to his master."

Alain arrived. "We have changed horses, lord. The others were tired."

"Good for you will need fresh mounts." I explained what I had planned. He grinned and nodded. "You and your men will pursue them all night. Do not get close enough for them to estimate numbers but keep at them. In the dark their fear of us will make them see double. I want them back inside Ċiriċeburh. Return to the farm of Bárekr. I will let you know when I need you next."

I led my men from the farm shortly before dusk. We did not ride through the bean fields. Instead I rode parallel to the woods and headed up the slope which had the spindly trees Erik had yet to cut. It also allowed us to approach from the east where it was already growing dark.

I formed my men up so that Alain and his men were the front rank with Gilles Bertrand and myself. We were not tightly formed. Folki and my men with the extra spears were behind us. I waited until it was almost dark and then I shouted, "Charge!"

We galloped up the slope towards the thin line of Franks. Folki and my other men just followed at a canter. The eleven of us hit the line of Franks and we surprised them. They were not ready. Some did not even have swords or spears ready. I thrust my spear into the thigh of a Frank and he was unhorsed. Gilles' spear took one in the neck while Alain unhorsed one with a powerful strike to the shield. The rest of the ones before us ran. I heard a horn from my right and then there was the sound of horses moving through the woods. Bertrand dismounted to end the lives of the two wounded Franks and I said, "Captain, keep your spears in their backs! We will see you when you return."

"Aye lord, this will be a hunt to remember. Come boys! We will have vengeance on our former master. Let us show him that running away is a bad habit to form!"

The three of us led the captured horses and headed back to Folki and my men. When we reached the farm, I said, "Erik, now is the time to bring your family in the walls. We need your sword arm on our walls."

"Aye lord. I am ready!"

We did not have far to go but it was night and we had women and children with us. It took us longer than expected. The Haugr was full. Erik and his family were the last to enter our sanctuary. Pepin of Senonche had helped my wife to organize them. We had many in our hall: that was to be expected for it was the largest building inside the Haugr. Others had taken in the smaller families. My wife greeted me warmly. "This was well don, husband. You people are grateful for our walls."

"Then let us hope they are up to whatever Philippe of Rouen can throw at them!"

Siggi Far Sighted ran towards the walls just before noon, "Jarl, we have seen the franks. They are heading up the coast towards us."

"Thank Sven for his warning. Have you enough supplies on your vessels?"

"Aye jarl and we can always sail north to Bárekr if we need more. He has a good harbor there."

A short while later Michel of Liger rode to my walls. He did not enter but shouted up to us, "Lord, the Captain says we chased the enemy back to their walls. We slew three more and took two horses. Alain of Nissa was wounded but he will heal."

"I will send to the captain when I need him. Tell him to rest and be prepared to come when he receives my signal."

We now had a gate at the north-eastern end of the Haugr. It was only wide enough for one man and there was no bridge across the ditch. If an enemy spied the disguised gate they would have to cross the ditch first. Pepin's bridge would allow us the opportunity to leave without being seen.

Ulf Strong Swimmer was the one who saw the banners as they approached, "Jarl, the Franks, they come!"

Philippe of Rouen was taking no chances. He had horsemen spread out in a long line before the main host. He was wary of ambush. It explained why he had come the longer way along the coast rather than risking the forest where he thought my archers might hide.

"Have the men and boys man the walls."

I did not think that we would be fighting this first day but I wanted the Franks to see that we defended my home. His cautious approach meant it took a long time for him to get close to us. He formed a long line of horsemen as his carts and wagons disgorged men and equipment. More than half of his army were on foot. I estimated something like a hundred and fifty men on foot and more than a hundred who were mounted. He came with tents and his men began to prepare a camp. It was more than five hundred paces from us and a hundred paces from the sea. He would not risk my ships attacking him. He and twenty riders rode closer. I recognized Charles Filjean and Hugo of Ċiriċeburh. They did not ride next to him but four warriors away. It showed their position. Had they displeased their lord and master? I saw that he had a fine chestnut coloured horse with a white blaze. It was bigger than the others. He was making a statement. His mail was also burnished until it shone as was his helmet. A real warrior just wanted mail and a helmet which did not rust. This leader was more concerned with the way he looked.

They came close to the stones which marked the limit of our Saami bows. They had been given to my best archers and Einar Asbjornson led them. He looked up at me and I shook my head. We would wait to let my new bows cause the most damage. The Franks came to within two hundred paces of our walls. That was a mistake for all of our bows had that sort of range. He obviously did not know that. I would not waste arrows. He wore a full byrnie and had a helmet and shield. He was flanked by two bodyguards who also had shields ready. It was a tempting target but I knew that we could wreak more damage if we released at a larger target. His standard bearer rode forward to the bridge over our ditch. "My lord, the Leudes of Rouen makes you an offer barbarian. If you board your dragon ship now and leave this land you can have your lives. You must leave every Frank and salve but my lord will, graciously allow you to depart his shores to save further bloodshed."

Those of my warriors who understood all of his words began to howl and jeer. Olaf Head Breaker turned his back on the Frank and dropped his breeks. I said nothing and waited for my men to quieten.

The Franks said, "Well? What us your answer?"

"I think you have had our answer but tell your master this. We are here to stay. I would have lived in peace with your people but that is impossible. If you make war on us then you will have to fight until every man, woman and child of this clan is dad for so long as one of us lives then none of you will be safe." I pointed to him. I wanted him to know that this was now personal. I shouted, "You have begun this but Hrolf the Horseman of the clan of the horse will end this. You have been warned. Now leave for if you remain longer this close to my warriors then you will die!"

He whipped his horse's head around and rode back to the others. Although our words had been heard by all I saw a conference. Philippe of Rouen stood in his stiraps and waved his fist at us. I laughed for it was a pathetic gesture. They turned and rode away.

We watched them as they continued to set up their camp. I stared at the burgeoning camp. The tents were soon erect and the horses tethered close to the sea. He did that for security. I would have made sure that they were closer to water but the nears stream was close to Rurik's hall. His men wold have to journey each day to water them. It was a mistake. There was neither ditch nor wooden palisade. That too was an error. He was relying on his sentries. There was a line of thirty men. Each was twenty paces from the next. In daylight, it looked enough. At night, it would not. Once they lit their fires to cook their food I left the walls. As I left I heard hammering. Arne Four Toes asked, "What is that?"

Reaching the bottom of the ladder I turned and said, "They are building their war machines. I saw them unloading the parts. We have until they finish them before they will attack."

I went to my hall to change from my mail. I sent Gilles to fetch some selected men. He returned with Rolf Arneson, Sven Siggison, Knut the Quiet, Audun Einarsson and Sigtrygg Rolfsson.

"I have sent for you because, of all my warriors, you are the ones who can move quietly and kill silently. Tonight, we go to the Frankish camp and we slit throats. When we have slit enough throats then we cut their horse lines and drive off their horses. Change from your mail. You will not need helmets or shields. We take swords, daggers and a halter."

Audun said, "A halter?"

"Aye for when we cut their horse lines we will each use a halter to help us ride a horse. Tonight's work will not win the battle for us but it will make their nights less easy and it will delay their attack."

They nodded and we prepared.

Gilles and Bertrand were unhappy to be left behind. "You two are fine warriors but you are not men who can kill silently. I have watched the Ulfheonar. I have hunted with Ulf Big Nose. I have chosen the five warriors I believe can damage the enemy and return here to fight another day. I want you two by the gate. When we return, we may be pursued. I need you to be by the gate. You are horsemen both and can judge the moment to open it."

We slipped out of the back gate. Finni and Rurik came as far as the ditch and then brought our bridge back inside. We headed inland. We ran, knowing the land well. When we had run a thousand paces we stopped and I led them towards the camp. We had blackened faces and hands. We would be hard to see but, as they had fires burning then their night vision was not what it should have been. We moved in a single line with Rolf Arneson at the rear. I moved obliquely across the land for I was heading for the end of the line of sentries. They had made a line which only faced us. Behind them were only friends. They did not bother to watch there.

We moved to the last sentry. He helped me by having his back to us. He was watching the fire. I dare say he was anticipating his relief and then he could join the others and eat. I could see the next sentry. He, too, was staring at the fire. I rose and grabbed the man by putting my left arm around his throat and squeezing. I plunged my dagger into his right ear and into his skull. His body went limp in my arms. Knut the Quiet rose like a wraith, took the sentry's helmet and donned it. I lowered his body to the ground. We crawled to the next sentry. We slew three and had three of my men in their place.

We crawled along and each of us lay close to the next three sentries. These were closer to the Haugr and they were doing their duty and facing my walls. We rose as one and three more sentries died. I led my men back to the end of the line and, leaving the helmets on the ground the six of us headed for the horse lines. I heard the sentries here. They were not watching for us they were guarding the horses. They were talking and, from their voices we knew there were three of them. We lay just twenty paces from them. The fires were some distance away and so their night vision wold not have been affected. I tapped Knut the Quiet and pointed to me and then one of the horse guards. I did the same with the other four. We needed two of us for each guard to make sure that they died silently.

Knut and I rose as one. I put my hands around his neck as Knut drove his dagger up between the Frank's ribs and into his heart. We laid the three bodies down. We had time now for all that we could hear was the sound of the sea and the horses as they moved, ate and snuffled. I spied the chestnut horse with the white blaze. I strode up to it and stroked its mane. I slipped the halter around its head. The others chose their mounts. The Franks had made a double line of horses. We walked down the line, leading our horses and untying the horses from the horse lines. We were half way down when the alarm was given. They had found the bodies of the dead sentries.

"Mount!"

We had not untiled all of the horses but this would have to do. We began to shout and to drive the horses towards the Frankish camp. The terrified horses galloped. The ones which were still tethered, reared and pulled at the ropes. They broke free and they, too, galloped towards the camp. I laid my body down flat along the back of the chestnut and kicked him in the flanks. He was a magnificent beast and he leapt forward. Using a weapon was out of the question as we had no straps. We just clung on. Men fled as the stampeding horses hurtled towards them. We made it to the fires before anyone saw us. Seeing us was one thing; stopping us was a different matter. I think the fact that I had stolen the horse of the Leudes meant that his men feared hurting their leader's mount.

One brave warrior grabbed my right leg as I galloped past. He was dragged along. I lifted by leg and kicked hard with my sealskin boot. He fell and I heard the crunch if his skull being crushed by Knut the Quiet's horse. The last obstacle was the line of sentries. Luckily, they had spread out to search for the killers of their comrades and we passed through them. Behind us I heard the sounds of pursuit. With just five hundred paces to cover we soon reached our gate. I saw Bertrand and Gilles standing, with drawn swords, on either side. We galloped through. I felt triumphant until I turned and counted. There were only four men with me. Audun Einarsson was not there. We had lost a warrior and all the joy went. It was a hollow victory.

Chapter 18

The next morning my men tried to cheer me up. Knut the Quiet had known Audun since he had first become a warrior. "It was a good death, jarl. Men will talk of what we did for many years to come." We were on the fighting platform above my gate and he said, "See, their camp is still in disarray. They have had men collecting horses all night."

"Knut is right, jarl. They have not the men to build their war machines. Tonight, they will expect you to return." Rurik spoke true but it did not give me any comfort.

"I know you are right but any loss is a grievous one. And see, they have put Audun's head on a spear."

"Then we will put ten of their men's heads on spears. Audun is in Valhalla. They despoil an empty body is all."

The Franks took all day to put their camp in some sort of order and that night they ringed their camp with fires and doubled their sentries. It mattered not for we were safe in our stronghold and we did not stir. The next day they began work on their war machines again. They were building three of them. It became apparent that they had been built and then taken apart. It would not be long before they were finished. I now had another part of my plan to put into operation. I looked at the position of our ranging stones. Their camp was just two hundred paces from the ones which were within range of the Saami bow. Ten of my archers and I had the bow.

That night they lit their fires. They had a ring of them around their camp to prevent us infiltrating again. They would prevent us coming close to them but we did not need to be close. I led Einar Asbjornson and twenty archers from the gate after dark. As we had done the last time we left without mail and shields. We wore no helmets. We slipped out of the rear door and then filtered around the outside walls. We moved through the dark silently. The fires of the enemy sentries gave us their position as clearly as if it had been day.

We halted at the last line of stones. We stood in two lines. The ones with the war bows stood before the ones with the Saami bow. We pulled back. It did not matter if we did not release at exactly the same time but once we began we would have to almost empty our quivers. Our second flights were released even as the first was descending into their camp.

The two types of bow meant that we covered a large area of their camp. We kept releasing as screams, shouts, cries and orders filled the air.

Beorn Fast Feet said, "Jarl, their sentries, they come!"

"Switch targets!"

We lowered our bows to use a horizontal rather than a vertical trajectory. We were still in the dark while the sentries who raced at us were not. Every arrow found flesh. The sentries wore no mail. For the powerful Saami bow it did not matter for they could penetrate mail at the range of less than a hundred paces.

"No arrows!"

"No arrows!"

"Then those without arrows back to the walls. The rest, we will fall back!"

I heard the sound of hooves in the distance. They had mounted some horses to close with the human insects who were tormenting their sleep. Six of us remained with arrows and we walked backwards. Einar's arrow took the Frank in the chest as he managed to loom up out of the dark. Now that they had left their fires far behind they were as hard to see as we. As we passed the hundred pace stones I saw a dark shape loom up. There were just four of us with arrows. Three horsemen hurtled towards us with their spears held before them. I had one arrow left and I pulled back as far as I could. The months since my wound had been ones where I had worked in my muscles and it paid off. I released at the Frank when he was twenty paces away. Any closer and I would have risked a spear. The arrow hit his chest with such force that he was thrown over the back of the saddle. The other three found the bodies of the ruminating Franks. One, who had an arrow in his shoulder managed to wheel his horse around and head back to the camp.

Shooing in the two horse we ran to the gate where Gilles and Bertrand stood. The archers who had first fled were now ready with fresh arrows and, as we approached the gate a flight of ten arrows soared over our heads and I heard cries behind as the franks who were following were struck. The gates slammed shut behind us and the bridge creaked as it was raised. We had annoyed them again. As my men congratulated one another and spoke of arrows they had released I knew that the arrow storm would not win the battle for us. We were building a wall and we needed foundations. We had laid sound foundations. The Franks had been hurt. They had lost sleep and we had twice breached their defences.

The Leudes would hasten his attack. He would hurry and in such haste mistakes were more likely to be made. We would exploit those mistakes.

My wife let me sleep longer than I intended. She meant well but I was annoyed. I needed to be on my walls so that I could see my enemy and his reaction to our attack. It was late morning when I walked my walls. Arne Four Toes pointed, "They have begun to move their camp further away and they are digging a ditch this time."

"They are learning. I would expect them to put a wooden wall around it too. It matters not. We will not risk another night attack. We will let them build their camp. I will ride to meet with Alain of Auxerre. He and his men have had enough rest. It is time for us to give them a new threat."

Gilles and Bertrand had the horses ready for us and, riding my new chestnut horse which I had named Odin's Gift, we left by the main gate. All work on the Frankish camp stopped. I heard the sound of horns as they prepared their defences for our attack. We had made them truly nervous. As we crossed the bridge I saw that there were just eight bodies lying close by our walls. The other dead had been removed. The eight bodies would begin to stink and to swell. When the Franks did attack, they would find themselves having to attack over the bodies of their own dead. It would not help their spirit.

Bárekr's farm was just six miles north of us and overlooked a small bay. It would be a better bay for our ships to use and the farm itself would have made a better stronghold but when we had come we had used what was already in place. In time, we would make the farm a second stronghold and we would move our ships there. For the moment, it was just a fortified hall with a ditch around it. The animal pens were filled with cattle, sheep, pigs and horses. If my enemy managed to get past us, then he would be able to slaughter them and our people would starve. I had a plan to stop that happening.

Bárekr and Alain greeted me as we rode up, "Have we won yet, jarl?"

I laughed, "No but we have hurt them, Bárekr."

"A fine horse, lord. A gift from the Franks?"

"Let us say I thought it too fine a beast to leave in the hands of such men. Have you ale? A horn will help me tell my tale."

As I drank I told them what had happened. "Now, Captain, I would have you bring your men each day and ride from my walls to the island.

Our animals here are a tempting target. You will stop them from spying them out. Vary your horses and your dress."

"You would have him think we have a larger body of horsemen to the north than we do?"

"I would. It will just make him and his men more nervous. Tomorrow he will be ready to begin his attack. Your presence will restrict what he can do."

"And when do we attack?"

"When he has eaten the supplies that he has brought and we have weakened the resolve of his men. Keep your men safe, Captain, when we do attack you and your warriors will be the spearhead who will help us defeat their horsemen."

"You have great faith in the eight of us lord. The Franks we fight will be lords themselves. They will not be hired swords."

"You do not give yourself enough credit. When you fought for Hugo of Ċiriċeburh then you were hired swords. The moment you joined me as freemen then you became greater than those you followed for you now fight for the clan and your people. If you wish to be a lord, then I will give you a title. It is not the way of our people but…"

He shook his head, "I did not mean that, lord. I am happy to be your captain. I just do not want to let you down."

"And you will not. When the eleven of us lead my horsemen, we will be fighting together. We will be the clan of the horse and the men from the north. The Franks will know they have a new enemy who will not be pushed back into the sea."

We reached my walls again in the late afternoon. I could see that they had almost finished assembling their three war machines. They had a ditch and stakes surrounding their camp and they had horsemen ready to ride to attack us should we tempt anything. As we entered the Haugr, Bertrand said, "They still have many more men than we do, lord."

"True but what of their hearts and minds? They have one dead Viking to show for their efforts and their dead rot and fester in the summer sun."

When we awoke the next morning, we could see that they were ready to begin their attack. Their three war machines were ready to be rolled into position. Folki had told me that they were fragile. He had seen at least one broken through wear and tear. I was counting on that. The Franks had two large wings of cavalry on the flanks and behind the three war machines were their levy. They had shields and spears. It looked to me as though they were going to attempt an old-fashioned shield wall.

Bertrand had good eyes. "Lord. See, just behind the war machines. They have twenty men. They look to have a strange weapon."

I saw what he meant, "Folki, what is that weapon they hold."

"I saw some when we attacked their walls at Caen. They do not use an arrow but a pointed stick like a dart. They can penetrate mail."

"Go and ask Pepin of Senonche to join me."

We had time for the war machines had to be pulled into place. They were not yet at the first line of ranging stones.

"Yes, lord? Do you wish me to fight?"

"No Pepin, I would use your mind and your knowledge. Those weapons you see behind the war machines, what are they?"

"They are called crossbows, lord. They have warriors from Brabant who are trained to use them. It looks like the men I see wear the garb of Brabant. They are mercenaries. The crossbows have a mechanism to wind back the string and they can reach four hundred paces, or so I am told."

"They are a war machine you hold in the hand?"

"They are. They do not have the ability to send their bolts quickly but they are deadly."

"Thank you." I had not expected that. It would affect my plan. I had counted on keeping them at bay by using our Saami bows. It seemed my enemy had anticipated me. "Einar, bring the men with the Saami bows here to the gate. Beorn Fast Feet take charge of the others and await my command."

Folki had told me that the war machines had a range of almost two hundred paces. They would need to be closer to us than that if they wished to hit my walls for they were higher than a man. The machines were pulled and dragged closer to us. They were soon inside the range of our bows. I could have ordered Beorn to have his archers send their arrows towards the enemy but I wished to see the war machines in action. The centre one was loaded. I saw that they needed eight men to load and release. Another ten had pulled them into place.

"Beorn be ready for my command. I want you to aim at the men close by the machines."

"Aye lord."

The first stone was accurately thrown but short. It hit the ditch where the bridge would have been. I saw the Leudes shout orders and the eighteen men on each machine began to pull. I let them start to move the machines and then shouted, "Now Beorn!"

Every man who had a war bow sent their arrows skyward. They sent wave after wave. We had plenty of arrows. The men pulling the machine had no shield to protect them and they fell. The machines stopped and the survivors raced back. It was then that the men with the crossbows moved forward. They were each accompanied by a warrior with a large square shield. Beorn's arrows hit the shields. It would be a waste to send more.

"Cease!"

Suddenly the shields were dropped and twenty deadly darts flew towards us. Three of my men were too slow to react and they were all hit. Salsi Salvison fell with one in the middle of his head. Erik Red Hair had one in his shoulder and Sven Bergilsson was pitched from the fighting platform with one in his chest.

"Take cover!" This had not been part of my plan. As I crouched behind the palisade I said, "Einar, we have one chance to kill the men with the crossbows. They had to emerge from behind their shield to send a missile our way. Folki said it takes time for them to reload. When they have sent their next bolts, we rise and await the dropping of their shield. Aim for those with crossbows."

The men with crossbows were confident of their weapons for they sent them at any target. I heard Rurik roar with rage as one hit his helmet and pinged off. "Let that Frank get close to me and I shall make his head ring... all the way to the sea!"

"Now." I stood with the others who had the most accurate of weapons. I held an arrow in my left hand ready to send it towards them. "Beorn, release another shower of arrows!"

As Beorn's arrows clattered into the shields I saw that one of those holding a shield fell. Einar Asbjornson reacted quickly and the crossbowman fell dead. As the shields were moved We each sent our arrows. Four more died before the Leudes had them moved back. He thought to use their superior range. As they moved back his levy were brought up with shields. They were trying to move the war machines back out of range.

"Beorn, concentrate your arrows on the men pulling the war machines. Einar our target remains the men with crossbows." They had fifteen left. As Beorn's arrows struck Frankish flesh the men with crossbows sent their darts towards my archers. Two more of my men fell but our Saami bows accounted to five more of the deadly hand held war machines. Sigtrygg Rolfsson, who had a Saami bow, was hit. The dart pierced his left hand. He handed his bow to Beorn Fast Feet as he was taken away to have his wound bound. It had cost them eight men but they managed to pull the war machines beyond the range of our bows. They were still within the range of our bows but I did not let them know that.

When he realised that his initial attack had failed the Leudes withdrew his men to his camp. He would plan something else. He still had ten crossbows. They could hurt us. Leaving Einar in command of the walls I went to see the wounded. Sigtrygg could fight for his hand had been bound and he could still hold a shield. Erik Red Hair could not hold a shield. They had made inroads into our men and I wondered what would come next.

Although we had plenty of food we were rationing what we had. We ate enough but not well. I knew that the Franks would be having it even harder than we were. We had seen them try to fish but Sven and Harold had taken the knarr with their ship's boys and discouraged them with arrows and stones. It was only the arrival of crossbows which drove them hence.

I returned to the wall at dusk. Arne Four Toes had taken over from Einar. "I have heard them in the woods yonder, lord. They are chopping down trees."

"They make a ram."

"That would be my guess. They also lit fires in the afternoon. They are planning something."

"But what?"

"Call me if you hear anything."

I did not sleep in my bed but in my chair before my fire and in my mail. When Gilles shook me, I was awake in an instant. "Lord, Arne sent me. The Franks are moving. He has heard their war machines creaking."

"Go get Bertrand, Rurik Gunnar Stone Face and Harold Haroldsson. Have horses ready." I ran to the fighting platform. I could hear the creak and rumble as the three war machines were pulled into position. "I expected something like this. We cannot see them and we are a huge target. They will not need to see us. Have water ready to douse the flames."

"Is that all we do, jarl. Put out the fires?"

"No Arne. I will lead men to end the threat of these machines once and for all."

When I reached the bottom Gilles and my men were there. They had saddled Night Star for me. He was jet black and the perfect choice. "Find a pot and tie a rope around it. Then fill it with coals. Prepare one for me." I saw Pepin, "Have the slaves fill five water skins with seal oil and have them brought to us."

I went to Night Star. And waited. Suddenly the night was filled with the noise of a crash as the first of the enemy war machines hurled its fire at our walls. Flames leapt up. The hiss of water and the column of steam showed that Arne had been ready. Soon, however, the other two released theirs and my walls were assaulted by three war machines. The Franks had their men with crossbows too. I saw a warrior pitched form the walls.

"Einar! Kill the crossbowmen! Use the light of their fires!"

"Aye jarl."

Gilles handed me my pot. "We ride out and throw the pots at the machines. Pepin will give each of you a skin full of oil. When you have thrown your fire then throw the oil. Return back to our walls once you have thrown your pots and skins."

"Aye jarl."

Pepin arrived and flinched as a part of the wooden wall erupted in flame, "Get that sea water here!"

I took my skin, "Lower the bridge. Open the gates!" The greased metal did not make a noise but I knew that the enemy had a chance of seeing the open gate. "Folki you and your men guard the gate while we are gone!"

The men working the machines had braziers with them and were picking coals to drop into the pots they had on the throwing arm of the machines. It was a slow process for they did not want the machine to catch fire. The braziers helped us to locate them. Night Star was fast and he was a warhorse. He was ready for war and we soon left the others behind. Our hooves alerted them. A crossbowman hurriedly brought up his weapon and loosed a bolt at me. It zipped over my head and then two arrows flung him to the ground. Cries of alarm brought men with spears from the dark. My own archers sent their arrows towards them. I threw my pit at the machine and pulled back on Night Star's reins to make him rear. His flailing hooves kept the crew from attacking men. The pot smashed and the coals began to burn. Without wind or oil, they would soon die. I whirled the water skin and threw it at the machine. The effect was spectacular. The flames leapt up and began to burn the ropes. The pot they were about to send toward us was half released and its colas added to those of my pot.

I had no time to admire my handiwork for men rushed at me. I drew my sword and charged towards them to allow the others to set fire to the other two machines. A spear gouged a line up the mail covering my right leg and my sword bit into the neck of the man. I heard a whoosh from behind me as another machine caught fire. I made Night Star rear and took the opportunity to look behind me. Both machines were on fire. Bertrand threw his pot but the rope broke and it hit one of the crossbowmen. My young warrior was quick thinking and he threw the oil over the man who burst into flames. He ran, blindly, towards his own lines. It was our chance to escape.

"Back!" The others galloped before me. I heard hooves pounding in the dark behind me and knew that they had sent horsemen. I leaned forward over my stallion and felt something strike my back. Stones and arrows were hurled and released form our walls and I heard a cry as one of the horsemen fell. And then we were safely within our walls.

The flames from the enemy attack had been doused but I saw that two more warriors had been struck by bolts. As I dismounted Gilles said, "Lord, your mail is damaged."

"Aye and I can see that your cloak has been cut. You were lucky, jarl!"

"I know, Rurik, someone is watching over me."

Chapter 19

The next day was almost an anti-climax. We woke to see the three smoking skeletons of the war machines. The Franks had cleared their bodies. When Alain and his men arrived for their patrol they were close enough to the Franks to see deep within the camp. They rode to the walls, "You have hurt them, lord."

"Aye but it is not over." I pointed to the rear of the Frankish camp. Men were busy making a ram. "When that is ready they will attack. Tomorrow, when you come, be ready for battle. You may have to do more than just watch."

"Aye, lord. We are ready!"

I went to my hall. Bagsecg had my mail and it would not be ready until evening. I took the opportunity to bathe. I used some of the sea water we had left. I did not think that there would be a danger from fire. I stripped off and poured pails of it over me. It refreshed me and washed away the smell of smoke and blood. May appeared with Matildhe in her arms she shook her head, "A Frankish lord would never show his naked body to his people."

I began to dry myself, "They are used to it and besides they have seen their husbands and sons naked."

"You are a strange people. Come, dress and we will feed you. You have not eaten enough over the past few days. Unless you get some food inside you then you will become a wraith!"

Ragnvald was waiting for me inside my hall. I had seen little of him over the past few days. He was eager to know of the battles I had fought. I told him what we had done and of the men who had died, "They are our people, Ragnvald, and their died for the clan. We should remember them."

He nodded seriously, "The boys who threw stones at the enemy told me that the Franks fled at your approach. Are they afraid of you?"

"They are afraid of us for we are not what they expect. When they destroyed Fótr's band they believed they knew how to defeat us. They did not and that is what they fear. Our enemies like us to be predictable."

"One of the boys said you were wounded last night."

"It was nothing. Others had wounds which were worse. Even Sigtrygg who had a bolt in his hand can still fight. It is why we wear mail. Soon, when you are a little bigger, Bagsecg will make mail for you." Mary flashed me a look of surprise. "It is just to get you used to wearing it. Then, when you become a warrior you will not even notice the weight."

Once he knew that he would be having mail made he was happy and he chattered on about what sort of mail it would be. When I was alone, later with Mary, she asked, "Why does he have to become a warrior so soon? When can he be a child?"

"Being a child is a luxury which a Viking does no enjoy. We have many enemies and we become a warrior or we die."

The next morning, we saw that the enemy had finished the ram and they were preparing to attack. We would have attacked at first light but the Franks were wary of our tricks in the half light of dusk and dawn. They wanted sunshine and the clarity of day to see what we would do. I wore my repaired mail and I stood on the fighting platform above the gate. Alain and his men were to the left of our walls. The Franks had the same formation they had employed when they had first attacked. The ram was in the centre and the flanks had their horsemen. The difference this time lay in the fact that they had dismounted some of their horsemen. I saw Hugo of Ċiriċeburh and Charles Filjean with some of their half-mailed men. There were in the centre of the line. Their line was four men deep and those in the second rank had their shields ready to shelter those in the front rank.

Our arrows would not help. The ram had men standing ready to pull it and others ready to protect them with their shields. There was no alternative. We would have to meet them, shield to shield. "Gilles, Bertrand, take our ten best horsemen and join Alain of Auxerre. I will make a wedge and we will destroy this ram."

"Aye lord."

"Arne, have every warrior with mail ready to make a shield wall. I want the rest on the walls with bows. I need every boy who can sling a ball ready to help us."

"Aye, jarl."

Gilles and Bertrand appeared with the warriors they had chosen. They each held a spear and two throwing spears, lighter javelins. "What you have the captain do, lord?"

"Stop their horsemen from interfering. If you have to run, then do so."

"We will not let you down."

The spears were stacked next to the gate and I took one. "Lower the bridge and open the gate. Clan of the horse let us show these Franks that we know how to fight! Gunnar Stone Face, you are the rock of the right. Olaf Head Breaker you are the rock of the left."

"Aye jarl!"

As I stepped out of the gate the Franks all roared. They began banging their shields. I placed myself ten paces from our ditch. We were well within the protective range of our stones and arrows. More importantly we could not be easily flanked. Gunnar and Olaf would make sure that the two ends were level with the ditch. My warriors began joining me. My most experienced warriors stood to the side of me. I had Rurik on one side and Arne Four Toes on the other. We formed a line forty men long. Behind us another twenty men gave us depth in the middle. Their spears rested on our shoulders and their shields lay in our backs. Knut the Quiet, Gudrun Witch Killer and Folki were arrayed with their oathsworn. We were fighting for family, friends and brothers in arms. What we lacked in numbers we made up for in heart.

"Close the gate! Raise the bridge!"

I heard Bagsecg shout, "Aye jarl!" His mighty arms would pull the chain and trap us outside. There would be no retreat. We would win or lose. There was no other outcome.

The ram rumbled towards us. The wheels were just crudely hacked logs and it was hard to move it in a straight line. Erik Red Hair might not be able to hold a shield but he could command he, without being asked, he took charge of the slingers and archers. "Kill the men on the ram!"

The ram was two hundred paces from the ditch and beyond the slings but our archers could hit the men pulling it. Despite the protection of the men with the shields the ram did not cooperate and each time it twisted another Frank died or was wounded. The ram was moving towards us but they were paying for each pace with a dead body.

I heard a horn and I saw that the two sets of horseman were advancing. The one to the left would face my horsemen but the one to the right would be able to charge us. Our only defence on that side were my archers. The Leudes was dividing our arrows and stones. We could do little about it save endure their attack and hope that we were made of the right kind of metal. I saw my thin line of horsemen charge. I knew that it was not reckless. Alain of Auxerre would not throw away my men. The ram was still a hundred and fifty paces from us. I saw that Alain and my men suddenly turned to ride across the front of the Franks. They threw their javelins. They did not throw them at the men; that would have been waste. Instead they targeted the horses. A horse has no shield nor does it have armour. Ten horses were hot and their riders pitched to the ground. Alain carried on his turn and rode a second time at the Franks who were ow trying to avoid the bodies of men and horses lying before them. Their second javelins caused almost as many injuries to the horses but even more confusion. When they galloped around a third time and raised their spears the Franks tried to forma mounted shield wall. Instead of throwing their spears they punched at the Franks as they charged obliquely at them. It stopped the enemy in their tracks.

Alain wheeled our men away and rode north. They had done all that they could. One wing of horse had been stopped. I did not have the luxury of seeing how the other fared for the ram was less than fifty paces from us. On one side of the ram Hugo of Ċiriċeburh led his men while Charles Filjean led on the other. They were not the levy. Th levy were to the flanks and made up the second and third ranks. The rear rank were the Leudes best warriors. I could see that they wore mail. He would sacrifice the others to weaken us and then destroy me and my best warriors when we were tired.

As we braced for the attack on us I heard Erik Red Hair shout, "Slingers, let us see how many horsemen you can unseat." There was a loud cheer from the boys and then the rattle of stones on metal. Horses whinnied and reared as they were struck. My slingers could not throw for long but while they did the horsemen had to endure a hailstorm of lead.

The ram was thirty paces from me. I saw the men preparing to rush it at us.

I shouted, "Wedge! Take the ram!" The two flanks remained stationary and I moved forward. Rurik and Arne stepped behind me and we had the beginnings of a wedge. The men at the front of the ram had their shields held high to protect them from the arrows. The first Frank knew nothing of my presence until my spear rammed into his eye and he fell to the ground. Arne stabbed the man pushing the ram and Rurik's spear took the next. The ram slewed around. It was no longer aimed at our bridge. More importantly the three of us had forced a hole in the ram's defences.

The three of us were able to jab and stab at men whose shields were held up to protect from arrows. My spear broke on the third man I killed. I drew my sword and hacked at the legs of the man at the rear. The rest of my wedge had now surrounded the wedge and those who were pushing and protecting were dead. The threat of the ram had gone but we were now in danger of being surrounded by the Franks.

Sometimes doing something quite ridiculous and unexpected works. I remembered that the second two ranks were the levy and not mailed warriors. They had a spear and a shield. Most had a helmet but they were not hardened warriors.

"Reform the edge! Clan of the horse, we attack!"

My men all cheered. I heard Arne Four Toes shout, "This is a good day to die! Let us make this a glorious day for we fight with Hrolf the Horseman!"

I began a chant as I stepped forward.

With mighty axe Black Teeth stood
Angry and filled with hot blood
Hrolf the Horseman with gleaming blade
Hrolf the Horseman all enemies slayed
Ice cold Hrolf with Heart of Ice
Swung his arm and made it slice
Hrolf the Horseman with gleaming blade
Hrolf the Horseman all enemies slayed

In two strokes the Jarl was felled
Hrolf's sword nobly held
Hrolf the Horseman with gleaming blade
Hrolf the Horseman all enemies slayed
Hrolf the Horseman with gleaming blade
Hrolf the Horseman all enemies slayed

It was my song and I knew that my warriors enjoyed singing it. It made us feel invincible for when we had fought Black Teeth it had been against impossible odds and we had won. The rhythm helped us to march and swing our swords at the same time. The line '*Hrolf the Horseman*' was roared at the Franks. I lunged with my sword as I parried the spear. The Frank was disembowelled in an instant. I slashed sideways as Rurik brought his sword over. We were in the second rank and the three Franks who faced us looked terrified. We could not afford to show mercy. Expecting a lunge the man held his shield low. Mt swinging blade bit into his neck showering those around him with blood. My blood was now up. We were all in the same rhythm. We parried and we swung. We seemed impervious to the enemy blows. I felt a spear head hit my mail but the links held and did not break. The covering of seal oil helped.

As I slew the last unarmoured Frank I saw that we had reached the better warriors. I readied myself for a stiffer challenge when a horn sounded three times. The Franks before us looked at each other in disbelief and then began to step backwards. Philippe of Rouen had ordered them to fall back. I think the warriors we faced might have disobeyed had not the levy heard the call and they ran backwards. They poured through the warriors on the flanks. Twelve stood firm. One, wearing an open helmet with a blue plume spat out, "We are not peasants. We are the warriors of Rouen. The rest might flee but we will take your heads; barbarians!"

I did not waste breath. I punched the boss of my shield at the hand which held the long Frankish sword. It smashed into the pommel and he reeled. I pulled back and punched again; this time at his chest. He was forced to take a step back. Arne brought his sword overhand at the warrior next to him. The Frank's shield came up but the blow split it. The Frank was left with a boss attached to a single plank. As the Frank with the plume tried to regain his balance I lunged forward. I aimed at his thigh. My sword slid through his breeks and into flesh before grating along bone. The warrior's face contorted in pain and I punched again with my shield. This time it was into his face. Already overbalancing he fell. I pressed my left foot against his should as I rammed my sword into his throat.

"Heart of Ice!" I raised my sword into the sky and shouted the name of my sword over and over. The other Franks were slain, one by one. The Leudes was using his horsemen, the ones who remained, as a shield to stop Alain and my men from charging the levy.

I was tired but I was filled with joy for we had driven the Franks from the field. Then I released that I had to end it. I turned to my men. I saw that not all had survived but there were more than I might have hoped.

"This is not over yet! We must get our horses and pursue these Franks!"

Arne Four Toes had a bloodied face and he had lost teeth. He grinned and it looked comical, "Aye, jarl! I do not want this day to end. We marched to what I thought was my death and we have won! What cannot we do now?"

I turned to Gudrun Witch Killer, "You and Folki keep your men here and make sure that the field is cleared of foes. Then guard the haugr until we return. The rest of you be ready to ride when our horses arrive."

"What do you intend jarl?"

"To keep our swords in their backs and to slay any Frank that we find. They will rue the day they tried to rid this land of us."

As we trudged back to the Haugr my horsemen rode in. "Captain, have horses fetched. We follow them."

He grinned. I saw that he too had been cut but he looked triumphant, "Aye lord! That was a battle to remember."

Walking through my double gates we were cheered by all. The men and the boys on the walls banged their feet on the fighting platform and women and children lined the path up the hill to my hall. Mary was waiting with Matildhe in her arms and a wide eyed Ragnvald next to her. "Well done, my husband. I did not watch but Erik One Arm and Bagsecg Bagsecgson told me all."

"It is not finished yet but when I have scoured my land of them it will be." I turned to my son. "Come, you can help me saddle Dream Strider."

He took my hand and gripped it tightly. "One day, father, I will go to war with you."

As we passed the forge I saw Bagsecg. I handed him my sword, "This will need an edge. This is not over yet."

"Aye jarl and it will be ready when you are saddled."

"Dream Strider is the oldest of your horses is he not father?" Ragnvald held my bridle as I put on the saddle.

"He is but all of my horses are relatively young."

"Then why choose him? Night Star and Odin's Gift are bigger."

"I have fine horses. Any one of the four is the superior of any other but Dream Strider was my first and we understand each other. It is as though we were as one. We understand each other and we might have far to travel today. Even when he is tired Dream Strider responds to every move. One day you will have your own horse. Always choose your horse. Do not let another give you one. You must look into a horse's eyes and know that he is the one for you. Speak to Gilles. He can speak with horses. He will tell you."

I handed my cloak to my son as I put my shield over my back. I knelt. "Fasten my cloak around my neck."

He did so very carefully. He made sure that the horse brooch securely held the cloak and that the chain was firmly held. I smiled, "When you are old enough you shall wear the sign of the horse. You will ride to war with the clan."

When I reached Bagsecg I saw that he held a spear. "I meant to give you this before, jarl. I found a longer piece of ash and I made a smaller, narrower head. The edge is a good one and it means that you have a longer reach than your foes."

I nodded, "Thank you Bagsecg but today we pursue. Keep it for me until I return."

Rurik, Arne and Einar took three of the recently captured horses as did Erik Long Hair and Sven Siggison. They followed me to the outer gate where the rest of my men waited patiently. Each had his saddle, reins and bridle ready. I saw Gudrun and Folki wandering the field and despatching the wounded. They were also stripping the bodies of their treasure. Without being told they would burn the bodies. It did not do to have carrion so close to our walls.

"Einar, ride to Sven and ask him to sail the knarr down the coast. Tell him we pursue the Franks and he can keep pace with us."

"Aye jarl."

We heard the drumming of hooves and my men and horses arrived from the north. "Erik One Arm, have the boys and any of the older warriors go to Bárekr's farm and bring the animals. They can graze here until their masters collect them."

The horses were soon saddled. I faced them as they awaited my orders. "The Franks are fleeing south. The Leudes hopes that, by saving so many of his men he can build another army and return here. He thinks we are barbarians who will drink ourselves stupid and celebrate our victory!"

Sigtrygg Rolfsson shouted, "And that is not a bad idea jarl!"

"There will be time for such celebration when we return. We will not let them rest. Save your horses. We know that most of their men are on foot. Thanks to the captain and our archers he has fewer horses anyway. Each warrior we kill means that they are less likely to return. Are you ready?"

"Aye jarl!"

"Then let us ride."

Chapter 20

We passed through their deserted camp. They had left tents and supplies behind. We would have another rich harvest there. I did not think the Leudes would head to Valauna but I did see the tracks of a large body of men heading through the woods in that direction. "We will deal with Charles Filjean when we have finished with the Leudes."

Gilles pointed to the ground. "The main army came this way, lord."

"You are learning Gilles."

We passed the bodies of men who had marched south with wounds and then succumbed to their injuries. Already our enemy was paying a price. As the afternoon wore on I wondered if they would stop and camp. I knew there were no settlements large enough for them to defend. The nearest place was Fótr's old stronghold. That was a long way ahead.

Had this been the Raven Wing clan then Ulf Big Nose and I would have been scouting ahead. I had too few men to risk losing a scout. This was the reason that we almost stumbled upon their rear-guard. The greenway passed through a wood and as it twisted down I saw their horses. They were just three hundred paces ahead.

I drew my sword and shouted, "After them!" Speed and surprise were as valuable a pair of weapons as a sword and a shield. There were only eleven of us who were confident when fighting on a horse. The Franks did not know that. I dug my heels into Dream Strider's flanks and he responded well. I had not ridden him to war for some time and he began to out distance the horses of the others. As soon as the riders at the rear heard our hooves, they turned and I saw panic. As the rear-guard their job was to protect the end of the column. They saw Vikings on horses and they fled. Or they tried at least. The greenway was choked with the levy. We were fifteen miles from the battle and they were weary. They had had little sleep and fought a battle. Some of the horsemen left the greenway and galloped across fields. Others ploughed through the levy.

I galloped up behind a Frank who was trying to force his horse though the mass of men. He turned and drew his sword as he heard the thunder of my horse's hooves. I brought mu sword down hard and the Frank's sword shattered under the impact. Perhaps it had weakened during the battle or perhaps it was badly made. The result was that my sword sliced across his chest and he fell from the horse. I backhanded my

sword to the right and laid open the skull of a Frank who was on foot. I
pulled back Dream Strider's reins and he brought his hooves up to smash
into two Frankish foot soldiers. As the rest of my men joined me so the
slaughter became greater. We might have ended the pursuit there and
then save that we could not get by the men who blocked our path. The
only way through was to slay them.

When the last of the forty men lay dead the greenway ahead was
clear. The rest had fled. Borki Silvisson had suffered a wound to the
hand. "Borki, collect the horses which remain and then the weapons.
Gilles ride to the shore," the sea was less than half a mile away, "signal
Sven to close with you and have him and his boys collect the weapons
and treasure form the dead. Then he can continue to sail down the coast
and keep in touch with us."

"Aye lord."

"The rest of you be ready to ride."

"If it is all as easy as this then we will all be the richest Vikings
ever!"

"Asbjorn Sorenson, do not count your treasure until you are safe in
your hall! The Norns are listening!"

Arne Four Toes was always wary of the Norns and his reminder
made my men hold their horse token and say a prayer to the spirits. It did
not do to be so overconfident.

Dusk descended. We were just walking our horses now. We knew
that we were following weary men who walked. There was no need to
exhaust our horses. And we knew we were catching them for we found
discarded helmets and shields. The levy wanted no more to do with them.
They only stayed with the body for mutual protection. When they
reached home, I doubted if any would stir again. We rested, briefly, at a
deserted village. There was a well and an empty trough. We filled the
trough and watered the horses. My men went into the huts and found
grain which we fed to our mounts. We ate whatever food we could find.
We did not sleep but we made water and unsaddled our horses. We
would catch the Leudes; of that I was certain. When we did I wanted my
small band of men to be fit to fight.

Dawn had broken when we found them. They too had had to rest but
they had travelled further than we had. The Leudes showed his
inexperience by halting in the open. They had passed farms and small
villages but ignored them. As the sun began to appear I saw that there

were still over a hundred men before us. I saw the banner of the Leudes and that of Hugo of Ċiriċeburh.

Alain of Auxerre said, "There are less than forty horsemen left, lord." We had managed to break up the large army which had been brought to quash us.

The sight of my men approaching stirred them to action. This time, however, they did not flee. As my men prepared to fight once more I saw a debate. The result was that Hugo of Ċiriċeburh and most of the horse formed a line. I saw the banner of the Leudes and a knot of horsemen gallop off. The levy began to disperse.

I looked at Alain and he nodded, "It seems, Captain, that your old master has been tasked with buying the Leudes time to reach his home."

"Aye lord. We will not catch him now. He will reach Caen easily."

"Then let us end this here. We ride boot to boot. Alain, you and your men with Gilles and Bertrand in the front rank. Rurik and Arne have the others form two ranks behind us."

"I beg a favour lord, let me be the one to fight Hugo of Ċiriċeburh. I owe to my dead comrades."

"You have earned the right." I raised my sword. "Forward!"

As soon as we started to move down the gentle slope the Franks formed a single line and began to gallop up the hill. I did not worry that they would overlap us. I had my warriors behind and they would deal with those who tried to outflank us. Alain still had his spear and he couched it beneath his arm. I saw that the majority of the men we faced wore leather armour with overlapping metal plates. It would be the tip of the sword which would do the most damage. The Frankish lord shouted encouragement to his men as he led the twenty-three of them up the hill. I think it was to encourage himself more than anything. He had fought us before and been bested both times.

I saw that he was coming for me and so I prepared my shield. I held it before me. Hugo of Ċiriċeburh swung his sword at head height. He whirled it to gain momentum. Alain did not give him the chance to strike me. Alain stood in his stiraps and punched hard with the spear. It hit the top of the Frank's shield and his chest took the force of the blow. His swing had made him unbalanced and he tumbled over the back of his horse. I had no time to see what happened to him as the next Frank hacked his sword at me. I flicked my shield to the left and deflected it with a punch. My shield smacked into his and he raised it slightly to help him regain his balance. As he passed me I lunged across my saddle and

my sword slid between two metal plates. Bagsecg had not only
sharpened the edge he had made the tip sharp too. It penetrated his
leather armour, his gambeson and then struck his ribs. I twisted as it
grated along bone and then pushed. I must have pierced his heart for the
life went from his eyes and blood erupted from the wound when I
withdrew my blade.

I reined Dream Strider in. The Franks were finished. Five of them
had baulked at charging us and join the levy who were streaming south. I
saw Alain raise his spear and ram it into the middle of Hugo of
Ċiriċeburh. He twisted it and pulled. He brought with it a snake of guts
and entrails. The young Frank twitched and then lay still. It was over.

"Do we pursue them, lord?"

"No Gilles. Ride, with Bertrand to the sea. It should be over that
rise. Light a fire and signal for Sven to close with us."

I dismounted and took off my helmet. "Arne, have the men strip the
dead. Alain, collect the horses. We will rest here and then you can head
back to the Haugr."

Rurik asked, "Will you not be with us?"

"No, I have a mind to speak with this Leudes. I will sail to Caen in
the knarr."

The knarr did not arrive until evening. My men chose to camp by the
beach. They ate the horse which had been killed in the attack. I waded
out to the knarr and was helped on board. The hold was filled with the
weapons we had taken from the Franks we had fought. My men would
take the rest back on the captured horses.

"Where do we go, jarl? Back to the haugr?"

"No Sven. Take me to Caen."

"There may be Franks there."

I laughed, "I am counting on that but I do not think any will bother
us."

We reached the mouth of the river after dark. Folki had told us that
there were no obstacles between the mouth and Caen and we sailed,
slowly, down the river. The wind was against us and we had to tack back
and forth. The crew must have been cursing me for my request. I rested
while we sailed. Sven's crew could keep a good watch. They woke me
before dawn, "Jarl we are here."

I washed and drank some ale. There was some two-day old bread
and ham which I ate. The river, close to the castle, was quite wide. Sven
turned it around so that we faced downstream. If we had to leave in a

hurry, then we could so easily and we would have both the current and the wind with us. I did not wear my helmet and so I combed my hair. The Leudes already thought that I was a barbarian. I did not want my appearance to confirm it. We were invisible in the river until the first rays of light picked us out. I heard a shout from the fighting platform of the stronghold.

"Take us closer, Sven."

"They may have war machines."

"I doubt it but we will take the risk. We should not appear afraid."

We drifted to within a hundred paces of the walls. I shouted, in their language, "I wish to speak with Philippe of Rouen!"

There was no reply but I was patient and we waited. More warriors appeared on the walls and they stared down at us as though we had come from a different world. I noticed that, on the mast head, Siggi Far Sighted had a bow and an arrow already in his hand. Sven was taking no chances. Any crossbowman who wished to try his luck would have to be faster than Siggi.

Eventually I saw the Leudes. He had a bandage around his head. Alain had not spoken yet of the battle he had fought. My men had done better than I might have hoped.

"I am Philippe of Rouen. What is it that you wish to say? Hurry for I am impatient!"

I nodded, "I can see that. I come here to confirm what I said when you attacked my people. I did not begin this war. You did. Now that it is begun I give you fair warning. Ċiriċeburh and Valauna will soon be part of my land. Your lord of Ċiriċeburh lies dead along with his warriors. Charles Filjean is no general. I will be happy with those two towns. However, should you or your king try to attack us again then you will feel my wrath."

"You dare to threaten the Emperor of the Franks?"

"From what I hear he is clinging on to power by his fingertips."

"Your brethren tried to take my city! What we did was an act of revenge!"

"Those men were not from my settlement. If the Bretons attacked me I would punish the Bretons and not you." I shrugged, and made the gesture large enough for him to see, "Perhaps I am cleverer than you. You slaughtered the ones who did attack you. What you did to my land was unnecessary and you have paid for it."

He was silent for a moment. "You will not attack my people?"

"I will not promise that for I do not break my word. I promised that I would not attack you once and yet it had no effect. I will say that If you do not attack us then it is unlikely that we will attack you."

"That is hardly comforting."

"I am not a Frank. I care not for your comfort. There are those who were Franks but they were ill served by your king. They now follow my banner. I welcome any Frank who comes in peace. If you visit with me then you are welcome so long as your hand stays away from your sword."

"Then there will be no war. Now farewell."

He disappeared and we were dismissed.

"Let us go home, Sven."

As we sailed away both Harold and Sven shook their heads. "I am pleased I never gamble against you, jarl. You have nerves of iron! What if he had declined your offer?"

"Then we would have fought them again. I saw nothing in our battle to make me fear them. We are few but we are strong. We will survive. When my son becomes jarl, he may even rule the land you see before you."

"Then you will fight him?"

"We have bought time that is all. He will not relish another defeat and when King Louis has ended his civil war then he will send another general to defeat us. By then we will be stronger. Besides this war is not yet over. We have Ćirićeburh to take and there is another Frank who wanted vengeance for his father's death. Charles Filjean and I have to settle this. I cannot have an enemy so close to Rurik's farm. I want Valauna to be our stronghold. We have more fighting yet before us."

It took a whole day to sail north. There were watchers on the beach and on the island as we headed north. It seemed that they were worried. As we drew close the Haugr seemed to disgorge every man, woman and child. By the time I stepped ashore I had to contend with their cheers and their warm greeting. Gilles was grinning, "What is this about, Gilles?"

"They feared that the Leudes would capture or kill you."

"No and I fear that this celebration is premature." I was a little annoyed. I wanted my men ready to fight. I could not leave Valauna as a threat. I had travelled the land and knew that if we held Valauna then we would have a safe southern border.

Mary smiled when I told her my thoughts. "They mean well, husband. You have succeeded where none thought that you would. Arne

Four Toes told me that he thought the clan would have a glorious but final end when you led the last charge. You have dragged them from the brink of disaster."

"I never thought that we would be defeated!"

She laughed and touched my hand, "I know! Do not forget, Hrolf, that I know you better than any. When we lived together on the island and there was just the horse sand Gilles I came to know and understand you. To the others, you were just a warrior with strange ideas about the future of the clan. I saw the mind and the leader. They are like children. Treat them as such."

The next day I summoned my warriors. Many had returned to their farms but the ones who remained gathered before my hall. I told them what I had told the Leudes. "Today we ride to Ċiriċeburh. If they resist us, then they will be attacked. I will give them two choices. Leave and return to Caen or join us."

Alain said, "Join us? They are our enemy!"

"How soon you forget. Pepin and yourself were all on the opposite side. Can we not give them the chance to make the same decision that you did?"

He had the good grace to look embarrassed, "Forgive me, lord. I have not yet learned to be a true captain."

"We ride now. For once we ride for war but hope for peace."

The gates were closed as we approached but the handful of men who came to the walls did not appear as a threat. "I am Hrolf the Horsemen. We slew your lord and I have told Philippe of Rouen that this stronghold will now be mine. You have three choices. Fight me and die. Leave with your arms and go to Caen or join my army. I swear that what I say is true. I give you until the sun is at its zenith to decide."

It took less than that time for the gates to open. An older warrior came out. I saw that he had a sling on his arm. "I am Charles of Honfleur. I command here. Some wish to go to Caen." He pointed to eight men. "The rest would like to stay here. We have families. I am too old to start again. I know that you have Franks who chose you over King Louis. We were ill served by our former lord."

I dismounted and clasped his good arm. "Then stay Charles, now lord of Charlesburh, you shall be my seneschal here. What say you?"

"I say aye."

The eight men began to troop out, "Ride to Caen. If my men see you at Valauna or on my land then your lives will be forfeit!"

Alain shook his head as they left. "I would not have believed it if I had not seen it. But tell me lord, why did you rename it as you did?"

"Two reasons: I found it hard to say the other name and if this old warrior was happy to speak for the others then renaming it after him would seem to be a prudent thing to do. It costs us nothing and if it buys the loyalty of these men then so much the better."

"Each day I learn something new. But tell me, lord, how do you know this?"

"I served Jarl Dragonheart of the Land of the Wolf. He was a great teacher."

As we headed back to my home I wondered if my visit to Valauna would go as well. We went with more warriors. Charles Filjean had fled with most of his men. He would not accept my offer. I did not relish the prospect of reducing the stronghold but I would if I had to. Finni and Rurik rode at the fore with me and Gilles. They, more than anyone, had a real interest in what happened at Valauna. Both were keen to fight for the safety of their home. I suspected that some of the Franks who had left the previous day had defied my command and ridden to Valauna. All of the nearby farms had been evacuated and the walls were heavily manned.

Arne Four Toes said, "It looks like we unsheathe our weapons this time."

"Perhaps. We will be a little warier. They may have crossbows." I had my shield held to my chest as I rode forward, flanked by Gilles and Bertrand. A crossbow bolt suddenly blossomed from my shield and I stopped. I have a message for the people of Valauna. It is the same one I made at the burh of Ćiriċeburh. Fight me and die. Leave if you wish or join my people. They are your three choices. The exception is the Seneschal. Before he can leave he must fight me."

There was one word shouted in answer, "Never!"

We withdrew out of range before any more bolts could come our way. The fact that only one had been released made me think they had just one of the weapons.

I rejoined my men. "There are four gates. Arne take a quarter of our men and guard one. Captain, take all of your men and guard the third. Folki and Gudrun take your men and guard the third. I will stay here with the rest. Make camp and use your archers to make life on the fighting platform unbearable."

"Aye jarl."

I turned to Gilles and Bertrand, "Return to the Haugr and fetch a wagon with food and a second with ale. I want the garrison to see us enjoying ourselves."

After they had gone Rurik asked, "How long will we need to be here? Soon we will have crops to harvest."

I smiled, "Not long. When the Franks returned here it was in a rush. They entered the walls and secured themselves. Do you think that they will have laid in supplies? I do not. I also believe that the Franks who disobeyed me have actually helped. They will tell the tale, no doubt of how Charles of Honfleur basely surrendered and joined me. They will tell of his elevation. While they might not approve, there will be others who will and there will be dissension."

Rurik nodded, "But we will have to sleep out under the stars."

"You are getting old and comfortable Rurik. Think of the times we slept on a pitching deck and were soaked by sea water."

Our camps were in the shade of the trees and were a hundred paces from the walls. The crossbow occasionally sent a bolt towards us but as the crossbowman had to expose himself to do so we had plenty of warning and his bolts were wasted. We were vigilant but we ate well and we drank well. The Franks did not try to leave. Our archers managed to hit at least six Franks. It was not certain if the men were killed or not but the fact that they could not walk their walls was a victory in itself.

I was woken, early on the third morning by Siggi. "Jarl, the gate is opening. People are trying to sneak out."

I drew my sword, "Then let us welcome them."

I saw the ten shadows move towards the woods. I had men waiting there too. They allowed them to enter the woods and then I heard a cry. We hurried to them. I found Erik Long Hair with his sword at a Frank's throat. "I nearly killed him, jarl" He pointed. "Half of these are women and children."

"You risked your families?"

"We wished to join those at Ċiriċeburh but the seneschal forbade us. This was the only way."

"Are there others who wish to do so?"

"There are many but they are afraid."

"Tomorrow my men will escort you north but first I need you to do something for me."

"Anything lord."

"Were you warriors?"

"We fought in the levy lord but we are all craftsmen. I make jewellery, Alfred here is a butcher and Gaston is a carpenter."

The next day I went with three of the men to within fifty paces of the walls. I shouted, "Last night these men and others came to my camp. They are unharmed. They wished to go to my new settlement. I will take them there later on. If anyone else wishes to join us, then come forth. I swear I will keep my word."

I heard a cry from inside, "You lie!"

Alfred the butcher was a big man with a voice to match. He shouted, "No he does not! We were treated well. We ate well last night and our children did not wake crying with hunger!"

There was silence and then I heard raised voices from within the walls. Fearing a sudden attack, we moved back into the woods. The noise seemed to go on for hours and then the gates were flung open and men, women and children flooded out. We had won! Then three horses with riders scattered the crowds, trampling one old man. It was Charles Filjean with two of his men and he was escaping. We could not send arrows for fear of hitting the townspeople. "Gilles, Bertrand, get our horses!"

Erik the Tall said, "I will come too jarl!"

The four of us were soon mounted. "Rurik take command of the town. Treat the people well and speak to the ones who first fled. Discover whom we can trust."

"You can rely in me, jarl. Take care. A cornered weasel is always dangerous."

"I know."

We did not gallop as the Franks had. They had a long way to go. If they kept the same pace for a long time, then we would find them besides exhausted horses. They would ride hard and then be forced to stop. Our siege had meant that the horses had not had good grazing and I doubted that they had had grain. Ours, on the other hand, were well looked after animals. We loped along at a steady pace. There was nowhere else for them to go but south. They used the greenways and then the road. The sound of our hooves pounding sent any other travellers running for racing horses only meant one thing, warriors.

Our pursuit was not purely for vengeance. Philippe of Rouen had accepted that we had won. Charles Filjean was a spoiled child who would never accept it. My men had told me that when we had attacked at the battle of the haugr and my wedge had carved deep into the heart of the Franks, it had been Charles Filjean who had broken first. It had allowed Alain and my horsemen to harass the right flank of the Franks and that, as much as anything, had enabled us to win. He was clinging to what little power he had and, I guess, he hoped that the Leudes would give him a new burh. If he did so then he would continue to plot against me and my people. He was a boil which, left alone, would fester further. The lance was the only solution.

The further south we went the flatter the land became and we spied the first of the Franks soon after noon. His horse was lame. He had driven it too far. We could not see the others but I knew they could not be far ahead. The Frank kept glancing over his shoulder. He suddenly wheeled his horse to the right to leave the road and enter a field full of wheat.

"Erik, Bertrand, after him!"

There was just Gilles and I left to follow the two men we pursued. I risked going a little faster. I gambled that the race was nearly run. If one of the enemy's horses had weakened to the point of exhaustion, then the other two could not be far behind. We ascended a small rise and passed through an, apparently, deserted hamlet. It would not be. The people would be hiding. As we reached the centre I spied the two Franks. They were less than five hundred paces from us. Charles Filjean had chosen the better horse for he was twenty paces further on than his companion.

"Gilles, let us catch them!" I drew my sword as we galloped down the slope. It was as though we were fishing and pulling on the line. With every step, we seemed to draw them two steps closer. The nearest Frank knew what was coming and he stopped his horse, began to turn and drew his sword. I did not break stride. I swung my sword at his chest. He brought his own sword to meet it. The shock shivered my arm but broke his sword and threw him to the ground. "Gilles, finish him!"

This was *wyrd*. I had defeated his father in single combat and the son had declined all of my offers. It would end now with the sea just four hundred paces from us. I recognised it as being close to the place where we had found the dead priest. The Frank's head kept turning. It demonstrated his panic. I saw him looking for an escape. He spied a greenway which went downhill. He took it and I knew I had him. His escape was an illusion. The path went down and then climbed, steeply to the dead priest's home. His horse would not carry him. He disappeared, briefly, as he turned the corner. Then I saw him. His horse had simply stopped. He could not climb the steep path to the cliff top.

211

Charles Filjean dismounted and began to run up the hill. I ride Dream Strider to the distressed horse and left him there. "Watch over this brave mount, Dream Strider. He deserves a better rider than the one who abandoned him." Dream Strider's head rose and he whinnied as though in acknowledgement. I left my shield on my saddle and headed after the Frank. I knew he could go nowhere. The hermit had lived isolated and surrounded by cliffs and seabirds. The path was not well worn for none came here any longer. I allowed him to waste his energy running while I strode purposefully after him.

The sound of the sea surging against the rocks became louder. I saw his head as he ran hither and thither. He sought an escape which did not exist. Then he saw me and I watched as his shoulders sagged in resignation. He would have to fight me. He had his shield with him and he hefted it around to his front and balanced himself on the flattest land he could see. I took out my sea and strode up to him.

"Think of all the lives that could have been saved had you fought me like this when I asked. And now you will die alone. None will mourn you and none will remember you. Your father had courage and he had honour. You have none!"

I deliberately insulted him for I wanted him to be angry and he was. Seeing that I had no sword he ran at me, swinging his sword in a wide sweep. With no shield for protection the blow, had it landed would have severed my left arm. I stopped, pivoted and swung my sword around back hand. The tip of his sword caught my cloak. Once again, the metal strip gave enough protection so that he merely tore a hole in my cloak. My sword continued its swing and found the frank's baldric and belt. It bit through them and severed some of the links on his mail. His baldric, belt and dagger fell to the ground. As he tried to race backwards he almost stumbled over them but just managed to recover his balance.

I stepped purposefully towards him. I waved the seax from side to side. It seemed to mesmerize him. I feinted at his hand and, as he brought his shield over, lunged with my sword. It pierced his bicep. He stared at the blood on the tip as though it was impossible for this to be happening. I kept moving forwards and he kept moving back. The edge of the cliff was just thirty paces from us and the ground before it was treacherous. I jabbed at him with my seax. He thought it another trick and did not react. My seax went through his gauntlet and into the back of his hand. He swung his sword at me again and this time it slashed across the front of my cloak and mail. I used the pommel of my sword to punch him in the face. His nose blossomed blood. I think his eyes watered for he waved his sword blindly before him whilst holding the shield as tightly as he could. I ducked beneath it and rammed my seax into his middle. It was not a mortal wound but it was one which shocked him. He looked down at the blood which seeped out. He took his shield and hurled it at me. I was forced to duck. He ran to the edge of the cliff.

"You shall not have the pleasure of killing me or claiming my father's sword!" With that he hurled himself from the cliff top. I sank to my knees. I felt deflated. This place of peace where a monk had died would now be forever haunted by the spirit of a man who had killed himself. Mary had told me that suicide was a mortal sin. The young man had paid a heavy price for his revenge.

Epilogue

The rest of the year was one of peace, growth and a growing friendship between my warriors and the news ones who had chosen to join our clan. Our church, on the island, became the one which the two new communities used. They travelled each Sunday to listen to Mary's priest and sometimes they stayed, during the afternoon to talk with us. Rurik moved his family, along with Finni and they lived in the town we had renamed Valognes. It was easier for us to pronounce and was close enough to Valauna for the Franks to be happy. Both of my warriors left their slaves, now freed, to run their old farms.

We also began to improve Bárekr's home so that we could use it as a port. It was safer for Sven to use. By the time the new grass was come we had a stone quay and our ships could remain moored all year round. We called it Bárekr's Haven for it was a safe haven for our ships.

Our dead from the battle were buried with honour in a barrow close to where they fell. Mary planted small blue flowers which came back each year. Eventually they made the barrow blue from first grass to midsummer's day. It helped us to remember them. We also remembered them by the many new children who would soon be born. Returning warriors celebrated well and most of the women were with child. Other, single men took wives. We had newly widowed franks who needed men and many young women had grown and were ready for husbands and families. Mary and Baugheiðr were also with child. For me it would be my third and for Gilles his first. Even Bertrand was now looking for a bride.

That Yule as we watched the Christians returning from the church on the island I reflected that we had come far in the last few years. We were now rich. We had made a new people and the revenge of the Franks had not weakened us; it had made us stronger. *Wyrd*!

The End

Glossary

Ækre -acre (Norse) The amount of land a pair of oxen could plough in one day

Addelam- Deal (Kent)

Afon Hafron- River Severn in Welsh

Alt Clut- Dumbarton Castle on the Clyde

Andecavis- Angers in Anjou

Angia- Jersey (Channel Islands)

An Oriant- Lorient, Brittany

Áth Truim- Trim, County Meath (Ireland)

Baille - a ward (an enclosed area inside a wall)

Balley Chashtal -Castleton (Isle of Man)

Bebbanburgh- Bamburgh Castle, Northumbria. Also, known as Din Guardi in the ancient tongue

Beck- a stream

Blót – a blood sacrifice made by a jarl

Blue Sea/Middle Sea- The Mediterranean

Bondi- Viking farmers who fight

Bourde- Bordeaux

Bjarnarøy –Great Bernera (Bear Island)

Byrnie- a mail or leather shirt reaching down to the knees

Caerlleon- Welsh for Chester

Caestir - Chester (old English)

Cantewareburh- Canterbury

Casnewydd –Newport, Wales

Cent- Kent

Cephas- Greek for Simon Peter (St. Peter)

Cetham -Chatham Kent

Chape- the tip of a scabbard

Charlemagne- Holy Roman Emperor at the end of the 8th and beginning of the 9th centuries

Cherestanc- Garstang (Lancashire)

Ċiriċeburh- Cherbourg

Constrasta-Valença (Northern Portugal)

Corn Walum or Om Walum- Cornwall

Cymri- Welsh

Cymru- Wales

Cyninges-tūn – Coniston. It means the estate of the king (Cumbria)

Dùn Èideann –Edinburgh (Gaelic)

Din Guardi- Bamburgh castle

Drekar- a Dragon ship (a Viking warship)

Duboglassio –Douglas, Isle of Man

Dyrøy –Jura (Inner Hebrides)

Dyflin- Old Norse for Dublin

Ein-mánuðr- middle of March to the middle of April

Eoforwic- Saxon for York

Fáfnir - a dwarf turned into a dragon (Norse mythology)

Faro Bregancio- Corunna (Spain)

Ferneberga -Farnborough (Hampshire)

Fey- having second sight

Firkin- a barrel containing eight gallons (usually beer)

Fret-a sea mist

Frankia- France and part of Germany

Fyrd-the Saxon levy

Gaill- Irish for foreigners

Galdramenn- wizard

Glaesum –amber

Gleawecastre- Gloucester

Gói- the end of February to the middle of March

Greenway- ancient roads- they used turf rather than stone

Grenewic- Greenwich

Gyllingas - Gillingham Kent

Haesta- Hastings

Hamwic -Southampton

Harpa- April 14th- May 13th

Haestingaceaster -Hastings

Haughs/ Haugr - small hills in Norse (As in Tarn Hows) or a hump- normally a mound of earth

Haustmánuður -15th September -October 14th

Hearth-weru- Jarl's bodyguard/oathsworn

Heels- when a ship leans to one side under the pressure of the wind

Hel - Queen of Niflheim, the Norse underworld.

Herkumbl- a mark on the front of a helmet denoting the clan of a Viking warrior

Here Wic- Harwich
Hetaereiarch – Byzantine general
Hí- Iona (Gaelic)
Hjáp - Shap- Cumbria (Norse for stone circle)
Hoggs or Hogging- when the pressure of the wind causes the stern or the bow to droop
Hrams-a – Ramsey, Isle of Man
Hrofecester-Rochester Kent
Hywel ap Rhodri Molwynog- King of Gwynedd 814-825
Icaunis- British river god
Issicauna- Gaulish for the lower Seine
Itouna- River Eden Cumbria
Jarl- Norse earl or lord
Joro-goddess of the earth
 Jǫtunn -Norse god or goddess
Kjerringa - Old Woman- the solid block in which the mast rested
Knarr- a merchant ship or a coastal vessel
Kyrtle-woven top
Laugardagr-Saturday (Norse for washing day)
Leathes Water- Thirlmere
Ljoðhús- Lewis
Legacaestir- Anglo Saxon for Chester
Liger- Loire
Lochlannach – Irish for Northerners (Vikings)
Lothuwistoft- Lowestoft
Louis the Pious- King of the Franks and son of Charlemagne
Lundenwic - London
Maeresea- River Mersey
Mammceaster- Manchester
Manau/Mann – The Isle of Man(n) (Saxon)
Marcia Hispanic- Spanish Marches (the land around Barcelona)
Mast fish- two large racks on a ship for the mast
Melita- Malta
Midden - a place where they dumped human waste
Miklagård - Constantinople
Leudes- Imperial officer (a local leader in the Carolingian Empire. They became Counts a century after this.)
Njoror- God of the sea
Nithing- A man without honour (Saxon)

Odin - The "All Father" God of war, also associated with wisdom, poetry, and magic (The ruler of the gods).
Olissipo- Lisbon
Orkneyjar-Orkney
Portucale- Porto
Portesmūða -Portsmouth
Condado Portucalense- the County of Portugal
Penrhudd – Penrith Cumbria
Pillars of Hercules- Straits of Gibraltar
Ran- Goddess of the sea
Roof rock- slate
Rinaz –The Rhine
Sabrina- Latin and Celtic for the River Severn. Also, the name of a female Celtic deity
Saami- the people who live in what is now Northern Norway/Sweden
Sarnia- Guernsey (Channel Islands)
St. Cybi- Holyhead
Sampiere -samphire (sea asparagus)
Scree- loose rocks in a glacial valley
Seax – short sword
Sheerstrake- the uppermost strake in the hull
Sheet- a rope fastened to the lower corner of a sail
Shroud- a rope from the masthead to the hull amidships
Skeggox – an axe with a shorter beard on one side of the blade
Skerpla -May 14th- June 12th
Sólmánuður-June 13th-July 12th
South Folk- Suffolk
Stad- Norse settlement
Stays- ropes running from the mast-head to the bow
Stirap- stirrup
Strake- the wood on the side of a drekar
Suthriganaworc - Southwark (London)
Syllingar- Scilly Isles
Syllingar Insula- Scilly Isles
Tarn- small lake (Norse)
Temese- River Thames (also called the Tamese)
The Norns- The three sisters who weave webs of intrigue for men
Thing-Norse for a parliament or a debate (Tynwald)

Thor's day- Thursday

Threttanessa- a drekar with 13 oars on each side.

Thrall- slave

Tinea- Tyne

Trenail- a round wooden peg used to secure strakes

Tude- Tui in Northern Spain

Tynwald- the Parliament on the Isle of Man

Úlfarrberg- Helvellyn

Úlfarrland- Cumbria

Úlfarr- Wolf Warrior

Úlfarrston- Ulverston

Ullr-Norse God of Hunting

Ulfheonar-an elite Norse warrior who wore a wolf skin over his armour

Valauna- Valognes (Normandy)

Vectis- The Isle of Wight

Volva- a witch or healing woman in Norse culture

Waeclinga Straet- Watling Street (A5)

Windlesore-Windsor

Waite- a Viking word for farm

Werham -Wareham (Dorset)

Wintan-ceastre -Winchester

Withy- the mechanism connecting the steering board to the ship

Woden's day- Wednesday

Wyddfa-Snowdon

Wyrd- Fate

Yard- a timber from which the sail is suspended on a drekar

Ýlir – Yule. The second month of winter (November 15th-December 14th)

Ynys Môn-Anglesey

Norse Calendar

Gormánuður October 14th - November 13th
Ýlir November 14th - December 13th
Mörsugur December 14th - January 12th
Þorri - January 13th - February 11th
Gói - February 12th - March 13th
Einmánuður - March 14th - April 13th
Harpa April 14th - May 13th
Skerpla - May 14th - June 12th
Sólmánuður - June 13th - July 12th
Heyannir - July 13th - August 14th
Tvímánuður - August 15th - September 14th
Haustmánuður September 15th-October 13th

Historical note

My research encompasses not only books and the Internet but also TV. Time Team was a great source of information. I wish they would bring it back! I saw the wooden compass which my sailors use on the Dan Snow programme about the Vikings. Apparently, it was used in modern times to sail from Denmark to Edinburgh and was only a couple of points out. Similarly, the construction of the temporary hall was copied from the settlement of Leif Eriksson in Newfoundland.

Stirrups began to be introduced in Europe during the 7th and 8th Centuries. By Charlemagne's time they were widely used but only by nobles. It is said this was the true beginning of feudalism. It was the Vikings who introduced them to England. It was only in the time of Canute the Great that they became widespread. The use of stirrups enabled a rider to strike someone on the ground from the back of a horse and facilitated the use of spears and later, lances.

The Vikings may seem cruel to us now. They enslaved women and children. Many of the women became their wives. The DNA of the people of Iceland shows that it was made up of a mixture of Norse and Danish males and Celtic females. These were the people who settled Iceland, Greenland and Vinland. They did the same in England and, as we shall see, Normandy. Their influence was widespread. Genghis Khan and his Mongols did the same in the 13th century. It is said that a high proportion of European males have Mongol blood in them. The Romans did it with the Sabine tribe. They were different times and it would be wrong to judge them with our politically correct twenty first century eyes. This sort of behaviour still goes on in the world but with less justification.

At this time, there were no Viking kings. There were clans. Each clan had a hersir or Jarl. Clans were loyal to each other. A hersir was more of a landlocked Viking or a farmer while a Jarl usually had ship(s) at his command. A hersir would command bondi. They were the Norse equivalent of the fyrd although they were much better warriors. They would all have a helmet shield and a sword. Most would also have a spear. Hearth-weru were the oathsworn or bodyguards for a jarl or, much later on, a king. Kings like Canute and Harald Hadrada were rare and they only emerged at the beginning of tenth century.

Harald Black Teeth is made up but the practice of filing marks in teeth to allow them to blacken and to make the warrior more frightening was common in Viking times.

The wolf and the raven were both held in high esteem by the Vikings. Odin is often depicted with a wolf and a raven at his side.

Hamwic (Southampton) was raided by the Vikings so many times that it was almost abandoned by the middle of the Ninth Century. Egbert's successor did not suffer from as many Viking raids as King Egbert. He did have an alliance with the Frankish King.

The Vikings began to raid the Loire and the Seine from the middle of the 9th century. They were able to raid as far as Tours. Tours, Saumur and the monastery at Marmoutier were all raided and destroyed. As a result of the raids and the destruction castles were built there during the latter part of the 9th century. There are many islands in the Loire and many tributaries. The Maine, which runs through Angers, is also a wide waterway. The lands seemed made for Viking raiders. They did not settle in Aquitaine but they did in Austrasia. The Vikings began to settle in Normandy and the surrounding islands from the 820s. Many place names in Normandy are Viking in origin. Sometimes, as in Vinland, the settlements were destroyed by the Franks but some survived. So long as a Viking had a river for his drekar he could raid at will.

The Franks used horses more than most other armies of the time. Their spears were used as long swords, hence the guards. They used saddles and stirrups. They still retained their round shields and wore, largely, an open helmet. Sometimes they wore a plum. The carried a spare spear and a sword.

One reason for the Normans success was that when they arrived in northern France they integrated quickly with the local populace. They married them and began to use some of their words. They adapted to the horse as a weapon of war. Before then the Vikings had been quite happy to ride to war but they dismounted to fight. The Normans took the best that the Franks had and made it better. This book sees the earliest beginnings of the rise of the Norman knight.

Books used in the research

British Museum - Vikings- Life and Legends

Arthur and the Saxon Wars- David Nicolle (Osprey)

Saxon, Norman and Viking Terence Wise (Osprey)

The Vikings- Ian Heath (Osprey)

Byzantine Armies 668-1118 - Ian Heath (Osprey)

Romano-Byzantine Armies 4th-9th Century - David Nicholle (Osprey)

The Walls of Constantinople AD 324-1453 - Stephen Turnbull (Osprey)

Viking Longship - Keith Durham (Osprey)

Anglo-Danish Project- The Vikings in England

The Varangian Guard- 988-1453 Raffael D'Amato

Saxon Viking and Norman- Terence Wise

The Walls of Constantinople AD 324-1453-Stephen Turnbull

Byzantine Armies- 886-1118- Ian Heath

The Age of Charlemagne-David Nicolle

The Normans- David Nicolle

Norman Knight AD 950-1204- Christopher Gravett

The Norman Conquest of the North- William A Kappelle

The Knight in History- Francis Gies

The Norman Achievement- Richard F Cassady

Knights- Constance Brittain Bouchard

Griff Hosker
December 2016

Other books by Griff Hosker

If you enjoyed reading this book, then why not read another one by the author?

Ancient History

The Sword of Cartimandua Series
(Germania and Britannia 50 A.D. – 128 A.D.)
Ulpius Felix- Roman Warrior (prequel)
The Sword of Cartimandua
The Horse Warriors
Invasion Caledonia
Roman Retreat
Revolt of the Red Witch
Druid's Gold
Trajan's Hunters
The Last Frontier
Hero of Rome
Roman Hawk
Roman Treachery
Roman Wall
Roman Courage

The Wolf Warrior series
(Britain in the late 6th Century)
Saxon Dawn
Saxon Revenge
Saxon England
Saxon Blood
Saxon Slayer
Saxon Slaughter
Saxon Bane
Saxon Fall: Rise of the Warlord
Saxon Throne
Saxon Sword

Medieval History

The Dragon Heart Series
Viking Slave
Viking Warrior
Viking Jarl
Viking Kingdom
Viking Wolf
Viking War
Viking Sword
Viking Wrath
Viking Raid
Viking Legend
Viking Vengeance
Viking Dragon
Viking Treasure
Viking Enemy
Viking Witch
Viking Blood
Viking Weregeld
Viking Storm
Viking Warband
Viking Shadow
Viking Legacy
Viking Clan
Viking Bravery

The Norman Genesis Series
Hrolf the Viking
Horseman
The Battle for a Home
Revenge of the Franks
The Land of the Northmen
Ragnvald Hrolfsson
Brothers in Blood
Lord of Rouen
Drekar in the Seine
Duke of Normandy
The Duke and the King

New World Series
Blood on the Blade
Across the Seas
The Savage Wilderness

The Reconquista Chronicles
Castilian Knight

The Aelfraed Series
(Britain and Byzantium 1050 A.D. - 1085 A.D.)
Housecarl
Outlaw
Varangian

**The Anarchy Series England
1120-1180**
English Knight
Knight of the Empress
Northern Knight
Baron of the North
Earl
King Henry's Champion
The King is Dead
Warlord of the North
Enemy at the Gate
The Fallen Crown
Warlord's War
Kingmaker
Henry II
Crusader
The Welsh Marches
Irish War
Poisonous Plots
The Princes' Revolt
Earl Marshal

**Border Knight
1182-1300**

Sword for Hire
Return of the Knight
Baron's War
Magna Carta
Welsh Wars
Henry III
The Bloody Border
Baron's Crusade
Sentinel of the North

Lord Edward's Archer
Lord Edward's Archer
King in Waiting

Struggle for a Crown
1360- 1485
Blood on the Crown
To Murder A King
The Throne
King Henry IV
The Road to Agincourt

Modern History

The Napoleonic Horseman Series
Chasseur a Cheval
Napoleon's Guard
British Light Dragoon
Soldier Spy
1808: The Road to Coruña
Talavera
The Lines of Torres Vedras

The Lucky Jack American Civil War series
Rebel Raiders
Confederate Rangers
The Road to Gettysburg

The British Ace Series

1914
1915 Fokker Scourge
1916 Angels over the Somme
1917 Eagles Fall
1918 We will remember them
From Arctic Snow to Desert Sand
Wings over Persia

Combined Operations series
1940-1945
Commando
Raider
Behind Enemy Lines
Dieppe
Toehold in Europe
Sword Beach
Breakout
The Battle for Antwerp
King Tiger
Beyond the Rhine
Korea
Korean Winter

Other Books
Great Granny's Ghost (Aimed at 9-14-year-old young people)

For more information on all of the books then please visit the author's web site at www.griffhosker.com where there is a link to contact him.

Made in the USA
Columbia, SC
26 December 2020